BULLET POINTS

Mark Watson was born in Bristol in 1980. A stand-up comedian, he recently gained international attention with the world's first solo 24-hour show, which won three Edinburgh Festival awards and was described by the *Scotsman* as 'one of the defining moments of fringe comedy, sure to become a cultural legend'. He had previously won the 2002 *Daily Telegraph* Open Mic Award, and been nominated for the Perrier Best Newcomer Award in 2001 with the show 'Far Too Happy'. He lives in London with his fiancée, who accepted his proposal on stage.

Mark Watson

BULLET POINTS

VINTAGE

Published by Vintage 2005

2 4 6 8 10 9 7 5 3 1

First published in Great Britain in 2004 by
Chatto & Windus

Vintage
Random House, 20 Vauxhall Bridge Road,
London SW1V 2SA

Random House Australia (Pty) Limited
20 Alfred Street, Milsons Point, Sydney
New South Wales 2061, Australia

Random House New Zealand Limited
18 Poland Road, Glenfield,
Auckland 10, New Zealand

Random House (Pty) Limited
Endulini, 5A Jubilee Road, Parktown 2193,
South Africa

The Random House Group Limited Reg. No. 954009
www.randomhouse.co.uk/vintage

A CIP catalogue record for this book
is available from the British Library

ISBN 0 09 946085 8

Papers used by Random House are natural, recyclable products made from wood grown in sustainable forests. The manufacturing processes conform to the environmental regulations of the country of origin

Printed and bound in Great Britain by
Bookmarque Ltd, Croydon, Surrey

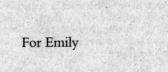
For Emily

1

Before They Were Famous

I first became interested in psychology in 1964, when I was fourteen and my English teacher stood accused of being insane. A tall, willowy man in a grey suit visited our school to investigate the accusation. He knew my father slightly, as Dad was the local police constable and they had worked together on a case once before. The man stayed at our house for a few nights and was soon introduced to me as a psychologist. Although I tried to remain impassive when passing him on the stairs, I naturally assumed that he could look into my soul.

If he had chosen to do this, he would have seen that my only major personality quirk was a blossoming inferiority complex. My best friend, Richard Aloisi, was the school's outstanding student and our interests collided with what sometimes seemed malicious frequency. The pattern for our friendship was set by our first meeting, at the eleventh birthday party of someone I no longer remember. I had just impressed a crowd of potential new friends by fitting three ping-pong balls into my mouth, a difficult trick taught to me by my uncle Tom on the otherwise uneventful Christmas Day 1961. Widely admired for my achievement, I was offering tuition to a narrow-mouthed acquaintance in exchange for part of his cake when in walked Richard, jaw impossibly stretched to accommodate four balls. My uncle had told me that the 'four-ball fit' was achieved only by a tiny elite; my heart sank at my first encounter in life with an obviously superior rival. 'Don't try four, Pete,' Tom had warned me gravely, removing the saliva-coated balls from my mouth like coins from a fruit machine as my mother watched unimpressed, 'and if you meet a fellow who can do it, stay out of his way.' That night, six girls collected Richard's phone number. Just two took mine, one of them (Jennifer O'Hara) later trading it for a can of Coke.

Richard and I would review this party with appropriate sentimentality years later, at another celebration: this time, the valedictory beerfest which marked our school leaving day. The guest list was almost the same, the same mannerisms and gestures now manifest in the bodies and faces of older, drunker people, as if all our school days had been a film in which the first occasion soft-faded into this one, only a montage of falling leaves and tumbling calendar pages marking the time. On this occasion, Richard – now, like me, America-bound – was asked what he would like on his grave-stone. After a second's pause, he said: 'I'd like to have no inscription at all, just my name. If you've really made it, they don't need to write who you were.'

This brought a chorus of appreciative murmurs. Even accounting for the hyperbolic emotions running wild through leaving night, it was the kind of comment that everyone could easily imagine repeating to awed children as Richard landed on the moon. When it was my turn to answer the gravestone question, I predicted: 'Mine will probably say, RICHARD ALOISI'S GRAVE THIS WAY.' The laugh that rewarded this comment was one of my proudest moments in secondary education.

The minor scandal over the controversial English teacher, Mr Paulson, was a rare taste of sensation in our home town, the last place in England untouched by the spirit of rebellion which would define the decade in the eyes of posterity. Witching was such an undistinguished place that an adequate summary of its history was printed on the bookmarks sold in its ailing, often closed library, where my mother had worked part-time for years. In 1682, the bookmarks revealed, the town earned its name with an act of superstitious brutality: three women accused of summoning the Devil were stripped naked and burned to death on the Green opposite the church, before an enormous crowd 'who in their excitement almost trampled each other to death'. The women protested their innocence, insisting that Satan had never visited them – he took one look at the place and walked twenty miles to Cambridge instead, according to a local joke – and it was said that they took revenge for their mistreatment by placing a terrible curse upon the town with their final breaths. If this curse existed, though, there was disappointingly little evidence of its working as I grew up.

No dreadful cries could be heard in the dead of night; no mysterious plague struck at the heart of the community; a documentary crew who arrived to capture a ghost on film were forced to make do with a sound engineer wrapped in a sheet. Richard and I once sneaked out at midnight on the anniversary of the witches' execution, undetected by both sets of parents – my young heart froze as I crept over the third stair from the top, which at the gentlest touch gave a creak as loud as a door in a horror movie – and headed for their deathspot on the Green, the meeting-place of all the town's disturbed spirits. Scorched into the grass was a large, ineradicable red-brown stain said by local legend to have been made by the witches' animal sacrifices, which mothers wheeling pushchairs and old couples on the way to bingo still studiously sidestepped. All we saw in exchange for our boldly executed plan, however, was a drunkard slumped against the low perimeter fence and a couple of shadowy figures groping each other in the half darkness. A year later, when I proposed repeating our investigations, Richard told me loftily that evil spirits were a product of the imagination, pointing to evidence in the *Children's First Book of Scepticism* which his parents had bought him for Christmas.

The only event that could be even fancifully attributed to the curse was the suicide in 1949 of the young son of a local painter-decorator. Nicholas Hirst was said by superstitious locals to have been born with an ugly birthmark in the shape of the witches' stain, and to have been driven mad by the voices of the condemned women. This sad death had happened more than two hundred and fifty years after the witch-hunt, which even by local standards was a long time to wait for something to happen, but it was close enough to my lifetime to excite my curiosity. My mother had been acquainted with the Hirsts and I pestered her with questions about Nicholas: whether he had really heard voices, whether he was mad. She refused, however, to discuss the subject, like (I used to think) most promising topics of conversation. I was driven instead to seeking drama in the humdrum crises that landed on my father's desk and were solved with disappointing simplicity and speed. 'The only curse of this place is the idea that it's cursed,' Dad used to say. So I was secretly quite pleased when my English teacher's eccentricity began to show signs of veering towards madness.

Well over six feet tall and racked by back pains which he vented in savage outbursts, Paulson was a colossus to the boys who held him in awe and the girls who regarded him with fear and hatred. Although he was only forty-five years old, he seemed to have a turbulent lifetime stored behind his hard, deep eyes, under which permanent dark circles gave the impression that he had not slept well for a decade. His lessons had always been distinguished by unpredictable flashes of temper – on his first day at the school he threw a poor piece of work out of the window, and even I (a cautious, solid pupil) had had my parentage questioned after scoring three out of ten in a spelling test – but he underwent a dangerous change after missing out on the school play.

The annual play was traditionally directed by the maths teacher Mr Tomlinson, although he looked as if the effort were gradually overpowering him. Tomlinson had a doleful way about him, but the specific disappointments of his life were more widely known – a cuckolding, an underachieving son. When Paulson presented himself as a rival for the directorship, he was snubbed in sympathy for the marginally more needful candidate. Paulson, whose ideas for the play had included a nude scene and a portrayal of female masturbation (he didn't say which play he intended to put on, but seemed determined to include these scenes regardless), was furious at the decision and began to plan a series of lessons which would showcase his sense of the theatrical in a manner never to be forgotten by his pupils.

He started in a small way, illustrating the conventions of Greek tragedy by teaching an entire lesson wearing a grotesque face mask, taping up the eye-holes halfway through to evoke the blindness of Oedipus, so that he could be identified only by the muffled voice emanating from the mask's enormous, distressed mouth. The following week, in a discussion of *King Lear*, he made the whole class follow him out on to the playing fields during a ferocious storm to convey a sense of Lear's similar predicament. Then, for a class on a fashionable branch of literary theory entitled 'The Death of the Author', the increasingly reckless Paulson used as a prop a corpse loaned from a friend at medical school. It sat slumped at the front of the room, unmoved by our distracted attempts at epistemological debate and by the front-row sobbing of Jennifer O'Hara, the class's most beautiful girl.

This stunt provoked a small-scale disciplinary inquiry, which Paulson survived by convincing the panel that the corpse had been a dummy. Many of those who had been present would always swear otherwise. I was sitting near the back and couldn't be sure, especially as I was far from certain of what a genuine cadaver might look like; Richard, whose opinion I would have trusted, had been absent, recovering from one of his periodical bouts of asthma, which represented his only apparent Achilles heel.

'This guy Paulson is a true performance artist,' remarked Mr Aloisi to my dad, during one of the awkward meals shared from time to time by the two sets of parents who had little other than their kids' friendship to unite them. Richard's father was a professor of social and political sciences from New York who had been lured to Cambridge by the kudos rather than the money, and spent a lot of time lamenting East Anglia's lack of glamour. The Aloisis had a huge house on the very edge of Witching, and held cocktail parties on the scale of those in *The Great Gatsby*, attended by minor celebrities from Europe and America and costing unimaginable sums. My parents, to reciprocate their invitations to these jamborees, had the Aloisis over to Sunday lunch so that the two fathers could make strained conversation about our school and Mrs Aloisi could request the recipes for dishes which she noticeably did not enjoy. I sometimes felt that the difference between our potatoes and gravy and the Aloisis' canapés and Californian wines encapsulated the gulf between my prospects and Richard's.

Referring to a teacher as a 'performance artist' was typical of Mr Aloisi, the sort of all-rounder who was equally comfortable discussing poetry and electoral reform. It was the kind of thing my father didn't know how to respond to. 'He certainly seems a strange chap,' Dad said on this occasion. 'I'd like to know how he's kept his job.'

'He must be sleeping with Kean, I reckon!' said Aloisi.

Mrs Kean was our headmistress. Richard's father cackled at his own mischievous suggestion, ignoring the pleading *not in front of the children* look which my mother angled across at him. Richard had had a *Children's First Book of Sex and Sexuality*[1] when he was eight; he was well at home with terms I only pretended to understand. This, however, was not enough to protect him from Paulson's next stunt.

When Paulson returned after a short 'holiday', he had the sense to rein in his chaotic instincts for a while, long enough for the expectation to dwindle. Nobody anticipated any trouble when he began a lesson on *Othello* by asking Richard about his health. Asthma had been troubling him again and he'd missed a week of classes – something he could easily afford, especially since his house contained more books than our school library.

'Without you, Richard,' Paulson declared, 'I'm afraid last week's lessons were lifeless.'

Like all great hyperbole, it contained a granule of truth, and Richard was snared.

'I'm sorry to hear that,' he replied, sounding smug.

'Yes,' Paulson continued. 'We all missed you. Everybody, a round of applause for Richard Aloisi.'

A little bemused, but cooperative, the class supplied the applause. Richard shuffled in his seat with modest pleasure.

---

[1] This book, and the *Children's First Book of Scepticism* mentioned above, are long out of print. The latter volume, which contained chapters entitled 'UFOs and Other Nonsense' and 'Death Is the End', was criticised by educationalists for its uncompromisingly harsh attitude towards childish fantasy.

Paulson, leaning back serenely in the manner of an impresario against the chalky blackboard, continued.

'Of course, there are some people who think you're an overprivileged, overconfident kid who gets all the breaks and takes all the glory away from harder-working pupils. But I'm sure those people are just jealous.' The atmosphere changed as abruptly as if Paulson had started yelling, though his tone was menacingly even, each syllable pronounced like the name of an enemy. I felt Richard stiffen; he glanced at me for reassurance but my eyes were riveted upon the speaker. 'So often, people *are* jealous of these kids whose fathers bring them over from abroad and spoil them rotten and give them the best possible start. There's a lot of resentment against wealth in this area, and when it's combined with arrogance . . .'

'Sir . . . ?' Richard tried to protest – he had the expression of somebody framed for a crime of whose exact nature he is unaware – but his tongue had become thick and fuzzy, his great reserves of confidence momentarily suspended.

Paulson was now enjoying himself.

'As for all those whispers about your sexuality . . .' he resumed.

A combined shudder and snigger passed like a draught through the room. The teacher had entered territory so murky that even the school's most celebrated bullies hovered on the fringes. The flush of pride upon Richard's face had deepened into something near its opposite: unfamiliar shades of indignation and embarrassment played across his features. Outside, there was silence; it was as if the whole school were listening.

'I can't *imagine* what those people are on about,' Paulson claimed with an exaggerated rhetorical shrug and head-shake. 'You're not a homosexual, are you, Richard?'

No sound could force its way out of Richard's throat. I

saw, for the first time, tears pricking the corners of his eyes as a press conference of turning heads studied his discomfort. Sneers crept around the edges of some mouths as the class's golden boy sweated in the spotlight.

'Well, even if you *are*,' Paulson went on, 'who are we to judge? Here, we might teach that homosexuality is wrong. But America is a foreign country. They do things differently there.'

'I'm not a . . . homosexual, sir,' said Richard in an unsteady voice. There were several barely stifled giggles, as if by repeating the word he had incriminated himself.

'Is that the line you always use?' Paulson retorted.

A gasp of guilty laughter swept perhaps half of the class along with it. I thought of the times I had mentally condemned my friend to a fate like this – jealous moments in which I wished he could be, as Dad might say, 'taken down a peg' – and I squirmed. Richard's face was now resigned to the unthinkable, like a nightmare-sufferer half aware that the only escape is to wait for daylight.

'*What are you all laughing at?*' Paulson suddenly roared, and the room fell silent before the last word had pierced the air. He turned his back and wrote a phrase on the board while, behind him, nobody dared even to exchange a glance. He stepped aside and allowed us to read the spindly capitals: FORTUNE'S WHEEL.

'You've just witnessed the workings of Fortune's Wheel, one of the mainstays of classical tragedy,' Paulson announced. 'The hero –' (here he gestured at Richard) – 'starts at the top of the wheel, and believes he will always stay there. The mob, the general public, believes the same. But then the wheel begins to turn, carrying him down and down, and the mob –' (here, with a contemptuous sweep of one hand, he gestured at us all, although I felt my inclusion was unjust) – 'the mob turns against the hero as keenly as it once supported him. "Call no man happy until he is dead," the Greeks said.'

'We've looked at a number of plays in which this pattern is played out,' said Paulson. 'I hope this little lesson has helped to give you a clearer idea of what those plays were about. And Richard, it'll be good practice for when you get your fifteen minutes of fame.' His voice was mild, as though offering an olive branch, but it was tipped with the instinctive jealousy of encroaching age. 'The rest of you can expect the alternative to fame: failure.'

The end-of-lesson bell rang just as Paulson had delivered this gem of encouragement. His knack of perfect timing only strengthened the suspicion that he rehearsed his lessons like dramatic performances. Lighting a large cigar, he dismissed his listeners.

Afterwards, Richard swore – as he would continue to swear – that he had understood the purpose of Paulson's attack and had gone along with the plan for the sake of the lesson. 'It's not as if I have anything to hide,' he said, and his throng of listeners hastily agreed, those who had sneered at him already regretting their fickleness, like people who have gloated at a fallen leader now returning to power. Mr Aloisi, however, saw the incident differently; his enthusiasm for Paulson's artistry seemed to have dimmed when he phoned my dad that evening. The sound of the phone always made Mum jump; my father had a guarded police-constable way of answering it which did little to reassure her.

'Kristal; who is this?'

There was no talk of gravy recipes on this occasion. Mr Aloisi shouted and ranted at my father for almost fifteen minutes, demanding a criminal investigation into Paulson's methods. He made similar calls to the head of the school's governors, and even (it was alleged) to the Education Secretary in London. Like many people given to overreaction, Aloisi generally got what he wanted. Within a week, the psychologist had arrived in our school for a series of 'informal interviews' with members of the class.

And this, as I have already said, was what first fired the interest in the study of people's minds, the study of why things happen and how they trigger more things and so on into infinity, which was to become one of the shaping forces of my life. The psychologist fascinated me: not just with the satisfyingly suggestive questions he asked ('Has Mr Paulson ever spoken to you outside the classroom?') but with the analytical calmness of his manner. His lean, close-shaven face gave the joint impressions of absolute attentiveness and sly detachment, as if he possessed the skill of devoting the halves of his brain to two independent tasks, like the uncle of Richard's who could write Latin and Greek simultaneously with his two hands. No doubt he sat impassively not just through my interview, but through the tearful recollections of the highly strung Jennifer O'Hara and the scrupulously even-handed testimony of Richard himself. When he spilt a splash of milk on to his jacket while breakfasting at our house, it looked as if he had done it deliberately; when he asked me a question about sports, I gathered that he was tacitly assessing my suitability for national service. In response to a wry remark by my dad about the Witching curse, he gave a short, sardonic laugh which made me ashamed that I had ever gone looking for witches in the night.

My generic mental image of a psychologist – before this real-life encounter – had been the popular caricature of the white-coated sadist who pumped electrical currents through the depressed; the symbolic jailer who appeared in films to cart the stricken hero off to a padded room. This man, however, was no mad scientist but (there was no other word for it) a *detective*. I longed to ask him how he had reached the peak of wisdom from which he declared, after five days of investigations, that Paulson was psychologically unfit to teach; but, although he sat up late with Dad, smoking and discussing cases and even on one occasion listening to Dad's Bob Dylan records – the two got on excellently – I could no more imagine initiating a conversation with him than I could see myself talking to Sherlock Holmes. On the psychologist's last evening before his return to London, however, Richard was staying the night with me. Though we had discussed the visitor in awed tones all week, Richard seemed quite unexcited by the man's presence in our house. Then, as dinner was finishing he asked, in the special voice he used for addressing important adults: 'Can I ask how you go about being a psychologist? What sort of skills do you need?'

The silver-haired mind-reader smiled slightly (something I hadn't seen before) and responded immediately as if he had been waiting for the question ever since he arrived.

'Well, professionally, it helps to go to the States,' he told Richard; and even though I was sitting next to him, I somehow felt I was eavesdropping as my friend nodded solemnly. 'That's where the best training is, and certainly the most opportunities to practise. I was fortunate to have the opportunity to study there at a time when it was very rare. It's not so rare now.'

In the next ten seconds several facts presented themselves to me:

- that Richard had already formed the same ambition as I had;
- that, with his academic prowess and a family who did not so much support him as physically heave him into useful niches, he would have a better chance of fulfilling it;

- that, unless I could defy precedent and probability, I would find myself for ever half a lap behind.

'As for skills,' the guru continued, 'just take an interest in the way people think and act. Think about cause and effect. Go to the roots of things. That's a good habit to get into.'

My dad, who had long been in this habit, nodded approvingly. He always liked to say, in relation to his police work, that there was never a single reason for anything, and in fact he adopted the phrase 'cause and effect' as his own after the psychologist's visit. I saw that these words were destined to have a profound effect upon Richard, as they would upon me; his imagination had been captured, as mine had. There were three years to go until we applied to universities and the race was on.

On the day that Richard announced his intention to become a mind-doctor, his parents bought him eight books on psychology – including a copy of *Understanding Understanding*, a seminal work of the period, signed by the author – and Mr Aloisi spoke to friends across the Atlantic who told him that Harvard offered what was probably the best psychology course. These friends also reported the first stirrings of what would later be known as the USA's shrink culture: psychologists were earning big money by lending their skills to the new art of advertising, plotting the fastest routes into consumers' minds and wallets; others were working for the Cold War intelligence effort; 'psychotherapist' and 'psychiatrist' were mutating from euphemisms for straitjacket-handlers into viable, even highly lucrative career choices.

'I've been thinking it would be a good idea to set up a practice in New York one day,' said Richard casually during a school museum trip, after we had escaped from Egyptology

13

to look at an exhibition devoted to the human brain. 'A friend of my dad's is a shrink in New York and he said he might be able to set me up if he's still going then.' *My* dad's friends were limited to Witching residents, as he had spent his whole life there; the only steps I had taken towards being 'set up' were working hard in biology lessons and occasionally browsing the *British Journal of Psychiatry*. Richard, who knew this, tried to offer me hope. 'I'm sure he will help you, as well.' But Mr Aloisi remained stubbornly, and quite reasonably, uninterested in my career development.

By the time I made that gravestone joke, at the leavers' dinner in the summer of 1968, Richard had secured his place at Harvard. He would undergo a four-year course called 'Psychology and Social Effects' and then, equipped with a stack of psycho-jargon and an ever thickening book of contacts, would move smoothly into the mainstream of American psychiatry. As for me, I'd applied to Harvard as well, and been turned down, but in any case I knew that my parents couldn't have afforded to send me there, and the rejection came as something of a relief in that respect. Moreover, one of my other applications was successful: Michigan State University offered me financial assistance to take up a place studying psychology and neurology. Like Richard, I would be in America for four years; like him, I would be trained as a scientist and prepared for psychiatric work; unlike him, I had no idea how I would survive so far from home, and still less could I imagine what I would do afterwards.

When I confided in Dad the difficulties of my unspoken, ongoing competition with Richard, he was his usual reassuring self.

'You might think, Oh, I wish I was as well off as Richard, or always came top of the class and suchlike, so I could take him down a peg,' Dad said, 'but the grass is always greener on the other side, you know.'

'But what if, this time, it *is* greener?' I asked. As it happened, the Aloisis' large garden was far better maintained than ours, because they employed a gardener while my dad could work outdoors only in short bursts, his lungs making prolonged exertion difficult. 'What if he's just always going to be ahead of me?'

'For goodness' sake,' Mum cut in. 'Why is this family always going on about the bloody Aloisis?' So often passive, my mother had a way of making these sudden, decisive interventions from time to time; in this respect she reminded me of my vision of God. 'Why have you always got to be competing?'

'I don't want to compete with him,' I protested, 'but . . .'

'Then *don't*,' Mum said, clearing away my *British Journal of Psychiatry* with a disdainful look. 'Do your own things. Otherwise you'll never get anywhere.' Surprised at herself, she backtracked a little – 'I only want to see you happy, Peter' – but the damage was done; incidents like this only bolstered the nagging feeling of distance which had always somehow separated us.

After she had left the room and we heard the lock of the bathroom door, on the inside of which there hung a faded photograph of a slim, pale young singer on stage in a London nightclub – the only memento of a thwarted career – I wondered aloud if it was Mum's own frustrated ambition which made her incapable of fully understanding mine.

Dad chided me for this ungenerous suggestion. 'Your mother would love nothing more than to see you succeed,' he said. 'It's just that she can't stand Richard's mum, so she doesn't like to hear you talking like that.' Mrs Aloisi had just appeared on national television in a cookery show, he explained; Mum had been in a bad mood ever since, muttering that she didn't know why we had ever bought a television set.

'I thought you said there was never a single reason for anything,' I said.

'Don't ever trust what *I* say!' Dad protested. 'I'm a policeman!' We laughed until he began to cough and Mum, re-entering, apologised for her outburst and made him drink a glass of water.

As the time approached for my departure to the States, I became increasingly nervous at the prospect, but it was, of course, an unmissable opportunity. Witching was as moribund as ever – Mr Paulson (who, we later learned, *had* been sleeping with Mrs Kean) was replaced by a kindly septuagenarian, the ghosts stayed in their graves, the police-station phone sat quiet for so long that Dad joked about disconnecting it to save money – and I feared that unless I made good my escape, I might become part of the fabric of the place. As for the fact that Richard would be racing, officially for the first time, on a faster track than mine, this could also be seen in a positive light. 'He'll be under an awful lot of pressure at Harvard,' Dad said, three days before we flew out. 'They work them hard there, famous for it. And his parents expect so much from him. I'm not sure he'll find it as easy as Mr Aloisi seems to think.'

But he did. Within a year of his honourable graduation from Harvard, Richard was working in a major psychiatric institution; by the time he was twenty-five, he was already behind the desk of his own New York practice, in an office so close to the heart of things that he could gaze out of his window at his wealthy clients jogging in Central Park. As ever, he had appeared in precisely the right place at the right time. Psychiatry was by now all but an arm of the entertainment industry, and the cult of self-analysis had made Manhattan a therapist's nirvana. A Wall Street banker who found himself without a lunch booking in a restaurant would try to get an appointment instead. Wealthier worriers who wanted to stay ahead of the craze employed whole squads of analysts: one client of Richard's saw a different shrink after each meal of the day (including brunch) and employed specialists to talk through problems with his clothes, his pets, his relationships with the other specialists. It had reached the stage where *not* having a therapist was taken as proof that something was amiss. There were two types of people, as the joke went at the time: those who were in denial, and those who wouldn't admit they were.

In such a shrink-hungry climate, and powered by his always ferocious devotion to work, Richard could hardly fail to become a sensation. By his mid-twenties – in the time it had taken me to land a job on a modest-sized psychiatric magazine – a steady swarm of actuaries, lawyers and professional idlers was choosing to lie on his couch rather than in a steam bath or on an executive sunbed. In 1976 he was named in the *New York Times* as one of the city's most successful people under thirty;[2] less official polls indicated that he was also one of the most popular and sexually fulfilled. When we spoke on the phone, clinking glasses and sophisticated big-city laughter soundtracked his wild but true tales of celebrity trauma and treatment. In response I could delve only into the shallow pool of anecdotes from my life at the *Michigan Psychiatric Journal*. Our phone calls were like communications between different planets.

And indeed, looking at him now from the vantage point of our middle age, there can be no denying that Richard has

---

[2] 'How Did They Get There Already?' *New York Times*, 5 May 1976

handsomely achieved every goal ever set for him, by himself or others. As for me, my career has been no failure by the usual criteria: I've run my own practice, met and treated many fascinating people, collected couldn't-have-done-it-without-you letters from most corners of the creative globe, and never been successfully sued by a patient. Nonetheless, I have never felt truly fulfilled. Richard thinks that I should stop thinking of myself as 'the less successful doppelganger that every great man needs',[3] and start blowing my own trumpet. 'You have a lot to teach people,' he says. He believes that a book detailing the key cases of my career might be interesting, even inspirational to read. I hope he's right. If not, I can only suggest buying one of his.

[3] A phrase I found in Julian Barnes' *Flaubert's Parrot* (Jonathan Cape, The Random House Group, 1984)

2

Bullet Points

I managed not only to graduate from university in America but to secure a job there, as a writer for the *Michigan Psychiatric Journal*. Sometimes I felt astonished at my own bravery, when I stopped to consider that I had fashioned a life for myself 5,000 miles from Witching. Mostly though, I was just relieved to have escaped. The *Journal* had a readership of about seventeen thousand: I had a greater audience for my articles than if I had called the whole population of Witching to attention. I researched and wrote up cases, interviewed people in the business and pored over survey results to discover how often people thought about sex.[4] Much as I still yearned for my parents' approval and strove to impress them in my weekly phone calls, monthly letters and Christmas appearances, the whole of Witching seemed to have shrunk behind me. The town became sleepier and more distant with every Christmas that passed and every small milestone of independence I left behind. Michigan was now my home. I lived in a small rented condo a few miles outside Detroit, socialised with people from the magazine – including my

---

[4] About every eleven minutes, according to the *Journal*'s 'Sex in the Seventies' survey (11/74), which also revealed that 20 per cent of men would be more able to identify their wife by her breasts than her face; and that 30 per cent had had a homosexual experience of which they were ashamed. The results may have been distorted by photocopied forms.

deputy editor, Simon Stacy, who took me out for a drink every Friday – and every now and then, jumped on a weekend train to New York to see the friend who was living our dream.

In many ways I didn't envy him his metropolitan lifestyle. For all the gloss and glamour and the sheer exhilarating scale of everything, which ensured that my first visit was one long open-mouthed skyward gaze, New York in those days seemed to me like a hell of a town in more ways than one. I could live without the sweaty subway rides, the air so thick and grimy you could feel it stick to your clothes, the twenty-four-hour music of restless vehicles jostling and honking on perpetually jammed streets. I enjoyed being able to park my car without finding my tyres on sale when I came back, and it didn't even trouble me that Richard – always, as my dad would say ironically, 'adequately well-off' – could now command five hundred bucks an hour without speaking a word. (In fact he had one patient, a successful artist, who paid him expressly to sit in silence while she made charcoal prints of her problems.) I never seriously thought of using my one, supreme 'contact' to establish myself in New York, although when he began to appear on network TV and in syndicated newspaper columns as 'Dr Rick', I began to wonder if I should abandon thoughts of ever going into practice myself and just launch a range of merchandise bearing the Aloisi name.[5] Richard now spoke in a voice remarkably like his father's – he had adopted the American accent, the way people adopted US citizenship –

[5] Perhaps not as far-fetched as it sounds. Oliver Sacks' books on psychology, including *The Man Who Mistook His Wife for a Hat* and *Awakenings*, gained him such a cult following that an unofficial Sacks merchandise catalogue was launched, featuring hats, spectacles and beard-trimmers. The company was closed down by a court order after making its founder, Harry J. Tiller, a small-business millionaire.

and it was becoming difficult to associate the slick face and voice on the small screen with my former playmate from a Cambridgeshire school with no famous alumni. Still, when Simon Stacy – who had a very competitive nature – attacked Richard for a self-satisfied appearance on CNN, I felt as moved to defend him as if he were a member of my family.

'I've known him since we were kids,' I said.

'He's from England too?' Simon asked incredulously.

'We grew up together.'

'Was he always a pansy?' Simon asked, draining his glass.

I couldn't be sure whether 'pansy' was a sexual insult – speaking like a Yank came slowly to me, although I watched as many movies as I could – but it hardly mattered. The days of Paulson's strange attack were long forgotten: Richard claimed hardly to remember the incident when I brought it up once. These days he was frequently photographed on the arms of New York's catwalk models; a different girl answered the phone each time I called.

And there in a nutshell was what made me begin to feel uneasy. As contact with Richard became more spasmodic, I realised that I had spent well over a decade relying on him for company and competition. Now that he was physically distant and professionally out of my reach, I had to redraw the map of my life and to decide what really interested *me*. The *Journal* was running a series of articles on the idea of the supernatural and I decided to write a human-angle story on the Witching people's idea of a curse. I wanted to convince myself, as much as anyone else, that between the esoterica of the psychiatric press and the celebrity sheen of the New York scene, there was a territory I could occupy, in which I might be able to help people see the explicable causes of inexplicable behaviour.

The idea for the Witching article posed itself in late 1977

when my Christmas visit home was extended to a month by the early-December death of Dad's brother, Tom. He died while staying with my parents and was buried in Witching because it was Dad who took charge of the organisation. Most people's first funerals serve as a reminder of mortality, but this was a particularly stark one: not just the age-beaten guests but the town itself seemed to be dying on its feet. The famous stain on the Green looked no bigger than the bruise left by a minor injection. The coffin containing the man who had taught me to stuff ping-pong balls in my mouth was carried by a quartet of haggard figures, each of whom looked as if he could easily have been the passenger himself; one of them, I realised with a chill, was Dad. My cousin Johnny, the stumpy-legged kid who had cried all night when he first spent Christmas at our house and was appeased only when I slid into bed with him, was an army corporal who took a last look at his father's eternal resting place with grim-faced military pride. As I was reflecting in this predictable way upon the ravages of time, my eye fell upon a simple stone commemorating MARY HIRST and, added later but dulling to the same shade, HER HUSBAND DAVID. There was none of the grandeur or tenderness of other graves – no DEARLY REMEMBERED or BELOVED – and, more importantly, no sign of the grave of their son Nicholas, the suicidal victim of the Witching curse.

'He's not buried here,' said someone right behind me.

I flinched as guiltily as a grave-robber and turned to look into the soft eyes of the increasingly unfamiliar singer in our bathroom. She seemed amused.

'Who?'

'Their son. That's who you're looking for, isn't it?' Mum looked up at me and I saw her thinking about how tall I was and, in her own way, about how time was passing.

'What makes you think that?' I objected, feebly.

'You were always interested in the strangest things,' she said, with weary affection. 'I'll never forget when you went out to the Green in the middle of the night with your dressing gown tucked into your trousers.' After a pause, she added: 'They don't bury suicides in the churchyard.'

If I didn't ask her now, I never would. 'How well did you know Nicholas?' I looked at the ground as I said it.

'I didn't know him,' Mum replied. 'I didn't move to Witching until he was dead. It was David I knew, the father.'

After each sentence there was a pause, and after the last, a very long one. The other mourners were all in the church hall, dutifully eating bad sandwiches; cousin Johnny would be answering questions about the army in cagey monosyllables. A spiteful wind disarranged my mother's fair-turning-to-grey hair; it seemed to blow through her without her noticing. It was graveyard weather, although any winter day in Witching delivered the same chill, straight from Siberia like an arrow across the North Sea and the flats of East Anglia.

'There was this rumour that Nicholas and Richard – the Hirst twins – argued over a woman, and Richard thought he was responsible for his brother's death,' Mum continued. 'So anyway Richard emigrated to Australia, he couldn't stand to stay around, and the father was left on his own with his two sons gone just like that, one the other side of the world, the other . . .' She shivered as if the cold had caught up with her all at once.

'And how did you know the father?' I asked, glancing down at HER HUSBAND DAVID.

'He used to come into the library. I'd just started working there and he was friendly, which not everyone was. I started going round and helping with cooking and cleaning,' Mum said. 'He was in a real state, you know.' Suddenly tired of the subject, she drew her coat tightly around her. 'Look at us, having hushed discussions at a funeral. Let's go inside.'

I followed her into the church hall where my dad was talking to his brother, Frank, the two of them alone on the earth for the first time. Mum had revealed more about the Hirst family in a five-minute conversation than I had ever gleaned from her before or would again. Later it would seem that I hadn't pushed her far enough; I learned when it was too late that some discussions can be deferred for ever, some topics never 'come up again eventually', however long you wait. The window slams shut and is sealed up permanently.

Still, the conversation – which, in its funereal setting and with my mother's reticence, had had the atmosphere of a TV detective movie – whetted my appetite for the forensic task of uncovering the facts behind the suicide of Nicholas Hirst, the lost soul who had been swept out of Witching's grave-yard. I suspected that the posthumous diagnosis of madness upon Nicholas, especially with the local supernaturalistic baggage, was impoverishing his memory and allowing the town to indulge its stuffy, old-fashioned claim to cursedness. My years on the magazine had taught me that 'madness' was a meaningless word. The twentieth century had shown that the whole world was mad; more detailed explanations had to be sought for the ways in which individuals fell apart. Almost as soon as Dad had driven a small party of selected relatives home from his brother's funeral and ushered them into the living-room where Bob Dylan growled quietly at them from the turntable, I began trying to find out everything I could about the Hirst tragedy.

It was a frustrating task. Though several locals recalled the family – David Hirst, his wife Mary who had died young, and their twin boys Richard and Nicholas – those who were old enough to remember thirty years back seemed able to retrieve memories of the family only in its complete, contented state, and were defensive when questions were asked about Nicholas's motives for suicide: any questioning of the witches'-curse theory was received like a slight to the town. Furthermore, the fact that Nicholas had killed himself in Cambridge, rather than Witching itself, meant that local people were vague about the very part of the Hirsts' story which interested me the most. Time, superstition and short-sightedness were conspiring to erode the footprints of Nicholas Hirst altogether.

But at least it was erosion, not yet deletion. From the recesses of aged memories I managed to salvage morsels of detail – Nicholas's brother Richard was a fine sportsman and all-rounder, the two were close but competitive – and from excavated local newspapers, school and university records I was able to glean more. Someone at the research lab where the twins had worked, in the early forties, was particularly helpful on the subject of their rumoured fight over a woman; sadly he hadn't known the girl concerned, nor had he kept in touch with Richard when he went to Australia: no one had, it seemed.

By the time I flew back to Michigan, I had amassed enough evidence to suggest that Nicholas, when he killed himself, was suffering from depression from identifiable causes. But the evidence was a jumble. So much was speculation or hearsay; the story was a pile of clippings, scribblings, conversations recorded or recalled. I didn't know how I could begin writing it up or why it would be of interest if I did.

Once more, inspiration came indirectly to me from Richard Aloisi. A feature of our conversations ever since his early days at Harvard had been his namechecking of famous psychiatrists and theorists past and present, who after my more practical course of study were no more familiar to me than foreign film stars. And so, still cherishing the hope of one day standing, if not shoulder-to-shoulder with Richard, then at least in the same room, I devoted long periods of my free time to speed-reading as much as I could of the canon. To do this I needed shortcuts, and I soon became dependent upon a series called *All You Need to Know about . . .* , which offered economical studies designed for ease of use. These guides were notable for their comprehensive indexes, which contained – in the most compressed form possible – a quick, bullet-pointed digest of all the information in the book. It soon dawned on me, as it has no doubt occurred to many students and other shortcut-seekers, that by looking up someone's index entry in their own biography, I could find a potted history of their whole life. In *All You Need to Know about Virginia Woolf*, for example – which I read because I had more than once been forced to feign familiarity with *To the Lighthouse* in discussions about Freud – I found:

Woolf, Virginia

- birth, 18
- appearance as a baby, 26
- childhood decision to be a writer, 29

And so on, through the formative experiences:

- sexual frigidity, 23, 37–9, 70
- experiences of madness in others, 51
- long-lasting psychological effects of:
    illness and death of father, 72
    death of brother, Thoby, 94

Until, inexorably:

- contemplates suicide, 220
- final letter to Leonard, 226
- death, 227

After following these rows of bullet points, I felt as moved as if I had conscientiously read the story they summarised. For all the complexity of lives, even the most remarkable could be distilled to a simple formula:

- born, 1
- achieves various things, 2–x
- dies, x+1

By looking them up in their own biographies, I became an apparent expert on the lives of Freud, Jung, Wittgenstein, Nietzsche, David Hume and (for a break) Walt Disney. Librarians would watch in sceptical amusement as I borrowed piles of *All You Need to Know about* books, ten at a time, and brought them back the next morning. Although the super-efficient précis of the bullet points left some scope for confusion (both Nietzsche and Disney had a 'believes he is God' entry, for example; fortunately only one could draw mice), its mapping out of cause and effect helped me to see that any story could be unravelled by stripping it down to a logical sequence of events. It was only a matter of time before I tried arranging what I knew of the Hirsts into bullet points and filling in the gaps to build up the story that Witching's unconscious pact of secrecy had always kept from me.

Hirst, David	Hirst, Richard (Jr)	Hirst, Nicholas
• born, 1904		
• desire to impress father		
• back injury		
• marriage to Mary		
• isolation from parents		
• moves to Witching, Cambridgeshire		
• wife expecting twins		
• painting/decorating job	• born, 1927	• born, 1927

• financial difficulties		• birthmark
• pressures of fatherhood		• suffers nightmares
• dislikes displays of emotion		
• Mary ill; hospitalised; dies, 1936	• death of mother, 1936	• death of mother, 1936
	• boys' absence from funeral	• distress
	• close relationship of brothers	
	• begins school	• begins school
• encourages spirit of competition between sons		
	• excellent pupil	
	• sporting successes	
		• victim of bullying
	• defends brother	
• takes on extra work		• skips school
• anger and frustration with Nicholas		
• excused from military service on health grounds	• made junior prefect at school	
	• youngest ever captain of school cricket team	
• pride	• frequent visits to rifle range, excellent marksman	• appears in school concert
• organises fishing trip for boys' 15th birthday		
		• no aptitude for sport, prefers music
	• scores 112 not out in junior county cricket match, watched by father	
		• feelings of inferiority towards Richard
• buys rifle for Richard to celebrate sporting success	• relationships with girls	

• financial constraints	• application to Oxford; offer of place to study sciences	
• guilt		
	• leaves school with excellent grades	• performs well in A Levels
• death of father		
• back pain; declines medical attention	• first year at Oxford	
• end of World War II		
		• concern at father's health
	• homesickness	• takes job in music shop, near Lincoln
• arranges 19th birthday celebrations for boys		
	• sexual indiscretion with married woman	• depression
		• meets girlfriend in Lincoln
• introduced to Nicholas's girlfriend		
	• confides in Nicholas	• visits brother at Oxford
	• settles down in second year	
		• dissatisfaction with job
• frustrated by physical infirmity		
	• graduates from Oxford	
	• takes research job in Cambridge	• relationship with girlfriend blossoms
	• creates job opportunity for Nicholas and finds flat to share	• takes job as lab assistant in Cambridge
		• shares flat with Richard in Newnham, Cambridge
• taken to football match for birthday		
• criticises temperament of Nicholas	• friendship with brother's girlfriend develops	• anxiety attack while driving car
	• promoted, works shorter hours	

	• plans Christmas at brothers' flat	
• at sons' for Christmas	• cooks Christmas dinner with Nicholas's girlfriend	• spends Christmas with brother, girlfriend and father
		• 27 December: plans to drive father back to Witching
• waits in car outside flat while Nicholas collects tools		• car problems; returns to flat for tools
		• suspicions aroused
		• enters Richard's room
	• panics, shields girl, pleads with intruder	
• hears gunshot and screaming		• seizes Richard's rifle and places in mouth

Though some of it was mere supposition, I found that this version of the story made sense. Where Witching tradition held that Nicholas had been 'not quite right' from the beginning, I was now able at least to guess what had taken place in his mind. I knew that David Hirst had been an awkward man, brought up in a highly competitive family; I surmised that he had passed this emotional repression on to one of his sons and transferred his instinct for competition to both of them. I could easily imagine how Nicholas had suffered the long-term effects of early bereavement; how in his developmental years he had felt himself undermined by Richard's constant successes; how Nicholas's birthmark had manifested itself as a psychological as well as physical blemish; how the combination of all these factors had brought Nicholas into the territory of psychosis.

At this point, the accepted version suggested that the unfortunate brother, under the gaze of the Witching spirits, 'lost his head' and blew his brains out; but the little-known detail supplied by my mother, of a woman who had caused a rift between the twins, suggested a final straw for Nicholas. It was the sight of his brother and best friend in bed with his one solace, rather than the invisible fingers of Witching's malevolent forces, that tightened his grip on the trigger. Nicholas, in other words, was a depressive, dependent individual finally felled by a sexual humiliation and fraternal betrayal. None of these elements was palatable to the audiences of the forties and fifties, but the story had a resonance for me – especially since by an odd coincidence the catalyst for Nicholas's collapse, his inspiration and his nemesis, was called Richard.

Although nobody could ever corroborate or deny my version of events – old David lay in Witching's churchyard, Richard was untraceable in Australia and the girlfriend had vanished many years ago – I felt that I had made a tiny contribution towards salvaging the memory of Nicholas. If I could publish my findings, perhaps posterity wouldn't catalogue him as a lunatic, but a victim; maybe in the future the same kind of reasoning might allow another potential Nicholas to be steered away from the path spelt out by his bullet points. And leaving all this idealism aside, it was something novel for the magazine. The Hirst bullet points were published in the April 1978 issue, with the briefest of commentaries detailing my thoughts on the case. It was the first article I had ever published without a single word being cut.

My miniature version of the Hirsts' story won some attention: it was reprinted in several places, including a New York-based journal where it caught the eye of Richard Aloisi, who called to congratulate me for 'putting our town on the map'. I even received a call from a British editor who took the story for fiction and wanted to put it in an anthology of avant-garde works compiled in memory of B. S. Johnson.[6] All this interest led me to make a regular feature out of bullet points. For each issue I would exhume a long-forgotten case and re-evaluate it by reducing its complications to the barest possible sequence of cause and effect. I showed that post-mortem verdicts of madness had often been used as a cover-up; that superstition and squeamishness (in particular with regard to the greatest of taboos, suicide) could lead to gross injustices. My mission was to restore dignity to lives which might otherwise have been written off as abortive exercises. For the first time I really felt that I might have something useful to say to the world.

All I needed now was to be treating my own patients, to graduate from defending the honour of the dead to saving the sanity of the living. In 1980, when I was thirty, a chance fell into my lap. Simon Stacy, my former colleague at the *Journal*, was working in the Lakelands Institute, a psychotherapeutic practice in Chicago. He called to let me know that a post had become available. Years of ambition flashed before me as he said that he'd recommended me for the job. I could hardly drive there quickly enough.

My parents were delighted, of course. I sent home photographs of my office, of our bland, brownstone building with the Stars and Stripes flying like a symbol of sanity outside, of the landmarks of Chicago and the towering

[6] B. S. Johnson, a British novelist, enjoyed brief fame for his anarchic novel-writing technique, most famously epitomised by *The Unfortunates*, a book published in the format of 27 loose sheets which the reader was invited to read in an order of his choosing. This 'book in a box' summarised Johnson's belief that the historical novel was now an archaic form: it achieved a limited cult status which still endures today. However, Johnson's other novels were underappreciated and, dogged by financial problems and self-doubt, he killed himself in 1973.

apartment block where I lived on the fifth floor. Sometimes, returning home from a day of grappling with the dangerous and deluded, I would fantasise that I could see somebody on top of the monstrous building, looking out desperately over the lights of the cold, vast city, and that any second I might be called upon to intervene, like the angel in *It's a Wonderful Life* (one of Dad's favourite films), using the weapons of common sense to deflect a tragedy from its course.

The idea of tragedy, despite Paulson's best efforts, had always left me cold: I disliked plays which seemed to have been written solely to demonstrate that the events they contained were inevitable, part of a plan carved into the firmament by whimsical gods. When I first saw *Romeo and Juliet*, as a nine-year-old, I was furious at having the story spoiled by the chorus's opening lamentations, and scowled at the chorus leader when I met him in the parking lot after the performance. I felt that something of the classical mentality – that tragedy reflected man's eternal, futile struggle against superior forces – still coloured the popular understanding of cause and effect. 'It wasn't meant to be'; 'it's in the lap of the gods'; 'it's not for us to know' . . . how often in Witching and the wider world had I heard these salutes to powerlessness? Although I never expected to change the world, I thought perhaps I could change the way a few people saw it.

The only thing I didn't send my parents was a copy of the Hirst article. I couldn't be sure what they would make of my efforts; I didn't want to make Mum think that I had taken advantage of her confidence, nor to give more credence to her conviction that I was forever sticking my nose into perverse areas of interest. I never forgot, though, that any success I might enjoy was as much theirs as mine. How easily, without Dad's encouragement, I might have re-enacted Nicholas's template of a mind pulled apart by comparison and competition. If just one of the bullet points in my father's life had been different, it could have changed ten of mine; and now I had the same responsibility to the people whose mental health lay in my hands. More than ever I believed that what mapped out people's lives wasn't chaos so much as a chaotic logic. It was possible to follow the system and anticipate some of the results; you just needed enough eyes to see all the dominoes and the people pushing them over.

I leave it to you to decide whether the theorising which launched my career amounts to anything in the real world. I hope at least I have convinced the reader that, whatever might have happened later, I started out with the intention of doing good.

3

Song for Whoever

INTERVIEWER: What are your songs about?

BOB DYLAN: Some of them are about five minutes, and some are about six.

When Dad, having ushered his brother's funeral guests into our house, sat in a corner on his own listening to Bob Dylan singing 'Romance in Durango', the scratchy sound rising insistently above the awkward nostalgic chatter and the still more awkward, tea-sipping pretences of normality, he was obeying the instinct of a lifetime. Many times since my early youth I had seen his hands fetch a record lovingly from its sleeve and lower the needle with the care of a surgeon. Sitting in meditative silence, sometimes tapping out the rhythm lightly on one knee but more often as still as a cat, he would shut out all distractions. Once, when my mother burst in because she thought she had heard a scream from next door, he made her wait for three minutes for one of Joni Mitchell's wailing choruses to finish repeating itself. And if interruption was unavoidable he would often restart the record from the beginning, even if it meant delaying paperwork by an hour. He was not a man to have music on 'in the background': if a record was playing he would listen to it as intently as he might listen to the tape of an interrogation. I never dared disturb him until I had reached the age where my concentration threshold matched his; then, from time to time I would take my homework into his study and sit quietly with him. By default, his musical tastes became mine.

It was unfortunate that my mother, having flirted with the stage lights in her youth, now had an aversion to pop music. At the age of nineteen, a promising singer and actress, she had won a prestigious talent contest with a rendition of 'Embraceable You' in a London club – the occasion of the photo now hanging in our bathroom – and was offered a paid, twice-weekly slot by the manager. Instead of becoming a stage icon, however, she became pregnant; the music industry turned its back, as did her family, who so disapproved that they disowned her. My parents never talked about how they had met, and in a way I was happier imagining the scene, in black and white: a smoky club, an entrancing singer on stage and – in the audience – my father, young, besotted. In any case, the repercussions of the romance were more down to earth: rather than the capital and its showbiz whirlwind, Mum ended up in my father's home town of Witching, where she became the local librarian, only getting near a microphone at five to five each day when she reminded readers that the building was about to close.

It was strange for me to think that by being conceived I had cut short her dreams. Sometimes I entertained it as another possible reason for Mum's frostiness towards me, though as I got older the idea that she would want to punish me for being born seemed less and less insightful. Still it was hard to meet the eyes of the young woman in the photograph without seeing in them a glimmer of reproach: for years I couldn't take a long bath because the effort of avoiding her stare was too tiring.

Sometimes I would overhear arguments which seemed to be caused by my dad's quirkily stubborn musical habits; more disturbingly, when I was thirteen, I heard my mother singing late at night over the wobbly notes of his untutored piano-playing. Padding across the landing, I perched on the treacherous third stair. The song came to a close and he took her into his arms; she pressed her face into his body. I went back to bed, chastened by the idea that my parents still had lives I only vaguely understood. The next morning at breakfast I was reprimanded for 'creeping about at night' and it was as hard as ever to imagine my mother as a singer, let alone a lover.

It was inevitable that music would retain a permanent, sentimental grip upon my affections. This survived my own dismal teenage attempts at songwriting (my lyrical models, even those at the tamer end of the scale such as 'I Want to Hold Your Hand', surpassed my own experience by too large a margin) and solidified in later life when I left home and had to start building my own record collection. Once past thirty, I felt I had reached the age where I was no longer eligible to follow the contemporary music scene, but had to wait for it to be filtered for me by younger friends; I did the same for Dad, coming home every Christmas with new records which I thought might meet with his approval. Scanning the folk-pop section of Chicago record stores (musical genres, at this point in the early eighties, were already beginning to bleed into one another, in preparation for the all-out schizophrenia that would follow) had brought me into contact with the name of Patsy DiMarco, a talented Illinois-based singer-songwriter beginning to enjoy nationwide exposure. Her first album, I saw from in-store publicity and from brief glances at the music magazine which I kept on my desk underneath psychiatric volumes, had won a spread of four-star reviews and comparisons with many of Dad's favourite artists. One morning during a lull between consultations, as I was toying with the idea of buying her album and taping it for Dad if it was good enough, she walked into my office.

Patsy's opening words – 'I'm having a few problems at home' – gave me the impression that she had come for relationship advice, something I was ill-qualified to offer. Fortunately, her case turned out to be at once more complex and (from my point of view) more manageable. She was married – like everyone over thirty, except me and the one other person I hoped eventually to track down. The lucky man in Patsy's life was Steven Rowlands, who, having signed her to his record label at one of her early concerts, soon managed to tie her to a more permanent kind of contract. As she gazed with charming interest around my featureless office, Patsy remarked that her recently released album had come to be seen as a chronicle of their fledgling relationship, and, by more romantic observers, as a kind of baby, the first fruits of their love. It was a fairy tale, however, to which reality had formulated a response – delivered, appropriately, by the postman.

DiMarco, Patsy	Rowlands, Steven	Ayer, Neil
• born	• born	• (childhood largely a
• learns guitar	• learning difficulties	mystery)
• rare talent		
• parents killed in accident when she is 13	• diagnosed dyslexic	
• suffers head injuries	• low self-esteem	
• makes recovery	• short-sighted	• (attends all-boys school)
• begins writing songs		
• wins local talent contest	• expectations of parents	
• learns how to use uncle's recording equipment	• love of music lessons:	• (drops out of school?)
	• piano	
• leaves school to become musician	• flute	

- favours pop rather than classical music
- works as backing and session musician
- works as roadie for various touring artists
- continues songwriting

- begins to play regular concerts

- talks with record companies; disappointment

- perseverance

- period of writer's block

- disillusion, considers quitting music business

- schedules new tour

- plays Dragon Club, Illinois

- meets Steven Rowlands
- signs for Kookaburra

- agrees terms for first album
- accepts romantic offer from Steven

- dates Steven

- oboe

- drums

- no aptitude for music

- pronounced a 'waste of effort' by father

- period of rebellion

- leaves home
- gets job at Kookaburra Music
- diligent worker

- promoted

- becomes talent scout
- annoyed by comments of fellow employees
- first signing, The Apples, break up after unsuccessful record
- pressures of work

- sees Patsy DiMarco at Dragon Club

- attracted to Patsy

- after deliberation, asks her out
- dates Patsy

- joins postal service

- sees Patsy in concert

- moves to Nelson, nr Chicago

• married	• married	
• buys house in Illinois	• buys house in Illinois	
		• first meets Patsy and Steven
• happily married	• happily married	
• highly productive period of songwriting	• insecurities	• conversations with Patsy
		• receives secret letters from Patsy
• records album	• happy with relationship	• writes to Patsy
• concerned by attentions of Neil Ayer		
• confides worries to Steven	• anger	• pays visits to Patsy
• album released	• fight with colleague in venue washrooms	
• warns Neil to stop visiting		
• headaches	• arguments with Patsy	
• protests innocence	• threats to Neil	
		• brings gift to Patsy
• panics, pleads with Neil		• mocks Steven
• watches, helpless	• fights with Neil	• fights with Steven
• meets Dr Kristal, through friend		

So now there were two men in Patsy's life, although only one by invitation. Somewhere along the mail round, Neil Ayer had developed not just an obsessive desire for Patsy's company, but the illusion that his love was reciprocated: an illusion fuelled by letters he claimed to have received from the star and hidden messages which he had found encrypted in her songs. Although in Patsy's account the two of them had never held a conversation on any subject other than the mail, Neil's fantasy quickly blossomed into an unsettling attachment. He had begun writing to her regularly and, to mark her birthday the previous week, had arrived with a bottle of perfume shaped like a woman and a novelty card almost as tall as Patsy herself. Steven was driven to fury by the sight of a gift more expensive than his own, and a small fight had broken out, which gave notice of the potential for more serious trouble. Steven was warming to the role of aggrieved husband; Neil, that of the romantic martyr. Patsy, becoming uncomfortable in the middle, had come to me for help.

'It's just that I've heard you're good,' said Patsy, winningly and perfectly on cue: I had been unconsciously inviting flattery by looking doubtful as she described her problem. 'A friend recommended you. She said you knew all about obsessions and delusions and that kind of thing. I thought you could maybe speak to Neil.'

'It sounds more like something for the police . . .' I began, continuing to play devil's advocate.

'I don't want the police involved,' Patsy replied swiftly. 'It's bad publicity, it'd make Steven more hyped up, and anyhow, nothing's really happened. It's all just kind of silly, but at the same time . . .' She passed me a note which Neil had written her and, as an aid to comprehension, the lyric sheet from her album.

Examining the letter, I saw the marks of obsession in the uncomfortable attention to detail: with its painfully scrupulous handwriting, even spacing, and identical letter heights, it could have been copied from a school blackboard. But, far from stifling the passion, the formality of Neil's presentation brought it into plain view.

Dearest Patsy
   I want you to know that I understand where you're coming from in your song 'Nothing Means Anything' and I'm sorry, I really am, that you had to go through this for me. I am working on a solution, all I need is a little time. I will get you

out of where you are and we will be able to start again with
everything you need. I want to tell you how much it meant to
get your letter, like all your letters. I hope mine gives you some
comfort. Things will get easier for us.

   Yours always
   Neil[7]

It was the idea that Neil was 'working on a solution' that Patsy found disturbing. Precisely what kind of a solution he had in mind, no one yet knew. It might be, as Patsy insisted, that he needed nothing more than a little professional help to purge him of his delusions and nudge him into a more productive channel of activity. The challenge was hard for me to resist, but that was only half the story: if I agreed to take on the task, would the postman consent to see me?

   'Well, he said he'd do anything for me,' said Patsy with a twinkling smile. 'But maybe you should meet my husband first.'

'The guy is just nuts, simple as that,' Steven Rowlands explained in our first meeting, which began with an awkward round of handshakes, during which he avoided eye-contact. On the sweaty hand which grasped mine, the nails had been chewed down to the cuticles. From the truculent comments with which he punctuated Patsy's fair-minded narration of events, it became clear that Steven saw me as a kind of pest control, employed to seek and destroy this threat to his peace and then to disappear. He was a relentlessly nervous man, quick-tempered but slow-moving with a large, childish mouth and eyes that narrowed each time I asked Patsy a

---

[7] The letter was elaborately signed, with a round flourish after the letter 'l' in which was drawn a cheerful face.

question which seemed to exclude him. The mere thought of Patsy in another man's company was intolerable to him: envy danced across his face when she mentioned that she had spoken to Neil to arrange our consultation. Other than this silent, scandalised commentary, Steven's only contribution to the meeting in their stylish living-room was to reiterate his diagnosis from time to time. 'The guy's a screwball,' he would say, gnawing moodily at his fingernails. 'He should be locked up.' The personal attack only sharpened my appetite for the first consultation with his counterpart.

I met Neil a few days later. I had perhaps imagined that he would view our meeting as an act of oppressive surveillance – I was well enough used to my regular patients edging away from me like prey from a predator – but for much of our lunch date he studied me with apparent amusement through cool, alert eyes, as if we were conducting an interview for a showbiz magazine rather than a preliminary assessment of his mental health. Several years younger than both Patsy and Steven, he was a far more relaxing conversational partner than Patsy's husband. But his assessment of their respective importance to Patsy's life was undoubtedly clouded by the *idée fixe* of his fictional love affair with the singer, and the resulting conviction that a jealous or uncomprehending world (its figurehead Steven) was persecuting him for his good fortune. There seemed no other way of approaching the matter than to win Neil's trust by humouring this conviction, at least for an introductory period. It was with this plan in mind that I passed him Patsy's lyric sheet and asked for his interpretation of some of her songs – an experiment I would later repeat on her husband.

The wild deviations in their efforts brought back memories of Paulson's Death of the Author lessons, in which we discussed the proposition that 'every reading is theoretically as valid as every other'. According to this school of thought there was no definitive reading of a text, not even by the person who wrote it. Even at the time I had found it an unsettling idea; much worse, though, if you were married to a songwriter and found someone else reading your love letters as his own.

A SELECTION OF PATSY DIMARCO'S SONG LYRICS

These lyrics are taken from the album Patsy *and appear by permission of Kookaburra Music. Interpretations by Steven Rowlands, her husband, and Neil Ayer, her postman and stalker.*

Patsy's lyric

Interpretations:

Steven

Neil

(1) *What I've Been Waiting for*

There's a hole in my life
   that's the shape of you
And the whole of my life
   has been a wait for you
Now the whole of the night's
   spent awake for you
Tell me loud and clear that
   you're
What I've been waiting for

Loneliness, in the end I
   confess, becomes a friend
I didn't want to free myself
From the pain of having no
   one else
Didn't want to know how
   good it could be
Just glad you forced your
   way through to me
There's a hole in my life,
   etc.

A reflection on the marriage. Patsy muses upon the defensiveness which she adopted to insulate herself against the pain and lack of love caused by the premature deaths of her parents; a defensiveness which was cut through by her meeting with, and subsequent marriage to, Steven.

Patsy's reaction to meeting Neil. The line 'the whole of my life has been a wait for you' may be a wry reference to his lateness in delivering the mail on that first morning. The rest is quite self-explanatory, dealing with the pact she made with Neil and his need to be persistent in 'forcing' her not to be content with a stifling marriage.

(2) *Something Bad Would Do You Good*

So concerned with being
   respectable
You can sometimes seem
   asexual

A frank look at the sexual politics between the newly wedded pair. Patsy, the artist, is

An explicit come-on to Neil, whose duties as a professional prevent him from displaying such

But to see you disarranged
Baby I'd like to make that
change
I know you wouldn't like
it babe
But something in you
would
The part of you that knows
That something bad would
do you good

perhaps not surprisingly painted as the more headstrong partner; but the passion on display comes as a shock – not least to the 'respectable' Steven, whose overall reaction to the lyric is one of self-conciousness.

passion to Patsy – hence the invite to 'make the change' from mailman to personal visitor . . .

(3) *Night and Day*

When you can't sleep at
night
And the streetlights seem
maliciously bright
Give the demons a chance
And they'll lead you in a
not-so-merry dance
Down the paths you didn't
tread
Past the things you should
have said
To the chances you have
wasted
The success you never tasted
Sometimes I can't be there
To scare those thoughts
away
But don't forget
It's never happened yet
That night didn't turn to
day

I know how it seems
When daylight comes to
rob you of your dreams
Like you're back at the start
Another day of troubles
clogging up your heart
And it feels like nothing
changes
But relief will come in stages

In this touching lyric, Patsy acknowledges the large part she has to play in boosting Steven's frail self-confidence. It was probably inspired by a separation of five days during which Patsy was away touring and Steven was left at home to take care of business. An attack of self-doubt during this period left Steven vulnerable to the pressure of his job, and resulted in a number of fraught late-night conversations with his wife. Patsy shows a deep awareness of the various insecurities haboured by Steven – who has never lost the feeling that he has something to prove, personally and professionally – and the message of support is both affectionate and powerfully optimistic.

Patsy here shows she understands Neil's torment as he waits helplessly, unable to express his love to Patsy except in their secret correspondence, and forced to face up alone to the unfulfilled life he continues to lead. Patsy reaches out to the lonely Neil, showing an acute awareness of his suffering and offering him solace: 'so soon' he will have the chance to experience this tenderness first-hand.

Don't let short-term
  worries blind you
So soon they'll be behind
  you
Sometimes I can't be there,
  etc.

(4) *Nothing Means Anything*

Sun didn't come up today
First time ever,
  weathermen said
It's just a little glitch, they
  say
Don't want us thinking
  the world is dead
Wish you could have seen it
Though there's nothing
  much to see
And nothing means
  anything to me

Saw a man on the news
  today
Learned to fly using only
  his arms
Cars flying down the
  interstate
Pigs and cows taking off
  from farms
But I don't want to fly
  right now
Don't care about being free
Nothing means anything
  to me.

Here Patsy gives us the other side of the story, focusing on her own feelings of loneliness without Steven. It probably refers to an occasion when Steven was forced to travel to Maryland to see a promising new act. While he was away, Patsy saw news items which could have provided inspiration for songs, but without the anchor of her husband, found it impossible to focus upon writing.

Patsy's testament to the loneliness she felt during an enforced period of separation from Neil. Though she initiated the split, for safety reasons, this lyric shows the insecurity she experienced with no way of knowing when she would next see Neil; an insecurity which for a short time rendered her incapable of taking an interest in the world.

Neil dissected Patsy's songs with remarkable assurance, one nicotine-stained hand tucked into a pocket while the other zipped up and down the familiar territory of the lyric sheet. The confidence with which he spoke was, although disturbing, also touching, like a child's description of an invisible friend. I almost found myself agreeing when he gave his breezy prognosis for Patsy's marriage: 'It's obvious she wants to get away from that dull guy, you know . . . it's just a matter of time before we make a new start.' But there was cause for real alarm: plenty of obsessive fans have stalked, kidnapped, even murdered their idols for the sake of a walk-on role in the lives they so eagerly watch.[8] Whilst there was little of the psychotic about Neil at first glance – he was no deranged fan playing records backwards for audio glimpses of his name – it was clear enough that he presented a threat to the marriage, even if only as catalyst for a dangerous overreaction by Steven or a trust-shattering argument. Neil's next letter was never far away, and according to Patsy they had been increasing in intensity. What started as a gentle one-way penfriendship was accelerating into a full-blown solo romance. The break-up was going to be painful for at least one of the interested parties.

Having arranged to meet Neil again in a week's time – and, again, on ostensibly casual terms – I drove home via KeyNotes record store (ahead of its time in its eccentric capitalisation) and defied the over-thirty rule by purchasing a

[8] Recently, for example, a married female tennis player was troubled by a stalker who changed his name to the name of her husband, forged ID papers with her husband's date and place of birth, and attempted to live under her roof, claiming that *he* was the real husband and the other man had stolen his identity. A survey of 1,000 American celebrities suggested that more than half had been put in danger by an obsessive fan, but the statistic is obviously questionable.

copy of Patsy's album. My route took me roughly in the direction of her house and, on an impulse perhaps triggered by her picture on the record sleeve, I decided to pay a visit. It was Steven, however, who met me on the doorstep. He was alone in the house and as uneasy as ever.

'I just thought I'd stop by to let you know I've been speaking to Neil,' I said.

'Well . . .' said Steven pensively, as if I had just made a difficult request; then his thoughts changed direction and he ushered me inside. 'I was going to call and ask you a favour,' he said, beginning to make coffee with the mechanical proficiency of a longtime addict. As we drank, Steven seemed to relax slightly – for the first time in my company – but he remained tight-lipped almost to the point of hostility. A couple of my attempts at small talk had sputtered out before he disclosed the nature of his request. He was about to go to New England on a three-day business trip, he explained, and Patsy had to stay behind, as she had a concert scheduled for Tuesday.

'Would you mind, uh . . . I'm not asking you to be . . . you know, like a bodyguard, but, uh . . .'

'You'd like me to keep an eye on Patsy?' I ventured.

'That's it,' Steven agreed, grateful as I was for an end to the guessing game. 'You know, I'm sure he won't . . . but I think she'd feel safer if . . . and I guess I would, too,' he finished, after a sentence of more pauses than words. I wondered how Steven ever managed to negotiate a deal.

Once I had accepted the assignment, he continued to warm to me, and we discussed his wife with an openness which had seemed unlikely. The reverent mumble with which he pronounced her name gave the first sign of a tenderness which emerged more and more as he expanded, with obvious gratitude, upon the theme of 'the love of his life': the one sure thing in a biography riddled with false starts and insecurities.

A clumsy, myopic and dyslexic child, Steven had struggled at school. He took up the guitar, hoping to claw back the confidence sapped by an impatient bully of a father, only to find (in a cruel parody of the traditional child-prodigy story) that music, the one thing that excited him, was also the one thing in which he was outstandingly inept. After abortive attempts to master out-of-tune instruments, he slunk into the music business by another, more accessible route – 'the back door' as he called it – finding work at Kookaburra Music. It was a job which suited him well, since he had acquired a good ear for quality from years of lonely musical evenings, holed up in his bedroom after parental tirades. Persistence had carried him gradually through the company ranks until he reached his current role as a talent scout. A large part of his professional responsibilities involved the unearthing of raw talents like the singer who had become his wife. 'Finding Patsy was the best thing that ever happened to me, in at least two ways,' he said.

But the run-up to her first release had put the heat on him again. As was always the case with an untried artist whom he had championed, his reputation hung in the balance, all the more so this time because of colleagues casting doubt upon his neutrality; one of these cynics made him so angry that he decked him in the men's room during a concert and left him bleeding into a washbasin. 'He yelled so much they had to throw him out of there for drowning out the band,' Steven said with guilty pride. When the album met with a stream of critical praise, Steven relaxed, only to have his peace ruptured by the news that his wife had made a besotted new 'friend'.

There was now enough of an understanding between us

for me to propose the lyrical criticism exercise which Neil had completed. After an uncertain warming-up period, Steven became lucid and even passionate on the subject of 'Night and Day' and 'Nothing Means Anything', the two songs in which Patsy reaches out to an absent loved one, in support and dejection respectively. As the summaries suggest, he was moved by what he justifiably saw as personal addresses to him, and identified incidents from the relationship's recent history as their 'inspiration'. Something about this flowery word, heavy in the hands of a man not given to discussion of the spiritual, rang a faint alarm, but Steven was into a groove now and began holding forth on his wife's work with escalating confidence. Where he came up against more abstruse language and slippery images, he tried to stamp a meaning on what he could of the lyric and sweep away everything else as details. 'Not too sure about these bits,' he would say, 'but the point of the song seems to be . . .'

And the point, in Steven's eyes, was quite straightforward. Patsy's album was indeed, to him, a chronicle of a young love affair. There was no room in those delicate poems for anyone else. It was difficult to blame him.

I tried some more general questions, mixing business with curiosity: how much he and Patsy discussed her writing, for example, and whether he had ever suggested a revision or supplied a rhyme for her.[9] This line of questioning pushed Steven into an abrupt mood-shift; his gaze lowered and he began shuffling the newspapers on the coffee table in an exaggeratedly absent manner. I understood that the personal

[9] Dorothy Wordsworth, the great poet's sister, is said to have supplied the rhyme 'vales and hills/daffodils'. See Joanna Culver, *Who Wrote That? 100 Masterpieces That Were Really the Work of Women* (Paper Fan Press, 1992).

revelations had taken a great effort and he was compensating for them with a renewed gruffness. It was time for me to leave.

I drove home not just with a clearer view of what Patsy responded to in this earnest, loving man, but also with a good idea of how slender a thread it was that supported his self-esteem. I was beginning to fear that Patsy's real husband was as much in need of psychiatric support as his usurper; and that bringing their territorial dispute to a bloodless end would be a nerve-wracking task.

That evening I settled down in front of the record player – exactly the same model as my father's, a Christmas gift from him to mark the beginning of my new life in America. This was my first chance to listen to the songs that had caused all the trouble. Patsy's album had been called many things in the music press, from 'a kaleidoscope of bruised, brilliant anthems' to 'a beguiling collection that's got no right to be as good as it is'. Perhaps because I had had a difficult day (having a toy fire engine thrown into my eye by an autistic patient and seeing Richard on TV given a round of applause for a joke I had told him years before), it had a quick, soothing effect upon me. The most impressive thing was the range of moods, all conveyed with equal force. In 'Something Bad Would Do You Good' Patsy was genuinely seductive: spiky vocals danced over a simple impertinent melody which lodged in my head for days to come. On 'Nothing Means Anything', and a similarly sombre track, 'Coping Well', she sounded vulnerable without adopting the doe-eyed mannerisms of less subtle female singers; the mood of sadness, evoked by a mournful slide guitar, hardly ever cloyed. But the record's real centrepiece was 'Night and Day', her song of support to Steven, appropriated by Neil and maybe many others. Lyrically it was one of her less original efforts, but with the demands removed from the listener's verbal ear, it packed an immediate emotional punch; I absorbed the impact, tiny hairs rising on the back of the neck, and thought of home.

The idea that the woman behind this sensuous voice was now a client of mine provoked a sudden stab of excitement. Who knew where it might lead? Perhaps she would record a duet with me and put it on her next album as a bonus track. Or she could dedicate a new song to me, called 'You Were There', or maybe just 'Peter' if she decided on a more personal tribute (the title would be down to her, of course). She might divulge that she was having creative difficulties – the second album is the toughest to write, I had heard – and enlist my help in penning new material. I would be nicknamed 'the singing shrink' and invited to appear on talk shows and documentaries about people who distinguish themselves in more than one field.

It took an effort to rouse myself from this spiral of imagination. The truth was that there was no failsafe way to measure the progress of Neil's obsession, and no way of knowing whether he would appear when Patsy was left alone. There aren't enough eyes in the world to provide a twenty-four-hour watch for everyone who ought to have one. Some things have to be left to the surveillance of the gods. I wasn't sure I trusted them.

It hadn't occurred to me on my previous visits, but in the quiet dusk of the following day Patsy and Steven's modern house seemed a promising site for a dedicated snooper. It was situated down a footpath off a leafy, isolated side street; there was any number of possible approaches and vantage points. As I snapped the car engine off, its jagged sound gave way to an unsettling calm which had me glancing around, as if Neil might leap from behind a telegraph pole to defend his stalking rights. A faint music, like birdsong, seemed to be emanating from the house; I hovered, unsure whether my imagination or my senses were supplying the data, and stood straining to catch the edges of notes as they drifted towards me. My finger wavered over the doorbell which, eventually pressed, rang loud and sharp like an alarm, making me jump – somehow I had expected something more harmonic – but the sound of the singing wavered no more than if it had been a record. Only after repeated rings, each one feeling more like an interruption, did the door swing open to reveal Patsy. Because one of her eyes was slightly lazy, I had a brief and troubling sensation that her welcoming, sheepish smile was directed at someone just behind me. Then her arms stretched out and took mine and we embraced like old friends.

There was a tactile generosity about her that contrasted with Steven's edginess. As she led me urgently to her studio, clutching my hand girlishly in hers, I grinned at the thought of what Steven would make of our apparent intimacy. The grin faded to a grimace of sympathy, one socially awkward man to another, as I imagined the two of them at a record launch or an awards party: Patsy a magnet for oily admirers, accepting their flattery with a sweetness easily mistaken for flirtation; Steven tongue-tied, toying with the edge of a tablecloth, waiting for it to end. There was no calculated charm about Patsy: the glimpses of slender breasts as she reached for and uncorked a bottle of wine, the appreciative glimmers as I made preliminary talk of no importance or insight, were born (I believed) of an appealing naivety about her own powers of attraction. Such ingenuousness, for all its charm, had obvious dangers. I wondered what mental treasures she had unwittingly left Neil in their early conversations, what routine but luminous affection he had translated into fireworks of passion exploding from her lyrics.

'I get into a little world of my own when I'm playing, it's like I'm a kid again,' she said, by way of a simultaneous apology for my long wait at the door and for the messy condition of her studio, where I was now sitting on a wooden stool as Patsy slid cosily into a beanbag. The windowless room looked like a museum of childhood, a transcript of the memory's record of youth. Though recording equipment and instruments dominated the studio, the few incongruous objects – a stuffed bear lying on top of an amplifier, a child's xylophone alongside its adult counterpart, a gaudily painted candle acting as a paperweight for a pile of songsheets – presented a goldmine for the psychiatrist, all the more when the gaze rested upon an enlarged photograph pinned in the bottom left corner of an otherwise gapingly empty notice-board. A pigtailed Patsy, eyes out of sync, smiled toothily from between the beaming faces of her parents. The picture was taken from close up, framing the heads alone, so that it was impossible to guess the setting.

Seeing me stare at the photo, Patsy smiled a softer, more knowledgeable version of the smile frozen on film. 'That's a couple years before they died,' she said. 'When I'm writing songs in here, it's just me and them. And, you know, a ouija board.' There was a half-second silence before Patsy burst out into a giggle. 'Only kidding.'

It was a timely joke, parodying her claims to artistic necromancy just at the point where they would make an outsider uneasy, but the shrine to her parents – killed in a car accident when she was thirteen – and to her curtailed childhood remained suggestive. What part did the loss of parents play in the formation of her psyche and to what extent was it still manifesting itself in her songs? Despite her tongue-in-cheek mysticism (and as time went by she produced more wry remarks to denude the various childish objects of any iconic significance), Patsy's songwriting environment strongly suggested some sort of psychic regression, and so did her methods: 'I get into a kind of trance,' she said, as if describing her journey to work. I waited for her to elaborate, but in vain; she looked surprised by her openness. 'That probably sounds like crap.'

Reassuring her that it didn't, I asked her about the writing of her recent album. The whole record had been put together in an amazingly short period, with the most productive sessions shepherding four, five, even six songs from the barest roots into a state of near-completion. 'I used to go in here for literally whole days,' Patsy recalled, indicating a small sofa-bed and, in a corner, an en suite shower room. It had clearly once been a regular bedroom and I found myself wondering whether one day it would house children of Patsy's. For the time being its function as a creative oasis seemed crucial to her productivity. 'Steven indulges me,' said Patsy affectionately, tugging at the sleeves of her blue and maroon sweater as if at the hand of her diffident husband. I suspected it would be truer to say that Steven accommodated her with a mixture of awe and incomprehension. The alchemy that turned feelings into song was a foreign craft to men like him, and like me.

'I don't really remember too much about how I did it, how I came up with things,' Patsy claimed when I quizzed her about these nights of intense inspiration. 'I just felt like a different person, or the same person but much younger, or something.' However seriously she took the idea – and it was harder to be sure the more we spoke – it sounded to me as if Patsy *was* in some sense transported during these rituals into some channel of frantic, almost hallucinatory, nervous energy in her brain.

As Patsy opened another bottle of wine (in spite of her

slight build, it seemed she could already drink like a rock star, and I began to feel embarrassingly light-headed) a clichéd observation swam into my mind: the peculiar kinship between her genius and – its traditional counterpoint – the insanity of Neil. Both visited fantasy worlds and brought back evidence: it was just that Patsy knew when the visit was over; Neil, on the other hand, was unable or unwilling to acknowledge the borders between the two regions. Without the benefit of an artistic vocation to coax people into joining his fantasy voyage, he was trying to force them on board. You could say that insanity is genius minus talent, I thought.

It was becoming clear, given the nebulousness of her writing methods, that Patsy herself would not be able to clamp meanings to her songs as readily as Steven and Neil had. She confirmed this when I asked about the roots of various lyrics, not for the first time using psychiatry as a cover for sheer nosiness. She was non-committal even as to the subject of 'Night and Day', the song her husband treasured.

'I wouldn't say it was "about" Steven as such,' she said. 'I mean, it is, in the sense that it's probably a response to something he was making me feel – I guess almost all of the songs are, in that sense – but I don't remember being inspired by specific things. They're not really about anything. They're just songs.'

I wished both Neil and Steven could have heard this, then quickly recanted the wish. Steven, the dogged supporter, would have found it hard to swallow; and Neil's convictions were too far entrenched to be shaken by something as trivial as the songwriter's own testimony. He could always claim, like Paulson's literary critics, to have decoded meanings hidden from Patsy's conscious will. For that matter, of course, it was possible at this stage that Patsy was withholding something from me – even (though I could not bring myself to believe it) that she *had* been corresponding with Neil. When, for the sake of openness, I half-jokingly acknowledged this possibility, Patsy's face lit up in amusement. 'That'd be funny, wouldn't it! If it turns out the reason he thinks I'm encouraging him is because I am!' White teeth peeped through briefly as her lips curled into a laugh. It wasn't the hollow laughter of a whodunit suspect trying to ridicule the charge, but an easy chuckle like a running stream. I laughed along, wondering all the same if the joke might turn sour before too long. She was too serene, Neil too confident, Steven too fraught. Rather than being Patsy and Steven versus Neil, it seemed to me as if all three were running on different courses, occasionally grazing each other on the way past, sending up sparks to warn of greater collisions to come.

Given the nature of a job which had accustomed me to listening far more than talking, it was a novelty to find myself wishing Patsy would say more. A lot of my patients had, in truth, less to them than met the eye: however hard they strained towards quirkiness or inscrutability, the basic normality of their motives and actions would keep peeking through the patina of craziness. Patsy, on the other hand, gave what seemed a genuine glimpse of the 'hidden depths' so many people tried to signpost; or if not hidden, then at least inaccessible to the general public. I was hungry by now to make the most of my commission to keep an eye on her, and when she dropped half a hint about the Chicago show the following night, I offered to be there. The prospect of seeing and hearing her, without the two men whose competing claims to her love were causing so much tension, occupied my thoughts for the whole of the next day: when Simon Stacy gave me a tape of a consultation to listen to, I found myself putting her album on instead, and had a difficult time bluffing my way through the subsequent meeting.

When I arrived at the club, a smallish knot of early arrivals was half listening to the opening act, an ageing country band dressed in checked shirts and sporting enormous beards. Throughout their slot a mixed crowd assembled, cool young regulars and (to my relief) people of my own generation filtering into the cellar-like room. With minutes to go before Patsy's scheduled start, I caught sight of a figure standing so close to the stage that he could have stretched up and played a few notes on the waiting piano; chain-smoking and running his fingers through hair too short to make it worth the effort, he looked like a café extra from a French movie. I don't know why I was surprised to see Neil – statistically there was no person more likely to attend a Patsy performance – but the sight of him unnerved me. The tension I felt for my new friend as she must have sat backstage, listening to the throb of the crowd, sent a current from my stomach down into my legs. Although it became harder to keep Neil in view as the audience thickened, the cigarette light gave me occasional flicker-glimpses of his face, which was aglow not so much with excitement or reverence as with pride. If Steven had entered at that moment, with his awkward hunch and his habitual look of a man about to be hit from behind, few would have guessed correctly which man was the husband and which the pretender.

If Patsy was conscious of Neil, she was too polished a performer to betray any emotion other than those framed by her songs. Whether sitting demurely at the piano, as she did after walking undemonstratively on stage to thunderous applause and whooping, or singing down into the upturned, thirsty faces, her every movement exhibited a star quality which instantly dissipated my anxieties. Later she would tell me that she had been scared for most of the evening –

especially when playing the slow, quiet songs in which her vocal muscles trembled like harp strings – but that certainly never came across. Hearing her live after listening to her record was like visiting a mountain range after seeing it on a postcard, and I couldn't help thinking how much Dad would have enjoyed himself. At the time I was always planning to take him to see Joni Mitchell on one of her irregular tours, but a convenient date never came until several years later, and by the time I organised things he was about to die.

I could feel Patsy lulling my mind into a blurry hinterland where thoughts surfaced and fizzed away unpredictably. The simple words '*The paths you didn't tread / The things you never said / The chances you have wasted / Success you never tasted*' provoked a strange tightness in my chest, as if my heart were being simultaneously pummelled and caressed; I felt as sure that Patsy was singing straight to me as if we had been alone in the room. And at the very moment this thought occurred, her head turned and our eyes met and stuck in an electric gaze which she held for five, ten seconds, and longer. She filled my field of vision completely, as if framed in extreme close-up; then the lens swung round and Neil crept into the shot. Unlikely tears were trickling down his face and he was mouthing the words back to her, or at her; and when the song ended, he stood still as a statue, head tilted up at the stage with a supplicant's gratitude. In a confusing moment I felt bonded to him, and at the same time even more isolated as I became aware of the intense solipsism of our reactions to the song. For each of us, it had been a secret dialogue with Patsy, just as everyone walking around at night can see the stars following him personally.

Searching the faces of other audience members, I could see how many were also gripped by the illusion, however thin and short-lived, of a personal pact with Patsy. If I – a virtual stranger – could buy into it myself so easily, it must be even easier for Steven to hear his search for self-esteem evoked in every song, and for Neil to read each word of 'Something Bad Would Do You Good' as an incitement to adultery. The difference, of course, was Neil's compulsion to move from fantasy into action; but all the same, as Patsy closed her set with a racy crowd-pleasing song called 'I'll Count You In', I thought about the gulf so often eagerly drawn between normal and delusional mindsets; at moments like this it seemed more like a stream, so narrow it could be crossed by a single excited footstep.

As the crowd belched out of the narrow doors past a bulky, obstreperous doorman whose cries of 'oneaddatime, oneaddatime' drowned out all post-concert reflections, I slipped around the back of the venue towards the dressing rooms which were unguarded. Somewhere Neil would be lurking, ready to approach Patsy; I wished that the burly official could be employed here instead. The whole area was ominously quiet: a couple of tour vehicles stood empty, waiting to receive Patsy's equipment and small entourage, but nobody was visible. Of course it was likely that members of this entourage were now with Patsy and that all was well. Still, with Neil's whereabouts unknown, Steven's disapproving face loomed into my head, frozen in its characteristic expression of suspicion and what I now believed was a quiet pleading for companionship. When the door yielded worryingly easily, I found myself in a tight, dim corridor which must have led back into the main venue. There were doors to the left and right; Patsy was behind one of them. As I wondered which, a woman's scream pierced the hallway.

With my stomach lurching in every direction at once, I reached the left-hand door as another, smaller, more pathetic scream backed up the first. I pushed it, to no effect; almost pulled the handle off before calming myself enough to turn it. The door swung open and a bizarre sight presented itself to my fearful eyes: three women, in various but advanced stages of undress, were sprawled in a row on the floor, each partly smothered by the lumbering figure of a brawny man. As two of the men's heads snapped up from the women to the doorway, I recognised the country band who had been on before Patsy. The drummer had his head between the legs of the thinnest girl and it was from her that the screams had come; in the thick silence that fell as I realised my error, she continued to make small noises somewhere between giggles and sobs.

'What the fuck . . . ?' began the bass player, but I was already backing away, hot with stupidity, incredulous that I had mistaken the noise of a backstage tryst for the cries of a victim. Perhaps these women *were* victims in their own way, but they seemed more than happy with their fate. Whilst the sight had nauseated me I had also – to my distaste – found it faintly arousing. Retreating straight away out of the door and into clean air, I ran headlong into Neil. We looked at each other with mutual guilt, two trespassers.

I could break the silence only with the obvious remark about the show. 'Yeah, she was OK tonight,' Neil agreed in an offhand way, staking an implicit claim to superior know-ledge, like a connoisseur dismissing a very good wine.

'Are you here to speak to her?' I asked, attempting an unthreatening tone.

'Maybe,' he said, thoughtful rather than evasive. 'I'm not sure if it's the best thing. She likes to just get away as quickly as possible after a show, so we often don't meet. But she finds it so frustrating just having to keep it all in when *he*'s around.' Neil, like Steven, did not dignify his rival with a name.

'Keep it in . . .?'

'Yeah.' Neil studied my face, as Steven had done, to assess its trustworthiness. 'I mean she kind of releases it when she's singing, but it's so temporary and then it's gone, and the best we can do is just send little notes and things. She has to push all these feelings for me under the surface.'

Challenging a patient's delusions head-on is as dangerous as shaking a sleepwalker, but maintaining the illusion can be even more dangerous: a boy in Witching had once broken both legs because his superstitious mother allowed him to sleepwalk out of a window rather than wake him. I decided to experiment.

'Patsy doesn't send you little notes,' I said. 'She doesn't want you to keep writing. She doesn't love you.'

'You don't believe me?' He reached into his jacket pocket, bringing out a neatly folded piece of paper. Having handed it to me and closed my fingers over it with theatrical care, as if handling a priceless relic, he watched my changing face. It contained the lyrics for 'Night And Day', in what I felt sure was Patsy's own handwriting. A closer look at the writing, which was smudged here and there and amended with crossings-out in other places, left me certain that it was a genuine original: it must once have nestled in the pile of songsheets which Patsy kept in her studio. I was dumb-founded. Neil grinned to acknowledge the shifting of power in the conversation.

'Where did you get this?'

'I told you, she sends them to me. Even the mailman gets mail,' he quipped with a dry laugh, holding out his hand to take the paper back.

My mind was spinning and I allowed instinct to steer me to my next move. 'Patsy said she wants this back,' I heard myself say, pressing the paper to my chest as he stretched out

63

for it. His face immediately screwed up in incredulity and he was about to refuse when I continued: 'She asked me to make sure you're looking after it.'

Each second now was heavy with tension as Neil assessed my face. I knew my ruse was a thin one, and had already begun to plan the next gambit, but to my relief he nodded.

'OK. Patsy seems to like you, so . . . OK. It's probably easier for you to give it to her than for me,' he decided, favouring me with almost a conspiratorial smile. The obvious irony, that Patsy and I had any kind of relationship only because Neil was seen as a threat to her, did not seem to trouble him.

'Tell her not to write back until it's safe,' he ordered me, watching approvingly as I pocketed the sheet with deliberate respect. 'And if she'd like to return the song to me, get her to leave it in the box as usual. I'll stop by early in the morning.' Before I had a chance to register these last words he was gone, and when I made my way back to the front of the building, he had evaporated into the city crowds as they swarmed noisily in and out of nightspots.

Curiosity almost killed the car on the way home as I glanced down again and again at the faded words of Patsy's song. All I had ever seen of her handwriting was a short note on which she gave me her address and phone number, and it was trying to fish this scrap of paper out of the depths of a crowded pocket that nearly made me swerve into a tree. When I found it and laid it beside the songsheet, one on each knee (the car by now stationary), any doubts were removed: if this was not the work of Patsy herself, then Neil was an international-class forger.

If, however, the songsheet was no forgery but a unique and valuable item, how had he laid hands upon it? All of a sudden Neil had ascended beyond the fan's realm and staked a genuine claim to be the subject of the song: the lyric sheet was, indeed, like a personal letter. Hard to believe, perhaps, but harder still to see how he could have obtained it if not from Patsy. A break-in, accomplished with no disturbance? Or could Patsy have somehow given Neil the songsheet without remembering? This was almost impossible to imagine, since the song was one of her most recent, part of the batch that Patsy came up with in her secluded studio sessions. In light of the harmless-looking piece of paper which sat on my passenger seat, Patsy's claim never to have encouraged Neil was unsustainable. Questions were crowding into my head, nestling uneasily with fragments of music. The next night, I went looking for answers.

Steven was just back from New England and his welcome was thick-edged with reluctance; indeed, when he offered me a drink it was in such a resigned tone that I hadn't the heart to accept. Although his desire to be alone with Patsy was only natural, his coolness irritated me after my attempts (however clumsy) at protecting his wife. His bear-like arm was draped proprietorily around her and, when I complimented her on her performance, his wry smile of reflected triumph wormed in under the skin of my professionalism. I would prefer to report that shaking this cocoon of domestic contentment was not my primary motive – at that time I still regarded my own lack of a partner as a temporary situation – but, whatever the reason, I found myself mentioning my conversation with Neil with undue relish. As Steven began to ask me why I had 'given that freak the time of day', I replied briskly, 'Well, he gave *me* something in return,' and handed over the songsheet. At the sight of it, their faces froze, a tableau of astonishment.

Patsy's large eyes tightened as if the sheet were a slander against her. Steven's stare interrogated both of us. I added helpfully: 'He said something about getting it from the box.'

The change which these words wrought upon Patsy's face was something I will never forget. Instantly losing the cloud of indignation, it became the face of someone painstakingly retrieving the details of a dream, and in the process finding herself uncertain where the dream yielded to genuine recollections. It seemed as if we were there for hours, Patsy frowning in concentration at a fixed spot on the coffee table and muttering to herself. As the clock ticked on accusingly, Steven and I looked on in helplessness, too aware of each other's presence, Steven's gaze not knowing whom to accuse and his arm uncertainly loosening around Patsy's shoulder. The odd non-conversation hung so stiflingly in the air that I began to wonder whether I should leave. The hint of a plea in Steven's eyes held me to the spot; that and, of course, raw curiosity.

At length – although it had perhaps been only two or three hour-long minutes – Patsy looked up with a new, artless vulnerability.

'OK, this is going to sound weird but I may have, kind of, given it to him.'

'What?' we chorused. Steven's mouth hung open but no more words emerged.

'Not deliberately, I don't mean deliberately,' Patsy went on. 'Maybe I'm wrong about this, I . . .'

'I don't want to hear this bullshit!' Steven suddenly exclaimed. Rising heavily to his feet, he brushed away his wife's restraining hand and rounded on her with a new, frenzied eloquence. 'How long have you been playing games behind my back?' he demanded. 'Do you really hate me that much? Why couldn't you have just told me right away, if you do?' Having finally tapped a vein of articulacy, Steven was relishing the performance; the emotional backlash was carrying him from one extreme to the other. Patsy, writhing in her seat, looked desperately to me to break his momentum.

'Steven, let her talk,' I commanded. Surprise was on my side and he was momentarily stalled. Having ushered Patsy back into the conversation, I waited for her to salvage herself. Steven looked at me like a traitor, but the wavering voice of his wife soon won his attention back. He was still in love, but it was a hungry love; I hoped that her explanation would satisfy him.

'I never thought about this before, but I used to always write things when I was a kid, you know, poems and stories and just . . . things, like everyone does,' she began haltingly, waiting in vain for a nod from the dyslexic husband and maladroit psychiatrist. She explained that her father – a publisher, whose bespectacled face I remembered from the photo in the studio – had the habit of saying 'I'd like to take a look at that when it's done' whenever he saw his daughter at work. In consequence, Patsy never considered anything to be the finished article until it had gone under her father's scrutiny; and when she began to write her first songs, at the age of eight or nine, these were duly submitted for his approval. Since she often worked on past her bedtime, it became her routine to creep out when she believed her parents were asleep and slip her work into the mail cage on the inside of the front door, where it would be found in the morning: a childishly idiosyncratic procedure which solidified over time into a formal arrangement. 'From eight or nine years old, I would put a copy of every song I wrote in the cage,' Patsy recalled, her face retracing the steps. 'Of course, they were usually still awake. They'd hear me creep to the door and back again. But it was all part of the game. Then . . .'

Then had come the motor accident which slashed

through her happy childhood: a head-on collision between her father's car and a heavy goods vehicle which, as well as leaving her an orphan, inflicted severe head injuries. Although eventually she made what was described as a full recovery, it was never clear how much her memory had been affected; her recollections of early life had always been patchy. No one could say for sure whether this was caused directly by her head injuries, by a repression of memories linked to her loss, by an unwillingness to cooperate with therapists, or (as seemed likely) by a combination of all these things. In any case, whether by an act of will or as a result of her head wounds, the memory of the mailbox routine remained buried somewhere in what Graham Rice calls the 'mental recycle bin',[10] a pool of memory still technically alive but inaccessible in everyday life. The problem was that Patsy's life had taken to making occasional forays outside the everyday.

Those trance-like phases into which Patsy lured herself in the writing of the album seemed to have begun the process of 'de-repressing' these memories, somehow loosening them so that they floated back, half formed, into her consciousness. The retreat into her psychic past which was such a part of her working method had also left her susceptible to involuntary reminiscences. (Patsy's eyes were still averted from Steven as I ran mentally through these explanations.) 'And then one time Neil said the same thing about my songs when we were just talking outside. I'd like to take a look at some of your songs, he said, and . . .' Some smothered impulse had awoken, surfacing

[10] Graham Rice, *Virtual Neurology* (Romany, 1994), a lively look at the analogies between human and artificial intelligence, which compares the brain to a computer with highly readable (if sometimes fanciful) results. His conception of the damaged mind as a 'faulty hard disk' is persuasive, though his series of jokes relating to 'floppy' and 'hard' states is unfortunate.

in the early hours of a songwriting morning when, as if sleepwalking, she went out to the mailbox (this one was at the end of the drive, rather than inside the front door, but it didn't seem to matter) and deposited a copy of the song she had just been writing, 'Night and Day'. 'I swear I never remembered doing it until just now,' Patsy said. 'It's like I was hypnotised and when you mentioned the box, it all came back . . . I guess I might have left copies of . . . of all the songs, but I didn't remember it, or I would have stopped, of course I would . . .'

Her voice now scratchy with defensiveness, she fell back into a volatile present, her eyes moving searchingly between us as she angled for reassurance.

'It's quite possible that memories can be de-repressed in certain circumstances,' I said uncertainly, hoping to ride through on a tide of terminology.

'I'm going to make coffee,' said Steven.

'You see, temporal-lobe seizures . . .' I persisted.

'Honestly, Steven . . .' Patsy began, but honesty was not the issue; her sentence faded away.

'Just give me a minute,' Steven quietly said. He stood up, shook his head gently and went out to the kitchen.

I was left to study Patsy in confused fascination. She was staring glassily ahead as a few tears snaked down her face; her hands were trembling. I coiled an arm around her and squeezed her shoulder ineffectually. She seemed not to notice and I withdrew it again before Steven could come back.

I felt sorry for her, of course, but was her bizarre story an effort of memory or imagination? The tale fitted perfectly with the shroud of mystery surrounding her art, and this raised questions. I had myself seen how consummate a performer Patsy was, how comfortably she could take on a persona on stage and discard it again afterwards. Was it plausible that she could have

- carried out this mailbox routine in childhood,
- only to forget doing so, after a car accident,
- then re-enact it in later life, under conditions of subconscious exertion,
- and then forget it again as the night faded?

There was no option but to give her the benefit of the considerable doubt; any other conclusion and I might as well make way for a marriage counsellor. Trusting to instinct, I was willing to believe that the legacy of her head injuries was a series of occasional and mild temporal-lobe seizures – the term with which I had attempted to silence Steven – during which she became what Dr Oliver Sacks describes as 'incontinently nostalgic':

> We surmise that our patient (like everybody) is stacked
> with an almost infinite number of 'dormant' memory-
> traces, some of which can be reactivated under special
> conditions, especially conditions of overwhelming
> excitement. Such traces, we conceive . . . are indelibly
> etched in the nervous system, and may persist
> indefinitely in a state of abeyance.[11]

Over the next night – having left a calmer Steven and a hesitantly defiant Patsy to reach a truce – I studied a mass of material on the subject of temporal-lobe seizures (most of it in index form). There was no doubt that Patsy satisfied the terms: the head injury, the lifestyle, the buoyant imagination all

---

[11] Dr Oliver Sacks, in a letter to the *Lancet* published June 1970, dealing with the effects of L-Dopa on post-encephalitic patients. The letter is reprinted in *The Man Who Mistook His Wife for a Hat* (Picador, 1985).

conspired to drill small holes in the mental screens that separated past from present, allowing occasional leakage in each direction. The old pair, genius and madness, were close enough to trade places and don each other's costume in her mind. Given how little I was looking forward to explaining this to Steven, it was a relief to find that he seemed to have reached the same conclusion when I returned the following day.

'I overreacted yesterday,' Steven confessed. 'It's just a hard thing to, uh, figure out.'

There were no signs of a leftover hostility. Steven, it seemed, was already on the way to toughening himself enough to grapple with the perennial uncertainties of the non-creative partner. For the sake of love he could endure Patsy's unconscious come-ons to an admirer, and resign himself to the knowledge that the weight of her past would continue to unbalance her behaviour in unpredictable ways. There was only one thing that really troubled him, as he confided to me while his wife was out of the room. 'You know, it's kind of petty, and I know the songs are just songs and whatever,' he muttered, weary with the subject even as he introduced it. 'But certain songs . . . the thought that they could have been written with *him* in mind . . .'

Though I reassured him that her reaction to Neil was sheer chance, his phrase triggering the memory, it was easy to see that in Steven's mind, the lyrics he had cherished as his own would always be tinted a strange colour. The realisation that no song could be claimed as his with any certainty was a more personal version of the truth of Paulson's Death of the Author – that no attempt at defining meanings could be sure to succeed. For a man so dependent on the acknowledgement of others, a man who had clung to the lyrics of 'Night and Day' like a legal confirmation of his supreme importance to Patsy's life, it was a painful pill to take. Common sense suggested, however, that there was still plenty for Steven to be proud of. 'It doesn't matter if she had you in mind as she was actually writing,' I told him. 'She couldn't have done it without you.'

Steven met this statement with a broad smile, perhaps his first in any of our conversations, and said, 'Thank you, Dr Kristal.' I had told him what he wanted to hear: a shrink's surest weapon. On the way home, I asked myself whether it was true, and realised I had no idea.

There was still the problem of Neil, and what should be done with him now that his delusions had been shown to be so grounded. It was my idea to play by his own rules and terminate the relationship in the same way that it had been conceived. Nervous of provoking Steven, I nonetheless proposed that Patsy should write a song aimed at Neil. 'Distance Makes the Difference' was written in their living-room by a collaborative team which would never be assembled again: Patsy, on the sofa with a notebook on her lap; Steven beside her, initially mute but later animated; and myself, overseeing the effort like a producer. It was a more prosaic method than Patsy had used before – instead of trance and flashback there were earnest editorial discussions between two men with no creative inclinations, and frequent visits to a rhyming dictionary – but everyone was happy enough with the result:

It's no fault of yours and it's no fault of mine
It's just one of those cases of wrong place and time
I think we know the truth, whatever we pretend
Distance makes the difference between a lover and a friend.

I don't want you to write, don't want you to call
That's not to say I don't want you at all
I just need space to breathe, give the bruises time to mend
Distance makes the difference between a lover and a friend.

This was a compromise: Steven's suggestion for the first line – 'Get out of my life, you're heading for a fall' – was adjudged to be too aggressive, and his idea of a third verse alluding to the postal service was rejected on artistic grounds. But my own contribution, 'give the bruises time to mend', survived the negotiations, and I felt like a genius as Patsy's handwriting sealed its immortality.

Patsy placed the custom-written work in the mailbox and it was duly removed; then the wait began. Days, weeks elapsed, fan mail and bills still arrived; but there was nothing from Neil. Relations between Patsy and Steven eased a little each day that he remained silent, until they were as relaxed as they had been before the stalking drama began to unfold.

When she was commissioned to write a one-off contribution to a charity album, Patsy again took the opportunity to widen the distance between her virtual lover and herself. Adapting a familiar Beatles riff, she came up with a song called 'We Can't Work It Out', the lyric reading like a relationship's post-mortem:

> You're not the one I need
> Much as you'd like to be
> You've too much sympathy
> I need an enemy
> You're so thoughtful, wrapping cotton round my precious
>   dreams and hopes
> But what I need's a sparring partner to knock down on the ropes
> Time to admit what we may have thought before
> We can't work it out any more

Three weeks after that record's release, Patsy received a long letter from Neil, sent from California, where he was 'beginning again'. He wrote that Patsy's decision had hurt him but 'maybe it was for the best', even going so far as to say that he had 'thought the same way himself' on occasion. Thanking her for her honesty, he remarked that he was glad the affair was ending with dignity, asked her to stay in touch and undertook to guard the 'little secret' with great care. It was a model break-up letter; nobody would have believed it was effectively a work of fiction. It seemed, as I had hoped, that the play-acted split had offered him the sort of closure which more abrupt action might have ruled out. For the first time Patsy was able to show Steven the letter with a light conscience. Steven read it expressionlessly and then screwed it up with a contemptuous smile. Patsy seemed to consider stopping Steven before allowing him to consign it to the trash with his last words on the matter: 'The guy's a screwball. He'll be locked away sooner or later.'

A postscript was supplied months later by the psychotherapist who treated Neil in California. 'Neil's claiming now that he is a homosexual,' he informed me. 'It doesn't seem logical, but he's very insistent.' We agreed that this was probably a red herring, but privately, with the dust now settled on a satisfyingly strange episode, I wondered. Could Neil have been overcompensating for a sexuality that he wanted to deny? Perhaps that explained the detached nature of his romantic campaign, the way he kept his distance so respectfully and slunk away so readily when given the imaginary elbow – almost as if he had always intended the fantasy to remain a fantasy, one in which the classic role of frustrated romantic could conceal his true (and guilty) sexual impulses. Pondering the question as I listened to 'We Can't Work It Out' on the otherwise appalling charity record, I also found myself wondering what Steven made of this latest lyric. Did he relax at what seemed a final affirmation of Neil's departure from the scene, or did he read into it the more ominous prediction that he himself would need to become more of a 'sparring partner' to survive the emotional skirmishes of a relationship?

These questions were theirs, not mine, to pursue. But before passing out of Patsy and Steven's life I did enjoy a moment of glory. Invited on to a show called *I Survived* (on which celebrities revealed details of hardships they had overcome, and won money for charity in proportion to the sympathy the audience felt for them), Patsy, as well as playing 'We Can't Work It Out', gave the first ever public rendition of 'Distance Makes the Difference' and credited me as her co-songwriter.

The specious idea of a Lennon/McCartney-esque meeting of minds between the singer and her therapist caught the public imagination. For a short period I found myself cropping up in the newspapers and music press, sending home new clippings almost every day; in one article, which Dad took with him everywhere and reread for the thousandth time two hours before he died, a Yale musicologist gave 'Distance Makes the Difference' eight marks out of ten (only one behind 'Hey Jude'). I even had an offer of a recording contract, although this turned out to be a practical joke by Richard Aloisi. If not an overnight celebrity, I had at least become a talking point.

Nobody knew the case's low points, however: how I had struggled to establish the truth and would never be a hundred per cent sure I had succeeded; or how I had found myself sympathising with the villain of the story and fostering a subtle antagonism towards the happy marriage; or how I had walked in on an orgy in a blundered piece of body-guarding and felt guiltily excited. All people heard was that I had saved Patsy's real relationship and killed a phantom one – how exactly, they never found out, as until now the details have been kept secret. And while I would have liked the emphasis to fall more heavily on the professional aspects of the case – in an ideal world unscrambling the puzzle of Patsy's neurological history should have won me more credit than rhyming 'mend' with 'friend' – acquiring a reputation among performers set up some of the seminal cases of my career. Meanwhile the pride-by-association continued as Patsy's career flourished.

When her third album won a major critical award, I mounted my personally signed copy in the office. I would laugh when patients asked if my name was concealed in the lyrics. Nobody knew that I had bought another copy of the album, on the day of its release, and played it backwards – just in case.

4

About Time

'It is improper for a psychiatrist to attempt to exercise power outside his recognised capabilities.'

T. Ferguson Rodger, 'The Role of the Psychiatrist'

Once I had acquired a reputation as a specialist in the private lives of public performers, my name rebounded around the small closed world of showbiz like a pea in a barrel. This had its good and bad sides. The inherent interest and glamour of even minor celebrities' lives made the next phase of my career an exciting one, full of colourful and extravagant characters who paid well and often demanded little more than psychiatric mumbo-jumbo: the more arcane and exotic the terminology I used, the more vindicated they felt in their claims to impending breakdowns and unique mental imbalances.

Of the substantial crop of well-known clients who came to my Chicago office between 1983 and 1986, as many as two-thirds were little more than recreational visitors, using me (as many of Richard's clients had always used him) as a stop-off between the country club and the health suite. So many were the architects and executors of their own difficulties, acting in the subconscious belief that their lives wouldn't be complete without hardship. Superstitions and perverse beliefs, unsubstantiated guilt, destructive time-fillers: they all poured in to fill the huge holes where the worries of a regular life should have been. I also saw many well-adjusted individuals whose minds were sagging in the nerve-cauldron of professional entertainment. The weight of expectation, the fickleness of success, sometimes even the intrinsic absurdity of a life spent pirouetting in a short skirt or telling mother-in-law jokes . . . any of these could sneak into the centre of a delicate talent and tug away at the knots that held sanity in place. Either way, whether the fault lay with the individual, the institution, or the strained marriage of the two, the tapes which catalogue my appointments from this showbiz period are full of bizarre stories, some of which would scarcely be believed if neither brevity nor libel laws prevented me from reproducing them in full. I met, among others:

- a Hollywood screenwriter suffering a crippling writer's block after the death of his muse, a golden retriever called Holly – 'It sounds silly, Dr Kristal, but she was as much responsible for writing those scripts as I was';

- a talk-show host who claimed sole responsibility for Third World debt; she sent a cheque for 1,000 dollars each week to the Ethiopian government, and interpreted broadcasts about African famine as personal attacks on her, until she eventually had to be stopped from watching the news;

- a millionaire TV magician who started lifting wallets because he needed a new challenge for his quick fingers, and soon found himself a kleptomaniac. By the end of our first consultation he had resolved to give it up. The next day he mailed back my wristwatch and passport.

From a professional point of view these were not especially stimulating cases. Where my training had prepared me to burrow to the bottom of cognitive defects and bring order to their victims' life stories, I now found myself little more than a major-league agony uncle. After all the effort it had taken to establish myself in practice, the realisation of my ambition was relatively unsatisfying. There were, however, financial compensations, which translated into time: time to take on less luminous but more rewarding cases, and time to go back to Witching. I flew home regularly to spend a week fishing and walking with Dad, who – having taken early retirement from the force, on health grounds – was beginning to convert our house into a one-man Hall of Fame. At the bottom of the stairs, where for years a school photograph had kept me imprisoned in a neatly pressed uniform and rehearsed smile, there were new exhibits: a framed and mounted copy of Patsy's LP, signed for Dad, a cut-out advert for the Lakelands practice, with my name highlighted; and, next to the school photo, a recent black and white picture of me at my desk, enlarged from the *Midwest Mind Monthly* report on the case of the dog-owning writer (who eventually brought in a replacement – a Labrador auspiciously named Orson Welles – but never quite regained the magic touch). The gap-toothed kid sat innocently alongside the paunchier, profes-sional Peter of today. Further along the hallway I hallucinated a continuation of the series: me with a shy, squealing kid under each arm, me receiving an honorary degree from Harvard, me and Richard on the set of our joint TV show, kitted out with microphones and complacent smiles.

But when, after amused preliminaries about my mutating accent and the cultural differences I had encountered, dinner-table conversation began to shine a gentle parental spotlight on my life, I found myself an uncomfortable subject for the quiet, probing questions I had become so used to posing: Are you happy in your job? What about everything else? How is home life? The major flaw in my routine was slowly exposed: I was lonely.

'I work long hours, you know, and it's hard to find the time to . . . meet people,' I would bluster. Or: 'It's all a question of priorities.' Or: 'There've been one or two people . . .' As my parents exchanged a wry look I would move the conversation along, with what was later to become known as reverse psychology: 'Richard's got plenty of girlfriends in New York, of course.'

'Well, he *would*,' Mum would say, and I would feel righteous by comparison.

Back in my Chicago apartment, however, the problem – suddenly, it felt like a problem – preyed on my mind. I couldn't ignore it for ever, any more than I could choose to stay at my current (and already advanced) age. My colleagues at Lakelands had their own families, or were absorbed full-time by the business of building them. The professional friendships I built up in my twenties had fizzled out into sporadic, pause-ridden phone calls, then twice-yearly invites to dinner parties at far-flung addresses, and finally Christmas cards with annual newsletters full of newly significant names: long-term girlfriends becoming wives, babies fast-forwarding into high school. I'd retained meaningful contact with a very small number of people; the others were reduced to nostalgic figures who might not survive another change of address book. Going further back, I barely merited a single bullet point in my school friends' biographies now, any more than they did in mine. The only exception was Richard Aloisi, and his time was stretched like a thin tent to shelter a crowd of interested parties. Even the voice on his new answerphone sounded distracted, as if recorded by a stand-in. After all the scrambling to position myself somewhere near Richard on the career scanner, to earn the right to talk to him in the language of a fellow professional instead of a Class of '68 hanger-on, I found such conversations harder than ever to obtain.

One Friday night, after six or seven calls to New York had been rebuffed by Richard's electronic double, I forced myself to accept the advice my dad had given me across the table on my last visit to Witching, in a tone between earnestness and play: 'About time you found a young lady, I should say.' He was echoing several Christmases' worth of increasingly pointed barbs from my uncle Frank and the inquisitive looks of Witching residents who saw straight past my transatlantic achievements to the space beside me where someone should have been. They all had a point. Whatever the reason – fragmented routine, limited social opportunities, natural diffidence – I had somehow reached the doors of middle age alone.

And so, at the beginning of 1986, I began placing notices in Personal sections and became accustomed to the pang of shame and excitement as I ran my eyes down the column to see my supposed qualities listed like those of the lawnmowers and unwanted gifts on the facing page. Over a period of months I hawked myself in several Chicago area newspapers, in magazines aimed at people of my age, and even psychiatric journals (in at least one issue of the *Midwest Mind Monthly* I was the only advertiser, so that it looked as if the whole section had been set up as an act of mercy to find me a companion). Some masochistic tendency made me keep hold of these periodicals, hoarding them in an ancient childhood scrapbook in the hope that one day they would make an amusing after-dinner distraction.

INTELLIGENT, VIVACIOUS PROFESSIONAL, 36, Chicago, thriving psychiatric career and spacious apartment, sense of humor, warm, good listener, slight and charming British accent, limited experience of relationships, enjoys theater, fishing and outdoor pursuits, literature, interesting discussions, open to new interests, friends include TV personality, WLTM similarly lonely person for companionship and potential romance. Can travel.

SPARKY, HIGH-FLYING GUY, thirties, Chicago area, prestigious career and big prospects, intellectual but grounded, English but emotional, generous but practical, loving but frustrated, good in a crisis, interested to meet like-minded individuals. Call in evening.

DON'T MISS THIS! For limited period, unique youthful college-educated man listening to offers of company and more in Chicago district and beyond (have transport). A real opportunity – don't just read this, do something about it!!! Money back if not completely satisfied.

GOOD CHESS PLAYER, tired of playing both white and black, looking for Chess World reader to stare down over a board, for one-off games or a long series, many other interests.

UPWARDLY MOBILE BLUE-EYED BOY, 36 but feels 21, looking for anyone 20–50, over 50 also considered, to share apartment and life.

PROBLEMS? Trade yours with mine, I'm a shrink and you could be my antidepressant!

I'VE PURCHASED AN EXTRA-LARGE BOX THIS WEEK, in the hope of attracting something more than the usual vague interest and fruitless exchange of calls. I am a devoted, witty, charismatic, reliable guy with a lot of stories to tell. I come recommended by TV's Dr. Richard Aloisi and when you meet me, you'll know why. I've gotten the wrong side of 35 with no credible record of romantic incidents, which I have to put down to the poor taste of the general public or (and this is hard) failings of my own. The usual strategy for reassuring people who've done a few laps without finding a partner is to make it sound like it's everyone else's loss: 'They just don't know what they're missing!' So here I am spelling it out without ambiguity. If you're single as you read this and you haven't yet got in touch, what you're missing is someone who might be able to change your life. Don't believe me? Try me!

OPPOSITES ATTRACT. So if you're stupid, ugly, callous and dull, step this way!

INCREASINGLY DEMORALIZED GUY, too old for this game, still holding out against better judgement for solution to solitude.

I'm not proud of this chapter in my publishing career and I reproduce it here only to purge myself of it. In my defence it has to be said that many of the desperate pitches were written in a spirit of self-mockery rather than indulgent melancholy, and one of them was composed by colleagues who took turns to supply a word during a quiet spell in the office. I don't want to descend into the overfamiliar vision of the tragic philosopher trying to be his own psychiatrist, the depression guru struggling against his own heartache, because life was never as romantically sad as that. While it never yielded much genuine excitement, the ongoing farce of my search for a soulmate breathed some colour into the days and weeks, and as more and more of my workmates tuned in, I found myself almost enjoying my role as the lovably unlovable serial bachelor. During one remarkable run of misfortunes (a perfect-sounding date that didn't show up followed by one who had an epileptic fit and a third whose ex-boyfriend arrived uninvited and threatened me with a meat cleaver), I had the sob-storytelling down to such an art that I could fabricate responses to the question 'Find love over the weekend, Pete?' and hold the audience as well as with a true story. There were moments when I even considered fictionalising my experiences for TV; I went as far as writing a preliminary script called *Getting Personal* for an acquaintance who worked as a script reader in Toronto. (He never got back to me, but years later, when *Frasier* was first aired and the world warmed to the ace psychiatrist and incompetent Lothario, I thought about calling a lawyer.) So it wasn't as if the single life had no consolations. Sometimes though the joke ran on a little too long in the hands of more malicious colleagues, and I started yearning for a break from Chicago.

The opportunity was waiting for me in a story which appeared in the entertainment section of the *Chicago Herald* one day, just a few pages forward from my latest inglorious appearance.

AUDIENCE ANGER AS TRAGEDY TURNS TO FARCE
Chicago Herald, May 4, 1986

William Shakespeare's play *Macbeth*, superstitiously referred to as "the Scottish play" to stave off disaster, has a long tradition of causing strange problems for players and directors. Now it seems the latest New York production is being struck by the curse.

Hundreds of audience members were left confused and angry at the Charterhouse on Tuesday after the last-minute cancelation of the night's performance of *Macbeth*, for which no explanation was given. A full house was simply told that the play "could not take place due to unforeseen circumstances". When the theater spokesman ventured a comment on the irony of this, given that the play deals with prophecy and the inevitable, members of the audience became restless and jeered the director, Julian Mackensie. Mackensie would not explain the mystery afterward, but speculation is rife that the blame lies with mercurial leading lady Lily Ripley. The 38-year-old British actress, a longtime friend of Mackensie's, has drawn criticism from audiences and colleagues for her erratic recent performances and unpredictable behavior: she disappeared for almost ten minutes at a key point in a recent showing, leaving her co-star Robert Langley (pictured below) to entertain the crowd with a stream of extemporized comments.

It is now suggested that Miss Ripley is suffering from performance anxiety, and may be replaced for an indefinite period by her understudy, Victoria Dobson.

The stage-fright story aroused a mild interest because I had once performed in *Macbeth* myself, like almost everyone to whom I mentioned the case,[12] but I would have forgotten it soon enough had it not been for Richard. He had been approached by the theatre company to treat Lily Ripley and, forced to decline on overwork grounds (he was the consultant psychologist on a high-profile court case), forwarded my name to the director. As I have already mentioned, after the

---

[12] *Macbeth* is one of the most produced plays ever. It is estimated that a performance begins somewhere in the world every four hours on average and so King Duncan dies about six times a day. See Ashley Kendrick, *MacBest and MacWorst: A History of the Scottish Play* (Aberdeen University Press, 1991)

DiMarco case I was billed, spuriously but flatteringly, as a specialist in 'creative difficulties', and a deal was quickly made. I flew to New York City with the pleasant feeling of walking into the drama I had been following in the news, like a character making his way from the wings on to the stage.

My research into Lily suggested that, whatever superficial similarities might exist between her case and Patsy's (and indeed, as we will see, deeper parallels later emerged), the two women were of very different dispositions. Lily had been in the movies and, according to several accounts, her Hollywood grounding still surfaced in her flamboyant lifestyle and unpredictable demands. I had heard, for example, that her dressing room at the Charterhouse had a special octagonal bed for an undiagnosed back condition; that she would be seized by pre-show cravings for date pancakes or incense candles; that her en suite bathroom contained manicure kits and rose-petal toilet paper manufactured by Tibetan monks. But at least – and crucially for someone who wants to get away with the prima-donna life – she could really act. I had once, on a failed date, been to watch her in a dismal film entitled *Hung Jury,* in which she played a female judge with what was thought to be a hilarious romantic dilemma. In spite of the lack of hilarity – the only people laughing were a crazy old man who also laughed at the safety announcements, and my companion, who accused me of being boring – Lily stood out as an excellent performer, making light of the moronic script and showing a talent for understatement which seemed at odds with the character profile I heard as, four years later, I prepared for the job of helping her to rise to her role in the umpteenth New York reworking of *Macbeth.*

The obligatory gimmick of this production was its setting in Stalin's Russia, but the real crowd-puller was Lily as Lady Macbeth, the destructive queen of the castle. For a while it had been plain sailing for the director Julian Mackensie. Then, as if the play had a reputation to keep up, strange things started to happen.

When I first met Mackensie for an overpriced lunch in the Charterhouse, he was on the verge of removing Lily from the show for a break of two weeks. Exhaustion would be the official reason for her proposed leave of absence, but everyone from the ice-cream vendors upwards knew that the problem was more complicated than that.

'As you know, she's been having these panic attacks on stage,' the director summarised, in the Brit-American drawl of a long-term expatriate, an unfortunate hybrid which would have made him sound like a foreigner on either side of the Atlantic, and which I suddenly recognised as my own. 'For a while it really worked to our advantage; you could see the fear, the emotions, the sense that she was losing control . . . all perfect. I thought I'd got the perfect Lady Mac.'

Regarding me with what I came to recognise as his standard expression – a soft, joyless smile that bore no relation to his mood – Julian tugged at his long, greying hair. With fifteen years as a London West End director behind him, he was confident in his understanding of actors' whims. However, he had been taken by surprise as Lily, with whom he had worked several times before, started to grow into her mercurial character.

Some claimed that her problems dated back to an unsettling incident in a rehearsal, in which a falling castle turret had almost decapitated Macduff, but Julian suspected that this was only a coincidental pretext for her behaviour, which had been irregular from an early stage in the production. An experienced actress with no history of anxiety other than the permanent adrenalin-rush of stage life, Lily seemed vague and distracted both before and after the show. She either wandered listlessly through performances or appeared, like some high-school actor, lost under the lights.

Looking ahead to a meeting with Lily, I had to concede that hearing about an overwrought actress's mini-breakdown did not whet my appetite the way exploring the psychic life of an upcoming songwriter had done. But the tale of Patsy DiMarco's creative sleepwalking had opened my mind to cases in which not all of the bullet points were on show at first, where some of them needed to be dug out of ground hidden even from the patient.

It was now twenty years since I had had the thrill of being urged into violence by a power-hungry wife, played by my beautiful classmate Jennifer O'Hara (who, by a strange coincidence, was later to marry a real-life murderer). The trouble was that I wasn't actually playing Macbeth, except in occasional rehearsals: I was the understudy to Richard, and unlike Lily Ripley's lucky understudy years later, I had little chance of being handed an opportunity by a lapse in the star's temperament. We were doing only a week of performances and Richard probably couldn't have suffered a panic attack even if he had wanted one. So conscientiously did he enter into his stage marriage with the girl routinely referred to as 'the beautiful Jennifer' that, during rehearsals, it was rumoured that they were researching their parts together backstage while Macduff and Macwhoever jabbered on about the state of the Scottish monarchy. Of the one hundred seats in our school theatre, forty had been booked by the Aloisi family for the first night. It was all set to be An Audience with Richard.

Then, on the eve of the show, the Scottish curse struck with playful malice at Richard's tragic flaw: asthma. Usually his attacks had been timed so as not to clash with any achievements he might have scheduled. In any case, everywhere he went he took a special inhaler which was twice as effective as a regular model, designed by an Aloisi uncle who worked as a medical innovator in Genoa. But on the Monday of the big week, after several months without a single wheeze, Richard started having trouble breathing and was sent home from school to recover; the crisis deepened when, despite an exhaustive search by the Aloisi family task force, the inhaler could not be found. The dress rehearsal was called off and Mr Tomlinson, the unhappy mathematician who had clung on to school-play duties, told me to make sure I was familiar with the lines.

At home I called an emergency reading of the play, with my parents covering the other characters' speeches. Mum's contribution, which began with a half-hearted attempt at the three witches and Banquo's wife, soon blossomed into a star turn as she took on more and more roles. Her delivery was impassioned and lyrical, her Scottish accent startlingly evocative; her eyes shone with the girlish joy I so rarely saw and longed, in vain, to inspire. Before long Dad and I felt almost like bit-part players – we were even eclipsed by a man who rang our doorbell to ask for directions and ended up in a cameo as Ross – and at the end I half expected Mum to take a bow to our non-existent audience. Instead, she shuffled off to clean the window sill, muttering that it was lucky she hadn't made it as an actress or nothing would ever get done around the house.

Although my mother had been the star, I had held Macbeth's lines together well; I was convinced, now, that I could play it as well as Richard. Whether I got my chance depended upon the appearance, or otherwise, of the inhaler. Over the next few hours the Aloisis would continue their search; Mr Aloisi was probably putting up a 10,000-pound reward and ordering local police to drain the river. But they wouldn't find it: I had it.

I didn't steal it, unless withholding something counts as theft. Richard had left it in my possession after we played football in my garden the week before. Sheer laziness and absent-mindedness had prevented me from returning it to him, although a more superstitious person would have called it fate. Suddenly it was an object of power as two visions of the future presented themselves. I had a moral duty to return it, and be a martyr to Richard's glory, but part of me felt that such acts of martyrdom had gone largely unappreciated in the past, as had so many of my attempts to emerge from the giant shadow of my serially successful friend. Richard's sudden incapacitation seemed like a leveller, a handicap for the stronger man, giving me the opportunity to taste what he was so accustomed to. The prospect of appearing in the play danced in front of me like a spotlight from the ceiling.

While I stared at the inhaler as if it had supernatural properties, Dad knocked on the door with the gusto of someone about to make a startling announcement. Perhaps because of the tiptoeing sensitivity with which he was sometimes forced to deliver news in his professional life, he relished this sort of opportunity.

'There's someone here to see you,' he reported. 'Shall I show her upstairs?'

The ominous 'her' was a favourite joke of Dad's, but this time he was able to back it up with a witness's description. Red hair, green eyes, about this tall. 'Not too bad looking, I should say,' he added, enjoying himself, as I threw panic-stricken looks around the room in which no woman unrelated to me had ever set foot. Jesus. It could only be the beautiful Jennifer, alias Lady Macbeth, come to discuss the play. She lived just a few minutes away but our paths never normally crossed; nor would they again unless I somehow seized the moment. I heard the creak of the third stair beneath Jennifer's light feet; there were less than twenty seconds before she would be standing here. Spontaneity, my weak spot, would be my only chance.

'How are you?' I blurted out, coming forward to greet her and blocking the entrance to my room with a clumsy gesture almost as incriminating as the sight of the inhaler itself. In a jumble of half-finished words I managed to suggest that we could sit out on the porch and have some food. 'It's a warm night, so, you know, why not?'

Jennifer agreed with me about the weather, to my relief since I had no idea what it was like outside. I was able to marshal her down the stairs without giving her any chance to see the inhaler perched on the table or any of the other objects that cluttered the place, each one suddenly laden with embarrassing potential, peepholes into a life which had never had to bear a girl's sharp scrutiny.

While I cooked hamburgers – the most glamorous food I could find in our house – nervously and inexpertly, snuffing out any potential silences with eager unnecessary remarks, she told me that she had just come from Richard. He was very disappointed (she reported) but resigned to missing the performances, and convinced that I would do a great job. During the rudimentary meal we went through the key scenes, testing each other, and I tried desperately to justify his confidence. Once relaxed, I rose to the challenge with only a handful of minor errors, and even on those occasions I found a wry backtracking remark which would prise a loud and dirty laugh from her lips. By the time two hours had slid by, she could have been in no doubt that I was a fine replacement for Richard, at least dramatically. My awe for Jennifer remained intact but I had, if not concealed it, at least managed it competently; she said she couldn't wait for tomorrow night. I wished her goodnight after offering to walk her home (there was no need, since she lived so close, but I didn't want to fall down on a technicality). In less than twenty-four hours, unless I threw away the chance, I would be standing next to her on a stage and treating her, for a short time, as my love.

It was hot that night and strange, indistinct sounds kept drifting in through the small window, pinned open in the vain hope of some fresh air. I floated in and out of dreams in which I forgot my lines, came on at the wrong time, was shot dead by Mr Paulson who had seized control of the play from his milder-mannered, mathematical colleague. In the long intermissions between the acts of this convoluted dream-play, as I shifted positions four times a minute trying to coax myself back off to sleep with light already dawning outside, a different version of events was taking shape in my mind:

- I give Richard the inhaler
- Richard, out of gratitude, is compelled to let me hang on to the role anyway, even for (say) just three of the six performances
- A double victory: the kudos of a selfless act without the bitterness of genuine self-sacrifice; three chances to perform, and with a clear conscience
- And Richard still gets three more shows than if I hadn't produced the inhaler
- Everyone's a winner

The obvious flaw: *would* Richard give me due reward for volunteering the inhaler, or would ambition overcome his generosity? It was a mini Prisoner's Dilemma: will he do the right thing if I do? Or should I do the wrong thing so that he cannot choose not to? As birds twittered outside to herald the end of a night which had barely begun, I knew that everything came down to a simple choice: take the inhaler into school, give it to Richard and hope for justice; or leave it.

Yet as so often when my life has demanded a tough call

between two possibilities, I solved the problem with a compromise pitched on a non-existent no man's land. At 7.30 a.m., over a breakfast I could not eat, my addled brain announced its decision: I would take the inhaler into school, but conceal it in a pocket, and make my mind up when I saw Richard, letting either guilt or greed strike the decisive blow.

Even as I arrived at the school gates I could see the cracks in this plan but, allowing myself to overlook them, I sauntered up to Richard, who was holding forth on some subject; he was easily identifiable by the packs of listeners clustered on all sides. I felt a throb of affection for him and realised that to deceive him would be almost as painful as to miss being in the play. As I neared, three or four of his audience wheeled round to face me and jostled to deliver the newsflash:

'Jennifer's away. She was sick fourteen times in the night.'

'I heard sixteen but apparently that's impossible.'

'She has to stay in bed for a week.'

'The play's cancelled.'

Nine or ten pairs of shining eyes looked at me expectantly, ablaze with the excitement of kids conveying bad news. Someone laughed mockingly to provoke me. Richard gave me an *I'm sorry you had to find out this way* look. But it was all wasted on me: I was numb. Losing interest, the newscasters moved on to spread the word, leaving me staring across the playground at nothing.

There was no understudy for Lady Macbeth. Maggie Francis was meant to be the deputy but she had refused to humble herself by learning someone else's part and relying on scraps from fortune's table. She was the only person I saw that day who looked more disappointed than I was, with the possible exception of the director Mr Tomlinson; and as he had already had the look of a thoroughly disillusioned man, it was hard to be sure how this ranked alongside his son's military desertion and his wife's sixteen-year affair with a Lutheran minister. My own emotions were not much easier to quantify. I didn't know what to feel first: relief that the dilemma had evaporated; crushing anti-climax at the big break gone astray; or anger at myself because in my haste to entertain Jennifer I had almost certainly undercooked the meat and served her a plate of poison. Chasing the random prizes of what I had allowed myself to think of as fate, I had overlooked the obvious cause and effect – poor cooking = food poisoning – that negated everything else. I derived no satisfaction from thinking that there was a certain (almost tragic) justice in the outcome, because I had created the chance for myself through dishonesty and destroyed it for myself through foolishness. Nor did it give me pleasure to forecast the epilogue to the tale, as surely as if the gods had written it all down:

- that Jennifer would never speak to me again without flashing me the special, hygienic look of contempt that passes between two people when one has given the other gastroenteritis;
- that, at the end of term, they would find time for a special one-off performance of *Macbeth* in the school hall where Richard and I would later drunkenly discuss our gravestones;
- that Richard and Jennifer would make a fabulous leading pair and a packed-in audience would call them back for four bows, the last one followed by a kiss, while a figure toward the back clenched his fists to beat off tears of envy.

Richard had offered to put me up while I was in Manhattan dealing with Lily Ripley, and we spent an enjoyable evening

94

in his Central Park palace sipping whisky and laughing affectionately at our young selves. Mr Tomlinson was dead, killed in a speedboat accident three days after his retirement; Jennifer O'Hara was married to the softly spoken Australian boyfriend whom Richard and I met at our school leaving party, and who in 1979 drove into an East London petrol station and shot eight people; and many thousands of amateur Macbeths had wrestled with their consciences for a brief moment in the limelight before going back to their real lives as bank clerks, dental surgeons and psychiatrists. Because the whole drama over a drama was now as quaint and distant as scores of other childhood episodes, we were amused by my being called in to treat a Lady Macbeth in the adult world. At the back of our minds, every play still took place in a school theatre with proud or indifferent parents filling red plastic chairs and paying threepence for a non-alcoholic drink at the intermission; every director was a weary algebra specialist with an unfaithful wife. I knew that to Lily and Julian and hundreds of other people in New York City, theatre was a job or a calling, but to Richard and me it was a charming distraction.

So I felt a smug, professional aloofness as Julian, giving me the director's angle on Lily's declining performances, delved into the pop-psychology barrel and pulled out a cluster of nebulous in-phrases like 'performance anxiety' (the deluxe name for stage fright) and 'panic attack' (the deluxe name for almost any public feeling of discomfort). I nodded absently as he described her outbursts in the dressing room, her disconcerted rambling and bouts of irrational nervousness. The most sensible measure seemed to be the one Julian had already taken, threatening to leave her out of the play until she took a hold of herself, and it didn't need a trained psychologist to figure that out. I was meeting Lily for Sunday breakfast in a Greenwich deli and I expected her to be a one-session patient: she would talk, I would ask some questions, make some trite suggestions and write down the names of calming pills favoured by the rich and excitable. I might get some flowers when she returned to form and my reputation could hardly fail to rise another half-notch. Being a shrink to an attention-seeking star is like being a fortune-teller with a credulous audience: the most general observations are greeted as piercing character insights, the most banal of predictions resound with the grandeur of an oracle's pronouncements. It looked like an easy assignment. My appointment with Lily was at ten and I told Richard I'd be done by one because he was taking me to the Guggenheim to see an exhibition of nude self-portraits by a family friend. Instead, I was with her for twelve hours.

Lily started it by being almost two hours late for breakfast, taking us right through into the brunch period. The café emptied, filled again for the mid-morning booster shot, then emptied all over again, and I was still sitting alone with the little tape machine I used for interviews and a book of yellow, blue and purple renderings of Richard's friend, which he had given me to whet my appetite for the exhibition. At half past eleven I realised I had been waiting almost ninety minutes and studied more than three hundred impressions of the female form (they made little impression on me, but perhaps you had to see the real thing). The waitresses were looking at me with either contempt or pity as late morning became early lunch; a businessman at the table to my right was earnestly tackling a vast omelette that looked like it would occupy the rest of his day. In normal circumstances I would have given it up, but there were no more appointments in my diary other than my date with Richard, and besides, I had very little energy. I had an incomplete night's sleep behind me because Richard and I had stayed up late talking about the old days. My limbs were heavy and stiff and my mind was stumbling along on autopilot, feeding me the occasional unchallenging thought like a TV station playing soothing music while technical problems are sorted out. With no cellphones or other instant excuse-makers available,[13] it was a simple battle between impatience and lethargy. I decided to give it till twelve, and at six minutes before the hour Lily showed up.

I think because of her reputation I had expected either to be smothered in an embrace or chilled by a frosty welcome, but instead she squeezed my hand with a shy smile and introduced herself, apologising for her lateness with a watertight excuse: 'I forgot what day of the week it was.' Then she slipped easily into a chair, ordered a coffee with various stipulations and turned her attention on to me with a generous smile.

I wasn't prepared for how beautiful she was, nor for the particular type of beauty she possessed. From the movie I remembered her as a blonde, and because of some inexplicable prejudice the stories of her cosseted behaviour had only strengthened this idea. But it was glossy red hair that hung long down her back, setting off implausibly green eyes that were brought further into focus by her well-fitting black outfit. I recognised her somehow, but not from the movies, and it took a while to make the connection: she reminded me of Jennifer O'Hara.

[13] Rosemary Sellars in *About Time* (Paradigm Press 2000) suggests that, since the first commercial cellular phone became available, US citizens are an average of 20 per cent later for appointments, because of the relative ease with which excuses for late arrival can now be made. In the UK and Japan, where cellphone ownership is higher, meetings commence an average of 40 per cent later than they did in the eighties. The figures are inevitably approximate.

It was many years since I had last set eyes on Jennifer, at the school leaving party. That night she hadn't given me a second look apart from when the meal was served, at which point she muttered something to her Australian companion and the two of them shot me a meaningful glance. Now, sitting opposite Lily, I could almost believe I was looking at one of those portraits in which the artist brings the subject into the present day, compensating for passing time. The small, quick, wicked lips, darting eyes and chiselled legs were all in place, but Lily's face and skin glimmered with the glow of experience where Jennifer had been 'like a ripe new fruit' (in the words of a school report which brought Mr Paulson another two minutes of notoriety, and which reportedly provoked his lover, our head Mrs Kean, into wild acts of sexual revenge).

Now that this strange lunch date is itself a snippet from the past, as I catalogue it from a distance of fourteen years, the intensity of my first gut reaction to Lily is as hard to understand for the older, duller Peter Kristal as it would have been hard to believe it beforehand. Looking back now is like watching the pilot episode of a favourite TV series, when the characters were still strangers. I can't be sure whether it was the Lady Macbeth connection that made me draw a straight subconscious line between the girl who had overwhelmed me (and whom I had incapacitated) at school and the actress who now sat across the table from me. If my memory is faithful and honest – neither thing a cast-iron certainty – the explanation wasn't as simple as the rekindling of a teenage flame that even at the time had burned with less than total conviction. There was something more complex about the spell which each of them managed to cast over me, although probably the complexity arose more from my perennially confused emotions than from any spiritual connection. In any case, barely five minutes after Lily's arrival I was already in danger of breaking the golden commandment of my profession: don't get too involved – also expressed by varyingly cynical shrinks as 'don't get too close', 'their problem isn't your problem' and (in the case of my down-to-earth workmate Simon Stacy) 'learn not to care'. But at this point, in 1986, I still had complete faith in my ability to avoid the pitfalls of personal politics. I was going to do my job and make sure Lily exposed more of herself to me than vice versa; and if any personal bond were forged, it would be on my terms. I just needed a little time.

In fact I had all the time I wanted, because as the lunch hour reared up and faded away, it became clear that Lily was in no hurry to leave or do anything other than talk. For about the first forty-five minutes of our meeting it was her interviewing *me,* about my (few, and boring) TV appearances, my role in the Patsy DiMarco case and then, our obvious common ground, the UK. For the first time in many months, I was meeting someone whose company I enjoyed; and I had the feeling that this was the beginning of a real friendship. It was with a conscious effort that I wrenched the conversation on to the stage fright that was plaguing her in *Macbeth.* 'Stage fright' was my phrase and as soon as it was uttered I knew I had made my first mistake. The brow clouded, the legs stopped jiggling under the table, the shoulders rose and fell in a polite sigh.

'People keep saying stage fright,' she complained with more than a hint of petulance, for which she then apologised with ungainly haste: 'It's just a little insulting . . . not that I'm insulted by you, but . . . when people seem to think . . . but then I suppose it's understandable, isn't it?'

For the first time she ran out of words, having talked herself into a corner. In the awkwardness that followed she tried to turn the conversation on to less charged aspects of the play, like the personal habits of Julian the director (reputedly a transvestite) and the mixed success of the Russian setting; but I was on the revelation trail now and, putting on the closest thing I had to a businesslike voice, asked for her account of the recent panic attacks.

'I can't really describe what's been happening,' said Lily with a slightly removed smile. 'It's not like I'm scared to go on the stage or worried about there being an audience there or what happens if I forget or any of that,' she began, back to full pelt. 'That's what stage fright is.[14] I've never had that. I played Joan of Arc in the National Youth Theatre when I was eleven, eight hundred people watching; I was in *Mr Imperfect* which took fifty-five million dollars box office and every one of those people saw me with a mole on my chin. So I'm not frightened, how could I be? Julian seems to think I am, just because I haven't been in a bloody Broadway show for a few years. The girl who's come in to replace me thinks I'm crazy

---

[14] Indeed, although there are many published works on the so-called 'audience effect' (see for instance Alan C. Dadowitz, *I'd Rather Die Than Speak in Public*, Raven Press, 1992), there is no definitive clinical definition of 'stage fright' beyond the obvious generalisations about anxiety apparently arising from a dread of performing in public. Most of us experience this to a mild degree: the above work takes its name from the statistic, publicised by the comedian Jerry Seinfeld, which states that a majority of people choose public speaking as their number one fear ahead of death itself. Given the personal and subjective nature of the condition, clinical research has inevitably sought to define stage fright by its symptoms rather than causes, and so case studies abound. Perhaps the most famous and baffling case in recent years is that of the concert pianist Roberto Ibrahimi, who, ten years into a successful career, was disabled by fear during a performance in Vienna and, discarding his prepared music, began maniacally playing 'Happy Birthday', which he completed 22 times before being led away from the piano.

because she's twenty-three or something and thinks what people tell her to think. People around the theatre look at me and I can see them thinking, Breakdown. But what does anyone know about what's going on in my head?'

She paused, for rhetorical effect rather than for breath: either her stage-training or some special gift had given her the skill of saying several hundred words per minute without taking in any new air. I took advantage of the silence to ask the obvious question: 'So what *is* going on in your head?'

She laughed with what seemed genuine admiration, as if this were the most ingenious thing I could have said.

'The last few weeks, while I've been performing, I've just had this terrible feeling of . . . not panic, well I suppose it is panic, but not like you panic if your house is on fire, more just this strong feeling that I shouldn't be there. I just feel I have to get away. I feel frightened. It's like claustrophobia. It's just annoying that it's *Macbeth,*' she added, 'because the last thing I want is people thinking I'm buying into, you know, the idea of the jinx and all that. I mean it's crazy, but people will believe what they read.'

As her speech ran out of gas, she took a long swig of coffee with a defiant expression, as if this action corroborated her words.

I could understand the frustration of the director if this was the best explanation Lily could give for going mentally and physically AWOL in the middle of shows. During one recent performance, as the newspaper cutting described, she had disappeared altogether when due on stage and was found sobbing in a bathroom only after ten long minutes, time that her co-star Robert had to fill by improvising a speech about Macbeth's childhood and marital problems. (Robert later said that if she hadn't returned in another two minutes, he was going to throw it open to audience requests or start a sing-song.) But there had been plenty of smaller frights – times when she had threatened not to go on stage, crucial lines preceded by nerve-shredding pauses while her eyes seemed to track her mind's journey to a completely different place. When Julian showed me the fashionably shabby black book in which he scribbled down notes during a show, it read like the diary of a madman. Enormous panicky handwriting spelt out desperate observations like 'LILY VERY LATE ENTRANCE' or just 'WHERE THE FUCK IS SHE?' underlined heavily enough to tear a slit in the page. I couldn't blame the people, and there were plenty of them, who thought the real cause of Lily's panic was that she was finding attention a little scarcer than it used to be, and surmised that the whole crisis was just a characteristically elaborate ruse by a woman overused to having care and admiration lavished on her. Then there were the stagehands who told me cheerfully that she was out of her mind, the same matter-of-fact diagnosis Steven Rowlands had once passed on Neil Ayer.

But neither of these explanations appealed. There was something about Lily that picked her out from the many cases of look-at-me syndrome I handled in this period. There could be no serious insanity verdict on a woman so fluent and self-aware: she was eccentric certainly, but in the field of serious mental disturbance she barely registered. As for the more cynical charge of crisis manipulation, it might be consistent with her character, but as an attention-grabbing trick it didn't make much sense. Most of her leading-lady spotlight had already been redirected to shine on Victoria Dobson, the twenty-three-year-old understudy whose rehearsals in the role had apparently been highly impressive and who might even now be ordering her own scented candles. While reviewers, audience members and even castmates prepared to embrace the new Lady Macbeth, Lily's profile was falling proportionally. The threat of being relieved of her role brought her a brief flurry of media interest, but not much of it showed her in a favourable light, and when I called her agent he told me curtly that he 'wasn't interested in talking about her'. So, although it was possible that she was playing for sympathy and pushing it close to the limit, I felt there was more to this story, something left unsaid in the stream of consciousness.

'I know people think I'm just making a scene for whatever reason,' said Lily, as if reading the thoughts recorded above, 'but why would I do that, why would I give someone else the chance to do my job? I get enough bloody attention being in the play without having to create a crisis.'

She wrapped her tongue around the 'cr' sounds at the end of this sentence with the easy musicality of a great elocutionist, but the chime was drowned out by a rumble of thunder and the hard patter of rain on the café windows. I recalled that it had been sunny last time I was out of doors, and by this indirect route realised that many hours had passed since I had arrived in the little diner, which now filled up again as rain-spattered couples jammed the entrance looking for shelter. Lily and I agreed to see out the worst of the storm and then arrange another meeting, before which she would experiment with a small dose of beta blockers to calm the panic which welled up before and during performances. I wrote down the name of a new fruit-flavoured brand of tranquilliser which I thought would appeal to Lily's taste for the exotic, only to find that she was already familiar with it. She seemed well acquainted, in fact, with the practicalities of clinical anxiety; and a cynic would have said that she had researched her part. But as the storm wore on and the conversation, staying in step, maintained its momentum, we found plenty of other things to talk about.

The subject of beta blockers segued first into a lively debate about the effectiveness of anti-depressants (Lily had used them almost throughout her twenties, like an astonishing percentage of women; I had only professional experience of them, at this stage). From there it was on to talking about the greatest disappointments we had known. Lily's was missing out on a part in *Annie Hall*, although I sensed what really hurt her was the movie's continued success. Suddenly the floodgates stood open and our conversation careered away. One minute we were discussing phobias (Lily's list included flying, doors with glass panes, large expanses of water, computer-generated voices, ice, beards and failure), the next, it was clothes (Lily made some discreet suggestions to improve my personal dress code). We debated the relative merits of American and British society, considered that living in Japan might be preferable to either, and then concluded that we were lucky to live in any kind of civilisation. I related some of my blind-date misfortunes to Lily and, plumbing the depths of unprofessionalism, allowed myself to get drawn into a mock-psychoanalytical role-play game in which I reconstructed a recent disaster. I was on my knees 'proposing' in a ludicrous burlesque of the hapless lover, when the spiky waitress who had been evil-eyeing me for almost eight hours asked the two of us quite firmly to leave.

By now, without even the excuse of drunkenness, I had far overstepped the accepted marks of doctor–patient familiarity. Lily didn't feel like a patient and, increasingly, I found I didn't feel like a shrink. I was enjoying myself more than at any time I could remember in the recent past and I had already burned my bridges, both by revealing personal information to a supposed client and by standing up Richard, who by now must have run the Guggenheim gauntlet of variegated nudes on his own and would be wondering if I had disappeared into New York's Bermuda triangle of crime victims. And so, when Lily invited me to come back to her apartment for a glass of wine – there was no performance that day – it seemed not so much a logical step as an inevitable one. The childish lust for excitement, which sometimes broke free of repression and made itself felt even in a heart as slow-moving as mine, kept telling me that great friendships grew from initial spontaneous adventures like these. The normally prevalent rational side of my mind was silent.

Her apartment was atmospherically lit with imaginatively angled soft-coloured bulbs, and filled with 'ethnic' objects – Chinese paper lamps, painted glass bowls containing mysterious shiny beads, apparently handmade musical instruments – all of them shrewdly positioned to give the simultaneous impressions of spaciousness and home comfort. The style of the place would be seen in the nineties as 'Third World chic', but this was 1986 and Lily was ahead of the game. The artfulness of the decor was occasionally undercut by an incongruous touch, like the poster on her kitchen wall that read YOU DON'T HAVE TO BE MAD TO WORK HERE – BUT IT HELPS! Below this bright red caption was the famous photo of workmen eating lunch on a metal gantry far above New York, but it had been doctored so that one of the mechanics was rolling his eyes and grinning inhumanly in a crude caricature of a lunatic. No sooner had I grimaced involuntarily at this cheery piece of madness merchandise than Lily apologised for its presence. 'It's a present from Julian,' she explained, 'so I can't really take it down, but I keep it in the kitchen which kind of makes the point, because *nobody* has posters in their kitchen.' Indeed, everything else in the apartment fitted into place with unselfconscious rightness. Her bookshelf brought Snoopy annuals and showbiz autobiographies shoulder-to-shoulder with volumes on syncretistic religions and the works of Eastern philosophers; the bottles in the cocktail cabinet were at the perfect levels between excess and prim austerity; the entire bathroom gleamed as if installed that morning. The contrived eclecticism of the whole place, like a film-set of a creative person's lodgings, reminded me of Richard's student rooms at Harvard; but here, the accrued paraphernalia of a life already strewn with anecdotes and experience gave off an air of authenticity, a confidence. Perhaps this itself was a pose, but if so it was a convincing one.

I was enjoying my sudden occupancy of centre stage in this new arena, and felt a tickle of wistful jealousy when Lily's answering machine splurged out a sequence of ten or twelve messages, a patchwork of mostly male voices inviting her to 'stop by' at cosmopolitan eateries. Many of the requests were delivered with such comicbook enthusiasm that I wanted to believe they were meant as jokes – one effeminate caller swore he would die unless he could have coffee with Lily before the end of the week – but none of them drew a laugh from their recipient as she poured wine into long thin glasses; in fact she seemed to see most of the messages as irritations. At some of them she sighed wearily, two or three were skipped altogether.

'I know it sounds terrible but I get really bored of being invited out,' said Lily at the end of the phone montage, after writing down the long number supplied in the final message and putting the slip of paper in a drawer from which it would probably never again emerge. 'The people don't really want to see me, they just want to get the inside story on what's wrong with me. It's not like they're real friends,' she added, perhaps noting my surprise. 'My real friends are great. But the people I know in New York, a lot of them are so . . . false. I'm surrounded by people so often and yet I get lonely. Do you know what I mean?'

I felt once again that I did know what she meant. I had come to New York, as I have already explained, with nothing to lose, and had expected to spend the week energetically meeting members of Richard's expansive friendship group, modestly fielding enquiries about the Patsy DiMarco case, trading repartee and revising my views on psychiatry minute by minute to adjust to the unresting brilliance of the New York scene. Instead I realised I would be spending most of my time reading casenotes in Richard's guest room, because he was so involved in his court case that he barely had a minute to spare. The reminiscing time I had managed to snatch with Richard, such as the night before, was as pleasurable as ever – like all great friendships ours could survive long separations and resume where it left off without any feeling of discontinuity – but even then I felt I was having to steal it from his girlfriend, Donna, whose expression towards me was always a kindly, understanding smile, as if I were Richard's child from another marriage.

'I don't know what I thought it would be like, really,' I concluded, as Lily nodded and murmured to complete the role-reversal. 'I wanted a break from Chicago, and that's what this is. I wanted to see Richard again and I've done that. It's just . . .' (I was alarmed to hear myself speaking what might have been a transcript from one of my consultations.) '. . . I suppose you can travel as much as you like, but if the problems are internal, then you'll never get away from them, you'll just be changing the canvas.'

'That's exactly how I feel about being here,' said Lily.

I persuaded Lily to show me the movie which had first brought her to the USA, a 'feelgood favourite' called *Mr Imperfect*. Originally slated for TV alone, the film's infallible formula of a young couple meeting, separating and meeting again, with an interim hour of frantic misadventures, made it one of the surprise box-office heavyweights of 1975. Lily, who (as well as conducting her romance) was accused of theft, mistaken for the First Lady and kidnapped in the course of the film's seemingly inexhaustible twists and turns, emerged from the experience into a blizzard of offers – frothy coffee-shop comedies and weepies about aspiring Olympians struck down by cancer – and before she knew it she was well positioned on Hollywood's wheel of fortune, her English stage-training irrelevant in the blur of breakneck six-week shoots. It was only in the past couple of years, once she had crossed the 'thirty-five threshold' and watched the Bond-girl offers turning into 'three scenes as the stepmom' roles, that she returned to her original master, the theatre. 'It was what I was meant to be doing all along,' she said, wincing as her permed twenty-something self slipped over unconvincingly and spilled drinking chocolate down the shirt of the café manager, a specially appearing Danny DeVito, who had helped to fund the movie's production, 'but films got in the way.'

Although she was half joking, aware that most of what surrounded us had been supplied by the silver screen, a part of her clearly clung to ideals of stagecraft, the idea of 'proper acting', a vocation rather than a profession. This made it all the more curious that I should be treating her for what most people regarded as sheer inability to stand her ground on stage.

I felt again that I was missing something, that the story of Lily's disturbance was a little more complicated than that of *Mr Imperfect*, which cantered along to an amiable conclusion in which the reunited sweethearts danced on tabletops in the café after hours, unknowingly watched by the secretly warm-hearted manager DeVito who was seen chuckling as the credits rolled. As an eager closing song reminded the viewer of the value of love, we agreed the picture was not one of Lily's career highs. However, when I added unthinkingly that movies of that genre never failed to depress me, she reacted with genuine surprise.

'Why would that make you depressed?' she asked, slipping tape into box and box on to shelf in what seemed a single easy motion. 'I mean, I know it's a bad film, but wouldn't you rather watch something that ends nicely than something like bloody *Macbeth*?'

'I would if I could believe it, or care about it,' I replied, caught a little on the defensive. For some years now I had been moving among people so cynical that an ideologically negative reaction to even the most uplifting films would be assured of a sympathetic response: Simon Stacy often walked out of movies at the first kiss. But Lily had made me wonder, fleetingly, why I couldn't just relax and enjoy a silly film in the appropriate spirit. 'I just can't buy into a vision of the world that's optimistic without being . . . well, measured about it,' I said, aware of the sound of each word. 'I mean, if you look at *Macbeth* . . .'

'Let's not talk about *Macbeth*,' said Lily abruptly and in such a clenched tone that it was impossible to argue. Whatever was at the root of Lily's *Macbeth*-specific panic attacks, it had left the nerve raw. Perhaps in order to crack the secret I would have to gamble on irritating the wound, but now was not the time.

'Maybe it's just bitterness,' I conceded, 'but I think a lot of movies present a vision of the world which is . . . well, unrealistic, but not in a fun escapist way. Unrealistic in a dangerous, my-life-could-be-like-that way.'

'Why *can't* people's lives be like that?' Lily retorted.

'Well . . .'

And here I tried to talk about all the millions of causes and effects which made up big events, skimmed over by directors anxious to get to the tabletop finale, and so ignored by audience members in their real-life pursuit of happiness. I wanted to tell her of the many relationship autopsies I had carried out in my professional life where the verdict was that people had wounded each other through ignorance of what life really involved. At the same time I felt like drawing her attention to the scores of single people of my own gloomy disposition who would not feel cheered by a cut and pasted happy ending, but even more disillusioned by the gap between their own experience and the alleged reality on the screen. But I made it only a little way down the third path before it became clear what I was really complaining about. 'You don't believe in love,' said Lily with an arch grin, as if we were talking about Santa Claus.

'I believe in love,' I objected. 'I just don't believe everyone can have it.'

A lot later, as midnight approached and I found myself at last making my way back to Richard's through the neon orange glow of New York's permanent daylight, I reflected that a film hero would have used that moment to move in for the kill. A line like 'Maybe you can help me to believe in love' would have set us up nicely to begin the next scene half naked in bed exchanging looks of delighted guilt. But there was no kill, just a conversation that ambled on entertainingly as Lily argued in favour of love and optimism while I spoke up for a realistic portrayal of crushed dreams. In truth, a romantic encounter would almost have taken the gloss off what had already been a memorable day for me: I had spent more time talking to Lily that afternoon and evening than to any other person in any twenty-four-hour period of my life. By the time I arrived back at Richard's, it was difficult to believe that I had not known her a mere few hours ago.

Having woken up in time to explain myself to a laconic Richard over a hasty breakfast – he was due for another long, lucrative day in court – my thoughts turned back to Lily, who would be on the stage again that night. In a confusing send-off she had presented me with a ticket for the upper circle, worth seventy-five dollars, and then begged me not to use it: 'I'll be awful, and you'll never want to see me again,' she explained with teasing sincerity. However, bearing in mind the complicated rules of feminine psychology, I interpreted this as a firm invitation to show up: staying away would indicate that I agreed with her forecast of failure and it might be taken as an insult. Even if I had misread the signs and Lily *did* want me to steer clear of the Charterhouse, there were obvious good reasons for seeing her 'in the office'. She sounded surprised when I called to confirm I was coming – for a brief moment I wondered whether I had hallucinated the whole of yesterday's encounter in a powerful flight of wish-fulfilment – but the arrangement was made and I could hardly wait.

In the afternoon I bought a new shirt along the lines suggested by Lily and sat in Central Park reading what was then the definitive anthology of works on stage fright.[15] At a

---

[15] Harold H. Humphries, *Don't Make Me Go Out There* (Raven Press, 1982), brings together more than a hundred accounts of stage fright, including a detailed breakdown of the Ibrahimi case mentioned above. This much-read and cited work suddenly fell from grace when, in its second edition, Humphries added a new preface suggesting that stage fright, 'like other anxiety-based disorders, can be overcome with the use of presently illegal barbiturates'. Subjected to an investigation, Humphries persisted in vaunting the medicinal properties of drugs ranging from marijuana to cocaine and eventually admitted that he had prescribed and even supplied them to patients. He was declared unfit to practise in 1988.

particular point, as the sun forced its way between clouds to brighten my small corner, I enjoyed one of the moments of perfect happiness that occur only once or twice a year, when for a short hazy period every impression that reaches the senses – in this case, a barely audible snatch of birdsong and a sweaty jogger labouring past with a complicated timing device – seems part of a specially orchestrated pageant. The jogger's jerky, determined efforts made me feel serene, as if we had a joint exercise target to reach for the day and he had agreed to take on most of the burden. Only the faintest note of unease sounded in the silence, and it took me a while to identify it: I was already nervous on Lily's behalf. Although I hardly knew her, it was an unbearable thought that something might go wrong for her.

The tension that night was palpable to every member of the audience in the Charterhouse, perhaps because each of them contributed a small personal wish to the charged atmosphere. To judge from the snippets of pre-show conversation, there was a roughly even split between spectators who hoped to see a perfect performance and those who longed for a catastrophe: some of the latter group seemed to have bought tickets with this sole purpose in mind. Then, as at any sports fixture, there were some who claimed to belong to one side while secretly rooting for the other: very soon after taking my seat I heard a voice behind me mutter, 'Let's hope she doesn't throw one tonight!' in a tone that indicated that, on the contrary, no outcome would be more pleasing. Turning my head to observe the speaker, I saw a well-dressed white-haired man with the air of a theatre buff, jabbing Lily's picture in the glossy programme with a critical finger. I felt the prickly sensation of resentment normally reserved for insults to close friends and family, and when the dimming of the lights made my stomach tighten I knew again that Lily – even before appearing – had found a way to knife through my professional objectivity.

In case anyone thinks that these memoirs are beginning to resemble 'a tale told by an idiot', I should say here that this book is principally intended to tell the story of the way my life and career have interlocked, rather than as a compendium of my 'greatest hits'. This compels me to focus upon the episodes which brought me into the public eye, and those which had the greatest impact on my own life, instead of rocketing the reader through a triumphant course of cracked cases. Unlike a lot of professional autobiographies, it's a story of failures as well as successes. I can say with an easy conscience that in ninety-eight per cent of all the cases making up my career, I have stayed clear of the dangers arising from too much personal investment. But it so happens that two of the exceptions form important parts of the overall story and cannot be omitted. Given more space I could list any number of cases which I handled with total professionalism, but (as Richard pointed out when I began writing) that might not sell as many copies. If the upshot of my honesty is that this book and, retrospectively, my career come to be regarded as amusing narratives of incompetence, like the videos of baseball players being hit in the genitals by a curveball, then I hope I will at least have provided entertainment.

The Soviet setting of Mackensie's production had the murdering Macbeth seizing control of his party from the old-school Communist Duncan and then picking off his rivals with shrewd internecine plotting, before being unseated by the friends he had betrayed in his rise to power. The three witches were Macbeth's political advisors, eventually revealed to be double agents conspiring with a foreign enemy; Lily was a seen-and-not-heard political widow who seethed with repressed passion and whose eventual suicide was a dark triumph for regimentation over expression; Macbeth's final ousting was executed by a lone assassin in a hotel room. To achieve all this without greatly altering the script would have been miraculous, and so Julian Mackensie had taken the usual liberties with the poetry, drafting in occasional spurious Russianisms like 'comrade', and adjusting the Porter's drunken ramble into a solemn hymn to vodka. Julian's Director's Notes explained that the intended tone was 'infinitely playful and grimly serious, revering the harsh splendor of Russian political tradition and attacking its excesses'. This sounded to me like an attempt to cover all the bases and leave no room for criticism; I had seen (and even written) diagnoses which ran for the same kind of cover. In any case Macbeth himself got away with claiming that the witches 'cannot be good, cannot be ill'. This just about summed up the production.

But, like much of the audience, my real interest was in the slender figure who first appeared in a white dressing gown reading Macbeth's letter in a voice cold and clear as water. Having somehow expected her to shrink under the keen headlights of the audience, it was with relief I saw that there was no trace of anxiety about Lily that night. I speak without bias (and at the risk of repeating, and cheapening, my earlier tributes to Patsy DiMarco) when I say she was the most impressive performer: she glided through the verse where others juddered, mispronounced or strained too hard. Her scenes with Robert Langley were sensual and unsettling; her breakdown was convincingly fraught without hinting at any real-life turmoil. Even after being reassured that this was one of her 'good nights', I continued to hold my breath each time Lily was expected on stage, but needlessly: tonight there would be no heart-stopping disappearances.

As she slunk off stage for the final time, the audience emitted a quiet sigh of mingled relief and disappointment and there was a telltale rustling as the elderly couple behind me vacated their seats early. When the actors assembled with mock-reluctant gestures for the curtain call, a sweaty Robert Langley leading Lily to the front with an expression of condescending affection like a husband congratulating his wife on a good dinner, I expected the audience to acknowledge what had been a compelling performance under considerable, if partly self-inflicted, pressure. Yet, beneath the splashing applause and good-natured cheers that came Lily's way, there was – it seemed to me – an undertone of cynicism, as if the audience, rather than having been entertained by her, was obliging her with its support. As had happened at Patsy's concert three years before, I had the fleeting impression of a direct contact between my eyes and Lily's as she gave a somewhat rueful wave to the auditorium before disappearing from view.

Eavesdropping on the departing patrons as they shuffled patiently between and around one another, through the giant ornate doors and into waiting cabs, I was perplexed to find that Lily's reviews were mixed, the number of positive assessments balanced out by what seemed baseless criticisms. 'All the words were there,' muttered a fat middle-aged woman from beneath an enormous hat, as I trailed along behind like a journalist eager for a snatch of incriminating gossip, 'but it's all about what you do with your face. *What you do with your face,*' she repeated forcefully to her conversational partner, a deaf old man who kept repeating 'Oh, yes, yes' in coerced agreement. 'You'd expect if someone caused that much trouble, they'd be worth it,' observed a tall man with a thick cigar, receiving several nods of agreement from his companions, which pleased him so much that he began preparing for an opportunity to repeat himself. 'You can kind of see why she's meant to be crazy,' concluded a woman on her way out of the bar with an extravagant pinkish drink in a glass decorated with the masks of comedy and tragedy. As well as a reprise of the protective indignation I had felt for Lily earlier, I now experienced a sensation of righteous annoyance. It seemed a classic case of the power of suggestion: these people had come to see a troubled star and, finding her coherent and untroubled, had read stress and strain into her face, panic into her voice, where there was none to be observed. But could it be simply that we had different ideas of good acting, or – more alarmingly – that I was the one distorting the evidence, hallucinating the polished performance that I wanted to see? I looked forward to hearing the most important assessment, that of Lily herself. I crossed the street, bought a bunch of flowers from a stall next to a newspaper stand carrying details of Richard's court case, and hurried to the stage door where we had agreed to meet.

Only when I had been waiting for more than an hour, in powdery rain which fell in soft sheets and was cinematically lit by the glare of street lights, did it begin to seem likely that Lily would not appear. This fear was hammered into a certainty by a thickset man with a moustache who appeared from thin air, like Banquo's ghost, clutching a jangling set of keys. He regarded me with a kind of disparaging compassion and I had a flashback to a humiliating childhood afternoon when Dad had forgotten to collect me from an after-school football practice.

'Nothing left to see round here, sir. I'm locking up,' said the janitor with an ironic grin, as if he were performing a clever caricature of his profession.

'I was meant to meet Lily Ripley,' I said. The claim sounded feeble and unlikely. 'I'm her psychiatrist,' I added.

'Sir, everyone is her psychiatrist at the minute,' said the janitor, slamming an outside door over the entrance I had been guarding in vain, and locking the whole conglomeration of doors with an elaborate flourish. The comfortable finality of his tone discouraged me from persevering. Probably there had been many other jilted visitors for Lily, perhaps even other psychiatrists. I thanked the janitor and went on my way, cursing theatre and its practitioners and lecturing myself once again on the dangers of emotional attachments. Walking past a homeless woman at the top of the subway steps, I made the mistake of offering her the flowers. As she turned away in contempt, a miserable two hours were complete.

The messages I left for Lily the following morning had to be conducted in relative secrecy – my supremely professional host, who would consider a ten-minute wait for a patient wasted time, was not in court until the afternoon – and even as the words came out I could sense them evaporating, overspill drops running off the surface of an already saturated answering machine. After plugging away fruitlessly for a while, I changed tack by calling Julian Mackensie, who answered first time and instantly but expressionlessly thanked me for my 'work with Lily'. I informed him briskly that this work had been stalled by her disappearance, but the news failed to elicit the remorse I felt entitled to expect.

'She was probably with her masseur,' said Mackensie.

'Her masseur?' I repeated.

'You know, she always has a massage after the show,' said Julian with a conspicuous effort at patience, as if the fact were so well publicised that nobody could be ignorant of it, even though in our twelve hours of talk Lily had not once alluded to this part of her routine. 'Then a couple of sleeping pills and God knows what else. *I* have enough difficulty getting in touch with her!' he added, laughing mirthlessly.

Something in the tenor of his voice reminded me disagreeably of the previous night's dealings with the self-confident janitor, and for a few moments I felt an immense irritation and antagonism towards Julian Mackensie which only grew in proportion to my awareness that he was not really to blame. I wanted to list the consequences of Lily's elusiveness, but honesty reminded me that my annoyance stemmed less from professional impatience than from a desire to speak to her again, and chagrin at the sudden plunging of my status from new, favoured confidant to stranded stage-door schmuck; from hotshot head-doctor to crumpled flower-offerer. This feeling was, in fairness, at least partly motivated by my work – Lily's case was intriguing and I felt capable of making real progress with her – but the personal slight was a major factor and for that I deserved no sympathy. Rather than share these thoughts with the director, I thanked him coolly and gave him a message to deliver to Lily: I would see her again whenever she was ready. I tried to place a sarcastic kick in the final word, but without real hope that Julian would deliver it properly.

Downstairs, Richard was sitting surrounded by cardboard files, loose sheets of paper covered in hand- and typewritten notes, and books, many held open at pages which had been attacked with a fluorescent pen: an Aloisi trademark since school, when his ink assaults on textbooks (a copy of which he always purchased himself rather than wait for the school to supply them) horrified some teachers but proved a devastatingly effective learning aid. Knowing the merciless stamina which Richard brought to any task that fired his enthusiasm, I would not have been surprised to learn that he had produced this entire mass of paperwork since I last saw him.

'It's a hell of a case, this one, Peter,' he said, grinning at me over expensive glasses. He had kept me up to date with the story over the past days, in odd moments, and now he filled in some of the background. A fifty-six-year-old man named Andre Genelli had allegedly murdered his wife, who was found dead in their backyard after a few months as a missing person. Although the investigation had struggled to find material evidence, Genelli had broken down in custody and confessed to the crime. Fighting the appeal should have been a formality, but Genelli's defence team had sprung a surprise, bringing in a psychologist who claimed that the confession was bullied out of Genelli by brutal interrogation tactics resulting in a case of Stockholm syndrome. Situated somewhere on the disputed territory between neurological imbalance and mere whim of the pressured mind, Stockholm syndrome affects people held as prisoners – in the original incident, the prison was a bank vault – who, in a subconscious attempt to ensure their own safety, develop feelings of blind acquiescence, affection, everything up to and including love for their captors.[16] Genelli's representatives, citing convincing evidence from a transcript of one of the interrogations, claimed that their innocent client had confessed in fear of police aggression. The NYPD laid themselves open to the accusation by suppressing further transcripts, and suddenly a mistrial verdict beckoned and Genelli could smell freedom.

Enlisted to swing the balance back towards the prosecution, Richard now held the key cards in a case that was gripping the attention of legal and psychiatric communities

---

[16] A fuller account of one of the late twentieth century's more intriguing 'syndromes' can be found in Jones, *Brainwashed in a Bank Vault* (Paradigm Press, 1979). A number of English translations have been made of the accounts of the original Stockholm prisoners, though these vary in quality.

alike; whereas I was treating a stagestruck actress who could not always be relied upon to see me. The contrast, as so often, was unflattering: we might both be intervening in newsworthy cases, but I was still playing games by comparison with the demands upon Richard.

With no contact from Lily that day to encourage me, I tried to follow Richard's industrious example and busy myself with further research into performance anxiety. I felt that if Richard were handling Lily Ripley, he would by now have compiled a history of every recorded form of anxious behaviour and perhaps everyone who had ever exhibited nervousness in public. I could neither read as energetically as Richard nor call upon his lightning-quick apprehension of theories, but perhaps by imitating the habits of a high achiever I could plant them in my own life; if I acted like a big shot I might become one, by means of the 'positive visualisation' which I was always encouraging.

Attempting to exhaust my brain with mental channel-surfing as night fell, I found myself thinking about Lily once again. Where had she been all day, and had it really not occurred to her to contact me? I half remembered a citation from an essay on stagecraft I had read years before: 'The perfect actor has no personality, or rather, has as many different personalities as he has encounters with others. Consistency of character is fatal.' Perhaps this nugget of pretentious wisdom contained a kernel of truth about Lily; perhaps she was living by the guidelines of *The Dice Man* – a book I had spotted on her shelves – and allowing the die to dictate her daily demeanour:

- 1 for flirtation
- 2 for indifference
- 3 for a complete disappearance
- 4 for an attention-seeking manoeuvre

And so on, each sixth of her arbitrary, die-driven personality independent from the others, so that a conversation with Wednesday's Lily had no place in the memory bank of Friday's. She wouldn't be the first person I had met who was happily resigned to complete inconsistency of character: *The Dice Man* seemed to have a lot to answer for among my patients. The difference was that normally I didn't take a client's recalcitrance as a personal insult.

And this brought me to another disturbing thought: what if I were being grossly unfair to Lily, and some disaster had prevented her from meeting me? Could what was troubling Lily, the hidden danger I had so far failed to grasp, be a personal threat of some kind: a dangerous or obsessed fan like Neil Ayer, perhaps, or a plot by a jealous understudy like the Peter Kristal of 1967? I felt a rush of affection, and a terrible desire to hear Lily's voice again. Although I had never yet caused the serious injury or death of a patient by sheer negligence, I felt worryingly exposed. With my last conscious thought I promised to devote the next day to finding her.

But even this modest aim was pre-empted by Lily's next move. I was shaken out of sleep by a red-eyed Richard who made me understand that I was wanted on the phone. A muggy light was half-heartedly dawning outside as Richard retreated to his room with a slam of the door; as my mind struggled to take stock, I realised that the telephone call might have inadvertently redirected his bullet points and those of the accused murderer Genelli. The missing half-hour of sleep might blunt Richard's argumentative tools; the loss of just a single metaphor would perhaps be enough to tilt the delicate balance of his case and puncture his treasured reputation as a courtroom shrink *par excellence*. I could not imagine who would be calling except my parents, with some momentous piece of news, and for the fourth or fifth time since the worsening of his chest problem I prepared myself for news of my dad's death. But it was Lily.

'Can you come round now?' she asked.

'It's —'

'I know what time it is,' she said, 'but can you come? I haven't told you properly what's been going on. I've realised that I need to trust you and tell you stuff so you can sort it out.'

'Why now?' I asked, though I was already warming to the idea; I felt inappropriately bright and interested.

'Because it's the right time.'

In five minutes I was in a yellow cab clinging to the inside door handle as a heavy-eyed driver licked around the side streets, apparently unconcerned whether sleep or death arrived first to bring him rest. By six o'clock that morning, while a dull sun rose over Manhattan, I was greeting Lily with a tentative kiss as she opened the door in a thin blue negligee and guided me inside.

I accepted a cup of syrupy coffee with what I hoped was a businesslike air, anxious to avoid the small-talk preamble which could lead us away from the promised revelations. The apartment was more or less as I had left it, although following her into the kitchen I was disconcerted to notice an addition to the Empire State Building poster: some hand had grafted streaks of red hair and a dress like Lady Macbeth's on to the raving individual, so that he now resembled a transvestite Lily. Too late it occurred to me that a neutral venue might have helped to create the atmosphere of a consultation, rather than a social visit. Instead, our demeanours remained comically out of kilter: Lily led me through to her bedroom where she perched like a bird on the edge of a large, oddly shaped bed, whilst I sat, with effortless awkwardness, in a small cushioned chair, forbidding my eyes from wandering over the smooth channels of her bare flesh. It could have been a scene from a porn film, the hapless professional about to be snared by the femme fatale. I began a joke to draw attention to the strangeness of the situation, then tried to squirm sideways out of the comment, and was finally forced to take refuge in the safe opener:

'So what was it you were going to tell me?'

'Listen,' said Lily. 'Do you trust me?'

This was the very question I often found myself asking difficult patients, because like a good chess move it forced the pace of events: if yes, then I was free to probe in any way necessary, if no then I could question their commitment to the whole procedure. ('You don't trust me? Then why are you speaking to me at all? What would it take to make you trust me?') Now I was the one being asked as Lily's generous green eyes glimmered like wet grass after a storm. Her face, uncomfortably flushed, bore the blotchy imprint of tears hastily washed away; her hair hung lopsided from uneasy sleep, her long hands were clasped together as if holding each other steady.

'Of course,' I replied.

'OK,' she said, 'I wasn't going to tell you this because it sounds stupid. It's probably the most stupid thing you've ever heard.'

'Don't forget, my job is to listen to stupid things,' I said, to put her at her ease. 'That's what it says on my business card, anyway.'

A bitter joke; two years ago I had unthinkingly drunk coffee from an I'M WITH STUPID novelty mug in the presence of a paranoid patient who had broken off his appointments in the belief that I was mocking him.

'Well, I've got to tell someone,' she said. 'And you're

the one person I've met that − I know it's only been once, but − I really feel I can tell you things.'

(A pause.)

'Basically, I've been warned to stop doing the play,' she said, looking down at her hands.

(A pause, to test the initial reaction. I remained inscrutable.)

'For two or three weeks now I've had . . . warnings that something terrible will happen . . .'

(I was silent, although now bursting with questions.)

'. . . in my dreams,' Lily finished.

This time I picked up the bait. 'In your dreams?'

'Well, not dreams, nightmares,' said Lily. 'Pete, I've had the same dream every night for almost twenty nights. The only way I can get away from it is drinking or taking things to knock me out. I'm terrified of it. I don't want to go to sleep in case it starts again. Do you know what that's like, being scared to drop off because you know something's waiting to scare the shit out of you?'

Her voice was low as if she feared being overheard. Stretching out, taking her clammy hand and setting it down carefully on my knee, I told her I did know what it was like, although the worst recurring dream of my life was several years in the future.

'Tell me about the dreams,' I said.

'It's . . . they're stupid dreams,' she said. 'They're not the sort of thing that's supposed to be scary.'

(Pause. I had known a bewildering range of themes serve as the basis for a nightmare. Just three months before the Lily case, a patient of mine − a banker − was driven close to insanity by a recurring dream in which he had become a water bird and was starving to death because he could not master the use of his beak. Like a horror film, a nightmare is a matter of atmosphere more than specific subject. However, I again remained silent.)

'In the dream, I'm normally just walking around and around, like I'm lost,' Lily resumed. 'I've got no idea where I am or where I'm walking. Sometimes I see something that looks familiar but it sort of changes shape so I can never be sure what's going on. Then gradually I notice that people are looking at me strangely. I try to talk to people and they ignore me. Someone spits at me and everyone laughs and claps. I start walking faster and faster but I'm surrounded, there are all these . . . sort of accusing faces around me, and they close in on me and start screaming at me, calling me a murderer. I'm trying to get away but they keep pressing in on all sides. I ask people what I'm meant to have done and they just laugh. I can't remember having done anything, nothing specific, but a part of me knows that I have.' She shuddered.

'Then suddenly it switches to something more like the present. We're in a room like this one. There's this woman who looks a bit like me. I ask her what's happening and expect her to shout at me like the others, but she's quite calm. She says I've got to stop everything, it's my only chance. I sort of understand she's talking about the play, about *Macbeth*. Then she loses her cool; she's shaking me, telling me to give it up. I ask her why it's wrong to do the play and then . . .' (this time, when she shivered, I felt her hand stiffen in real fear as if conducting electricity) '. . . then I look into her face and it's *my* face, but dead. It just stares back at me with, sort of, hollow eyes. Then I wake up.'

She sniffed.

'And then I go and perform in the play, and . . . everything brings it back. It's stupid, but weird things do keep happening. You can't comment on it because the *Macbeth* thing is such a running joke, but . . .'

'What sort of weird things?' I asked.

'Well it started when James was nearly killed by the turret. That was the day after I first had the dream, which could have been coincidence, but . . . another time the dream was particularly bad, the next day I felt this pain around my heart and couldn't breathe on stage. Robert was there doing his speech and I was thinking: Just keep talking, because if I have to talk, I'll only be able to choke. And then the day I disappeared, when it was in the papers, I was throwing up,' she added, almost proudly, in the manner of a child vindicated in a dinner-time tantrum. 'For no reason. I was just doing the bit where I tell Macbeth that he'll be a man if he kills Duncan, and I thought, Christ, I'm going to be sick before I can get these words out. I had to rush through the last four lines and then people say "Oh, she can't act" while you're coughing up your guts backstage.' The recollection must have been strong: pallor passed across her face at the memory.

'Just little things like that have been going on since this play started. And I haven't been able to tell anyone, because how would that sound? Ooh, I've been having terrible dreams.' She laughed. 'They'd think that was a perfectly reasonable excuse for fucking up their show.'

The most interesting part of the tale was the persistence of the dream. Although I had known recurring nightmares before, a run of more than twenty nights – longer than some Broadway shows – was unprecedented in my experience. Even accounting for tricks of Lily's memory which might have exaggerated the frequency, it was a freakishly resilient dream, and the strands of subconscious data which combined to produce it must have been very central to Lily's mental make-up. Again, it was probable that Lily's mind, shaken by the frightening main thrust of the dream, discarded small plot variations from night to night, but the central features – the jeering crowd, the warning, the ghastly face – were obviously firmly embedded. Each of these features was a common enough anxiety-dream component and I had no doubt that the accompanying daytime symptoms could be put down to coincidence, psychosomatic processes or the all-over fatigue of a mind and body deprived of proper rest.

The question, however, was how to address the root cause and drive these nightly visitors out of Lily's mind.

'The thing is, I know it *is* a warning,' said Lily, before I could present this rational view, and not for the first time I had the impression that my brain was supplying Lily with a copy of my thoughts at the same time I myself received them. 'All my family have been accurate dreamers, like, scarily accurate.'

This was unpromising: naturally, I shied away from any analysis of dreams that treated them as specially arranged picture shows, coded prophecies from another dimension, rather than suggestive but random collocations of thoughts. Still, I stuck to my policy of minimum intervention for a little longer, hoping that Lily would not pilot us too far towards the region where Freud makes way for five-dollar guides to the supernatural informing the reader that a dream of vegetables portends wealth but a cypress tree may spell disaster.

'My grandfather dreamt that his brother was in terrible danger,' Lily recounted, 'and four days later he died in the First World War. He was in the catering department so it wasn't the sort of thing you could ever predict. He was blown up by a shell fired by one of his friends as a practice. And Mum has all kinds of dreams. She dreamt that she would marry a left-hander and she did, she dreamt he was having an affair when he was, she even dreamt a phone number once and phoned it when she woke up, and it was a school friend she hadn't seen for twenty years.' Pride wrestled with unease on Lily's face. 'So you can see why I'm scared. I can't just ignore dream after dream telling me not to do the play. If I could, I'd just leave. But I need the money and I need the exposure. I've got casting people coming in a few days for a film. I can't not do it.' She paused. 'I need your help.'

Lily's appeal to hereditary powers of dream prophecy seemed like a double corruption of the idea of cause and effect: drawing shaky lines between dream and subsequent 'predicted' event, and then longer lines between the Nostradama of her family and herself, meant taking obvious liberties with the philosophy of consequence. Like any such claims, the stories of nocturnal revelations were impressive enough until viewed in the context of all the wayward predictions that went unreported. It was hard to know at this stage, however, whether pointing this out would calm Lily's superstitious impulse or imply exactly the disrespect she had feared. For now, I decided that someone who had suffered twenty nightmares deserved the benefit of the doubt, and asked: 'What would you like us to do next?'

'Would you sleep here tonight?' Lily asked.

This should have presented a dilemma, but I was now so far over the red line of doctor–patient relations that it was barely visible in the distance as I looked back. For a while it had been apparent that this would not be a standard case with delimited consultations: ten o'clock to eleven, coffee, an hour of professional neutrality. My flight back to Chicago was booked for a week's time – the theatre company's budget for 'cast mental health' ran out at that point, and so would the patience of all my rescheduled clients at home – but in the meantime anything seemed possible.

We arranged that I would come at eleven, after that night's sold-out performance. I was halfway through advising

Lily to have a relaxing day when she gleefully answered the phone, shouting the caller's name – it sounded like 'Margot', perhaps 'Marco' – while giving me a conspiratorial look that suggested she had been dreading this conversation. A brief exchange followed in which Lily apparently agreed with everything the caller suggested, and which concluded with her arranging to meet him for breakfast in an hour. Replacing the phone, she explained that one of her friends was 'desperate' to see her. 'He wants to talk about this book he's written, he's being sued for a hundred thousand dollars or something,' she said casually, kissing me lightly on the cheek and moving off to begin her preparations for this and other appointments. Trying to follow Lily's social map was like joining a TV series in its fifth season, I decided; the ground would be made up eventually, but for now I was content to let the minor characters come and go. Outside, a beautiful morning was unfolding itself and fatigue had not yet returned to claim back the energy I had taken on loan. I could see a long day stretching invitingly ahead of me, each hour leisurely but full.

I shaved in the restroom of a café, using a tiny disposable razor, among many gifts lavished upon me by the airline which had flown me to New York in first class, unnecessarily but at the theatre's expense. I now realised that with the money squandered on the trappings of airborne luxury (the deer steaks, 1962 wines, executive breath-freshener and office golf set), the theatre company could have paid for me to treat Lily for another week. When the case originally came up I would probably not have agreed to shelve my Chicago appointments for two weeks or longer, but that was before I met her. Splashing water on my face, I looked into the grimy men's-room mirror and saw a confident, clean-cut man in his early thirties with a fine romantic pedigree and no history of inferiority. My self-image was slowly being overhauled.

That day I continued my Aloisi-style study course by devouring as much of the history of dream theory as I could. It was an area I had been interested in at Michigan, and had delved into many times in my clinical career – most recently when working with the banker terrified of turning into a bird, who was so sensitive to the subject that close friends at the bank stopped referring to 'bills' – but in my new-found lust for back-to-basics research I felt compelled to work my way through an anthology of dream psychoanalysis, even the fifty-page introduction which taught me that Chaucer refers to dreams more than forty times and that the Inuit word for 'dream' is the same as for 'truth'. Among all this trivia there were grains of crucial information, much of which I memorised, in the old style, by visiting the index. Reassured by my revision, I felt that I had a sound clinical grasp of the phenomenon of dreaming; but in the realm of psycho-therapy, as we have seen, person-management is equally important. Logic and theory alone wouldn't be enough to convince Lily that her dreams were not premonitions of fast-approaching disaster: it would take artful persuasion and frequent acknowledgements that she was right to be afraid.

There was, of course, the chance that the recurring dream would stop if I could put her at her ease before sleep, but the 'warnings' had been so often repeated that it would be a long time before Lily's fear subsided altogether. As for using medication which would make dream recall impossible, it wouldn't be without precedent, but the side effects were uncertain – besides, this seemed like the stopgap solution of a hack doctor. It would take real skill to guide Lily away from her fears, away from the idea that onrushing disaster was being signposted by her dreams. It was a challenge I relished and the thought of seeing Lily through the night lightened the hours of the afternoon. Late was certainly better than never.

In the evening, as I packed an overnight bag like a seventh-grader preparing for a slumber party, my ear was caught by a familiar name on Richard's ever-active TV. Although he watched hardly any television, even missing his own appearances, his girlfriend Donna – a freelance graphic designer – would leave it on all day for fear of missing something interesting (one of the seven reasons which Richard was to cite when, in 1988, he ended their relationship and moved in with the twenty-four-year-old editor of a fashion magazine). Between endlessly cycling gaudy commercials, a 'breaking newsflash' whisked the viewer off to a courtroom where a jury was about to pronounce a verdict on Andre Genelli. A scanning shot took in rows of captivated faces, among them Richard's. On this hyperactive station, even the stately activity of the court was presented with the breathless image-jumping of a sports event: while a lugubrious judge ventured some moral platitudes, a whispering anchorwoman kept up a frantic commentary. The mishmash of voices and images was almost impossible to follow, but the end result was clear enough: the bloodless lips of an official spelled out the word 'Guilty' and the room erupted in pockets of jubilation or despair. Cinematic cuts served up personal cameos: the defendant shaking his head in defiance, miscellaneous relatives and onlookers adopting looks of studied dignity, and a pack of slick-haired interchangeable prosecutors congratulating each other with gentle high-fives and handshakes. In the middle of this pack, already turning his mind to the next triumph, was Richard.

I took the long way round to Lily's that night, planning

to be twenty minutes late. I had calculated this carefully: it allowed time for her inevitable unpunctuality, but not enough time to seem slapdash if *she* ended up waiting for *me*. Tonight was a night, however, when my habits of cautious premeditation and introspection had to be put aside; initiative, boldness, improvisation, all the tools I was never issued with, must come into play. There were prizes at stake.

There was a surprise in store right away, although it was a minor tremor compared with what was to follow: Lily arrived, not just half an hour late on top of the time I had allowed – nothing surprising so far – but accompanied by one of her castmates, a very tall man who was playing Donalbain. Lily introduced him as Liam and explained that he had 'come back for a drink'. As she sat down away from both of us, hands on knees and feet up on the edge of the chair like a child watching late-night TV, I enquired brightly about the night's performance (it had gone well) and engaged her lanky co-actor in dutiful conversation. Everything he said irritated me, in particular the jovial references he made to Lily's recent problems. I conceived a dark suspicion that it was he who had amended the poster in the kitchen. By this stage it hardly needs to be said that my impatience with him was really a trick of my natural predator, jealousy, an emotion which accounts for so many incidents in this story that I am increasingly afraid to highlight them as we go on. The jealousy made me feel, in turn, restless discomfort as if I were hoping to get away with something dishonourable. In any case, it was half past twelve before Liam had been shown to the door after a lengthy exchange of in-jokes (between them) and civilities (between us). By that time Lily was 'pretty much knackered' as she put it, and within half an hour we were in bed.

It was the same bed, as nobody will be surprised to read.

Yet the relationship between us remained as pure and platonic as is possible between two bed-sharing eligible adults, one of them needing protection and the other eager to provide it. We arrived between the same sheets by an innocent route: Lily remarked that the spare room was very cold at night (this was true; I verified it for myself) and she had lent all her blankets to her political writer friend who had sold his house that day as security against his 100,000-dollar lawsuit. I volunteered to sleep on the floor in her room, she offered me the bed; and so we compromised on a bed-share.

'I think maybe I won't have the dream tonight,' said Lily as she undressed while I looked at the curtains. 'It's good not to be alone.'

I agreed with this, levering myself on to the extreme edge of the baffling, eight-sided bed so that I was as respectful a distance as possible away from the woman I was still trying to refer to as a 'patient'. By the time unconsciousness came – claiming Lily first – I had got closer, but not much closer. In my whole life, I realised, I had slept only a handful of nights with other people. A smattering of short-term relationships and one or two meaningless incidents after the few blind dates that had not ended in disappointment or worse. But this intimacy meant more than simple sex, I told myself as Lily slept, breathing softly through her nose, her long eyelashes fastening down the lids, keeping danger at bay. Years fell away from her face as she slept; she looked at peace. Just by being there, I was doing my job. The theatre company was getting more than it paid for. I watched her eyelids flutter until the warmth and her proximity lulled me into a fuzzy acceptance of sleep.

Five hours later those same eyes were opening and closing frantically as Lily writhed in the grip of another nightmare. She had sat straight up in the bed and was mumbling an indecipherable word over and over, with an insistence and animation terrible to watch. Torn between shaking her out of the dream and letting it run its course, I watched as she slid out of bed and took strange, faltering steps around its perimeter as if trying to avoid falling into a ditch. She continued to enact the dream for two or three tense minutes, occasionally making a timid but desperate gesture like someone trying to fend off an attacker. I remembered reading about a French experimenter who had made lesions in the lower brains of cats to release them from the paralysis of an REM sleep and watched as they acted out their dreams, jumping on to tables and out of windows, no doubt waking up puzzled. When Lily's dream-play was over, she sat down on the edge of the bed, her back to me, the curve of her buttocks faintly visible against the nightdress, and I relaxed momentarily; but then her shoulders heaved in a huge sob and, still asleep, she began shuddering and weeping to herself again. Gingerly, like an animal-handler, I took her by the shoulders and coaxed her into wakefulness. She looked around confusedly for a brief time before wiping her eyes and leaning back, exhausted, against the bedstead.

'Well, there it was again,' she said at last.

'The same one as usual?' I asked, embarrassed.

'Yes, the same,' said Lily.

'The warnings were the same, to stop doing the play?'

'Yes. They said something terrible would soon happen.'

'It'd be useful if they could specify a day for us.' It was the wrong comment and I immediately began trying to repair the damage. 'I didn't mean to sound . . .'

'Don't you take me seriously?' she demanded with not quite enough energy to be truly angry, but enough to make me repentant. 'What are you here for, if not? Just to sleep with me?'

'I'm not here for that at all,' I said.

'So this is how you usually treat patients, is it?' she asked, with an expansive gesture around the bedroom. I was disconcerted and so, I think, was she. There was a pause.

'We're going to cure you tomorrow,' I said, rashly.

'How?' She was struggling to keep the hard edge in her voice, but still there was pressure on me to say something authoritative, to give notice of some plan for her delivery.

'I'm going to hypnotise you,' I said, to my own amazement.

'Does that work?'

'I think it'll work,' I said, picking up the gauntlet I had thrown down in front of myself. 'I'm going to get you to tell me what it is that's causing these dreams. They must be coming from somewhere in your unconscious mind.'

'And the warnings . . . ?'

'Maybe we'll find more clues about them too,' I said diplomatically.

'Well, it's worth a try,' she agreed. 'Listen, Pete, I've got casting people coming to watch me in a few days.' The businesslike talk cut a contrast with the setting: tousled bedsheets lay all around, scattered in Lily's skirmish with the mystery invaders. 'I've got to decide whether I can do the play. Whether it's safe.'

I wanted to object to this irrational talk of risk, but we had traded (light) blows already and besides, the 'prophecy' of the dream message could easily prove self-fulfilling: if Lily maintained the belief that her involvement in the play was cursed, her performances would continue to be blighted by it. Her big night in front of the movie moguls was in danger of being ruined by another dose of anxiety-related illness. It would also be my last night in the city. The nature of my race against the clock was clear and the next lap would be the hypnosis.

Lily, sitting obediently opposite me the next day in the lounge with phone disconnected and curtains drawn, was an eminently hypnotisable subject. My concern had been that her penchant for the mystical might overcook her mind with ideas about contacting 'the other side', but her concentration was immaculate and she followed my commands rapidly and surely, as if I were directing her in a rehearsal. It took a short time to put her into a hypnotic trance, a condition which I tested in the usual way by conditioning her to respond to set commands only. When a fire alarm went off briefly in the next-door apartment, she didn't twitch a muscle.

Her face was blank, waiting to act as a screen for signals from unknown territories. 'Just allow yourself to slip back into the dream,' I said soothingly. 'Don't be frightened, you're going in deliberately this time.'

A hypnosis is not so different from a dream: it has been described as 'a kind of interactive dreamstate in which the subject is like the character in a video game played by the hypnotist'.[17] Under these controlled conditions I hoped to be able to pilot Lily through her subconscious, allowing us to observe the region through a clear window rather than the manic distorting lens of dream logic. It would be like

---

[17] Rice, *Virtual Neurology*. An otherwise enlightening passage on hypnosis is unfortunately complicated by Rice's insistence upon maintaining the 'human brain as a computer' conceit, which underpins the whole work. His description of the hypnosis of a prisoner is obfuscated by constant, confusing reference to the patient's 'RAM', 'ROM' and 'floppy drive'; and his conclusion that 'hypnotizing patients of this type is like playing *Super Mario Brothers* on a Pentium' leaves the reader baffled. Rice has also been taken to task for his comment that 'while in some cases we can upgrade a patient chip by chip, at other times it seems more advisable simply to replace them with another model'.

revisiting a feared stretch of woodland in daylight and finding it almost disappointingly free of real dangers.

Lily was a natural dreamer, for better or worse, and in twenty minutes she was in a dream state as profound as an REM sleep. I have the tape of myself affirming this, and however peculiar Lily's report from the other side was, I do not think anyone who listens to it could honestly deny its validity.

Things started to happen when, after a little meandering through minor curiosities of her subconscious, Lily announced that she could now see 'the same woman'.

'The woman you always see?' I asked.

'Yes.'

'And who is it?'

'It's me,' she replied promptly.

'You?'

'Yes. Myself.'

'And who are you?' I asked.

'I'm Elizabeth,' said Lily.

At this point, to avoid accusations of embellishment, I submit the transcript of a conversation which, for large portions, was more of a monologue. On the Dictaphone tape you can hear the hum of traffic, the occasional shouts of children, the belching and coughing of water pipes, the scream of a police car, all washing over the apartment as I sat, mesmerised myself.

TRANSCRIPT OF CONVERSATION BETWEEN LILY RIPLEY AND PETER KRISTAL, 21 MAY 1986.

PK's comments: Subject — 38 years old, of sound mind — under hypnosis for approx. 45 minutes at beginning of transcript.

PK   Tell me about Elizabeth.

LR   My first name was Elizabeth. I lived in . . . *(inaudible)*. I died there too.

PK   Died there?

LR   Yes.

PK   When was that?

LR   Years ago now. Before anyone we know was around.

PK   And what did you do?

LR   My father owned land and I worked for him. I was married to . . . *(inaudible)* . . . but everyone called him Jacob. My friend Rebecca lived just outside the village on her husband's farm. She was my only friend. We went everywhere together. I helped her with picking berries and she helped me cook for my husband because she could do it better than I could, she knew about getting the flavours. My husband said I spent too much time at her home.

PK   How long did you live like that?

LR   Till we died.

PK's comments: At various points I studied the subject's face for signs of self-awareness, but there was no fluctuation in her expression. Her voice, also, remained expressionless throughout.

PK   And how did you die?

LR   There was a fire at the old farm.

PK   You died in a fire?

LR   No. The fire was at Rebecca's farm. The barn burned down, people said it was the witches.

PK   Witches?

LR   They said there was witches in the village [because] of all the queer things happening, children getting sick and dying, one mother had nine children die in a week. And other things. People with strange diseases. And at night people could hear . . . singing and *(several inaudible words)* fires and things like strange animals. So everyone knew about the witches. And Rebecca was meant to be one of the witches.

PK   *Was* she a witch?

LR   No, she was my friend. But she kept these dolls, just things that she had since when she was a baby, and people said it was dolls like witches used, and then some people saw her by the barn on the night of the fire. So they said she did it and that they would burn her.

PK   But she didn't do it?

LR   Jacob did it.

PK   Your husband?

LR   They were fighting, Jacob and Rebecca's man. Jacob said I knew her husband too well.

PK   Was it true?

LR   *(After pause)* So Jacob, my man, he went to the barn and set it on fire. Killed all the chickens and the place was ruined after that. All because of a jealous thing with him and Rebecca's husband. And then he said Rebecca did it because she was a witch.

PK   And they burned her?

LR   *(Pause)* I could have told them she wasn't a witch. They asked me, did you see who did it?

PK   And you said . . .

LR   I told them no. I knew Jacob did it. But I was scared,

he'd find out I said something and kill me. So I told
them nothing. And they asked me was Rebecca a
witch. I said I didn't know. I didn't say she was a witch.

PK   But you didn't tell them the truth about the barn?

LR   *(More forcefully)* I didn't say she was a witch.

PK   But they burned her?

LR   Her and two others. Said they were a gang of witches.

PK   Were there many people there?

LR   Rebecca's family. Her husband. Her brothers and sisters.
Tom, James, Arthur, Lauren, *(inaudible)*, Frances, Jemima,
Steven and all the others . . .

*PK's comments: At this point Lily reeled off the names of almost
sixty villagers and described their occupations, also supplying physical
details and trivia for many of them. This information – amounting
to approx. seven thousand words in total – cannot all be reproduced
here. A discussion of the historical credibility of Lily's story follows
the transcript.*

LR   . . . all these people, all pressed together so they nearly
couldn't breathe, and at the burning I saw them all and
they were jeering and spitting at me because they
thought *I* was a witch and should have been in the fire
with her. And I couldn't look at Rebecca up there on
the pyre. And I wasn't there when she died but they said
she cursed me, said I would never live to be older than
her, nor would my children, or their children. And I
knew the curse was true. So there was nothing I could
do and I would come to a terrible end because I had
lied. So I had to die, too. And I went into the barn, what
was left, all burned, just the remains, and I hanged
myself by the neck that same night so I would die too.

PK   You hanged yourself?

LR   I did it with a rope, and I stood on a bucket.

PK   And how long did it take for you to die?

LR   I . . . *(becoming increasingly incoherent, she slumps down as if asleep.)*

TRANSCRIPT ENDS

My first task was to make sure that Lily had not dramatically fulfilled the curse by dying under hypnosis, since she had lapsed from the unconscious narration into a sleep so deep that dragging her to her bed was like moving furniture. Slumping her carefully against a pile of pillows like a doll, I went to make coffee. My mind felt as crammed and creased as an old notebook; the inoffensive Dictaphone tape had taken on properties so sinister I hesitated before playing it back, turning down the volume as Lily's emotionless voice recounted her past life story a second time, jumping at the slightest sound outside. I had just witnessed either an astounding feat of imagination and performance, or – if it had all been genuine – a remarkable example of recall under hypnosis. But what was Lily recalling, and how had her mind come to be stuffed with the minutiae of a centuries-old incident? As I gazed up at Lily's books on reincarnation and the soul, they beamed back like religious evangelists: *It's never too late to change your mind*. There must be an explanation that did not require her to have lived and died before, but for the time being I felt extremely baffled. As for the large coincidence which tied together her story of a witch curse with the formative myth of my home town, that was even more bemusing.

Ours was not the only town in history to hear the bitter last wish of a dying scapegoat, but her story was uncannily close to the tale which was always brought out at Witching Hallowe'ens: most memorably by Mr Paulson, whose gruesome school-assembly re-enactment of the lynching had been a sign of things to come. I strained to recall the details of Paulson's courageous adaptation, but all that would surface in the memory was the horrendous burning-flesh sound effect that Paulson had got from his brother, a TV production assistant; the younger children leaving the hall in tears; the undisguised envy of Mr Tomlinson. Tomorrow, I resolved, I would look up the details of the Witching trial, because I suddenly realised that in spite of all the childhood tales I knew nothing of the actual witch-trial story. Nor did I know anything more about the history of witchcraft than what could be learned from *The Crucible* (which was performed at school the year after *Macbeth*; I didn't audition). At times like this, I felt I knew nothing about most things. But I had heard a unique testimony, whatever its provenance, and I owned a piece of Lily nobody else had ever seen.

Watching Lily listen to the playback, I scanned every flicker of her face, from her confusion when she entered the room to find ghosts from her past filling the airwaves, through horrified engrossment, to speechlessness at the climax. Neither of us moved or spoke for a full two minutes after Lily's recorded alter ego had finished her dire pronouncements and hidden herself again. The click of the run-out tape sounded as loud as a pistol shot. Lily shook her head vigorously as if doing this would change the scene, like a snowstorm in a jar. I was reminded of Patsy in the moments after she had relived the songs-in-the-mailbox drama. The same profound confusion, that same sense of not being able to trust either the emerging memory of the past or the senses' account of the present; of being suspended, somehow, between the two. Again, the hardest of cynics would have struggled to say there was anything feigned about her manner.

'So that's it, I can't do this any more,' Lily said calmly, and moved towards the phone with the usual haste, the desire that her erratic decisions should be carried out before common sense could put a red line through them. But I had the pen ready.

'Hold on. You're going to leave the play because of this? What about the casting agents?'

'Casting . . .! Pete, my life is in danger.'

'Slow down. Let's discuss what we heard there.' As I had done with energy a day earlier, I now took a loan of confidence, hoping that it would prove to be justified when I understood the contents of the tape better. 'So you don't remember anything about the hypnosis?'

'Of course not,' said Lily.

'You don't remember saying any of it?'

A brief, hard stare. The balance between ensuring scientific integrity and not appearing to challenge Lily's *personal* integrity was a delicate one.

'How could I?'

'And now you've heard what you said, does it make sense to you, does it explain things?'

'Well, you heard it,' said Lily. 'I've had past lives, I sort of knew that. In a past life I was a bitch and I let my friend die, I suppose I could have guessed that. I've always had a fear of fire, and I've always had this thing about hanging . . . and drowning, too . . .'

(I had to suppress the comment that a fear of agonising death was not the most unusual I had come across.)

'. . . and there's a curse on me. How old was Rebecca?'

'You didn't specify,' I said.

'But not old,' said Lily, her voice falling away. 'I'm going to die really soon. While I'm doing the play. That's what the curse says. It must be because I'm doing a play about witches and killing and stuff that the dreams have come.'

She spoke as if these facts had been established beyond reasonable doubt. Her voice, tremulous but calm, conveyed both horror and resignation, like some Shakespearean heroine grimly aware that she has taken a draught of poison. But despite the undoubted vividness of her 'memories', I could not believe that this intelligent individual, with whom I had found so much in common on our first meeting, was

144

committed to this classically fatalistic idea of tragedy: something ordained by the inescapable processes of fate, maintained by endlessly cunning patterns of inherited misfortune, signalled by obscure pointers and clues.

'Lily, I know these dreams have been terrifying, but don't you think they could just be dreams? And what you said under hypnosis could just be things that are lodged in your head somehow? Instead of the whole thing being a . . . dire warning?'

'But what about all the stuff I said just now? How could I know all that, about the burning and the curse? Do you think I made it up?'

'No,' I reassured her. 'I just think it might have come from somewhere other than memory. I think you might have had this psychic baggage from . . . well, from . . .'

(And here inspiration, a rare visitor to my plodding mind, struck.)

'Whereabouts does your family come from in England?'

'London,' she said, 'but my father's relations are all in East Anglia. What has that got to do with anything?'

'I'm just wondering,' I muttered excitedly, 'whether you might have . . . so to speak, inherited these memories from an ancestor.' The feeling of being propelled by inspiration was exhilarating: what half-formed conjecture would I hear myself come out with next?

'What, through my genes?'

'Yes,' I said. 'There's a lot we don't know about genetics, transmission of information and personality.' (Here I was gaining momentum; a psychiatrist, even a doggedly rational one, never feels safer than when talking about how little we know.) 'It's been known for people to produce information under hypnosis which they could never have possessed unless someone had . . . handed it down to them.'

A mysterious ancestor in Witching, a sense of shame

invisibly passed down through the generations, sitting un-attended in the attics of consecutive Ripley minds and now stumbled upon by chance? More credible than the idea of a real curse, it was nonetheless a witch's brew of fact, fiction and supposition, stirred into a mix almost as haphazard as a folk tale. As Lily seemed halfway to being placated, however, I pressed on.

'Why don't you give it one more night?' I said. 'Do the performance tonight. Maybe now you've released the knowledge of the curse, things will be easier.'

Her fingers were still cradling the phone receiver, but with less conviction.

'Also, you need time to think about this . . . all this,' I said, gesturing at the Dictaphone tape and by extension at the disarranged mind which it now represented. 'Let's meet after the show. I'll spend the rest of the day thinking about a treatment, and if you still feel that you need to do something more drastic, we'll . . .'

I left this unfinished, a blank cheque for her to inscribe with the promise of any spiritual solution that might comfort her. We embraced for a long moment and she thanked me, gripping my hand. I stared into her eyes and wondered if what lay behind them would ever make sense to me. It still seemed possible, but I needed to find a way of convincing her that science could account for the apparently supernatural; and before that, I had to work things out for myself.

Today I could go away to the Internet and lay my hands on the entire Ripley family tree in less than the time it has taken me to type this sentence. In the mid-eighties, though, trying to find a single name in the slush pile of the world's accumulated trivia felt like combing a beach for a contact lens. The Fullman Library contained thousands of English parish records on microfilm, and there was nowhere near enough time to sift through the information. Not only was I looking for a needle in a haystack, as I scanned the grainy records for traces of Lily's heritage; I wasn't even sure where the haystack was. It was two o'clock already: Lily's make-or-break date with the casting agents was looming, and I would be flying back in forty-eight hours.

Several times I had to extricate myself from the mental catch-22 of wasting time by worrying about the lack of time. My concentration was rewarded in part: among the mountain of interesting witch titbits I dug up were several accounts of the Witching trials. Although most were condensed into a few short paragraphs (as I had always feared, the town wasn't quite important enough even to be a big player in the field which supplied its name) and some central facts were contested, three sources identified a woman called Rebecca Pelley or Pulley as one of the executed parties. None of them could corroborate Lily's story of the burning barn – all the records divulged was that the women were 'Burnt to their Deaths upon a Pyre, for having been found to be Witches, and to be engaged in Conjurations, Spells, and Magick, with the aim of establishing the Devil within the towne'[18] – but it was a link nonetheless and a satisfying one. Furthermore, a couple of calls to genetics specialists confirmed that there were plenty of precedents for Lily's generation-spanning recall. Many psychiatrists regard genetic transmission as the best explanation for the hundreds of cases in which claims of past lives are supported by mystifyingly accurate facts.[19]

[18] Cited in, among others, Joanna Culver, *Scapegoatess – A History of Wronged Women* (Paper Fan Press, 1981)
[19] See for example J. A. Dawson, *Blue Genes: Why Old Songs Can Make Us Sad*. The theory is, however, contested in Aloisi, *Paranormality*.

Locating a possible member of the Ripley family in seventeenth-century Witching was interesting for more than one reason: if Rebecca's curse had really been directed at a single enemy, a treacherous friend, rather than the whole town, then Witching's long love affair with the idea of its own cursedness might be destructible. It would make a nice postscript, almost ten years on, to my Hirst analysis. 'Further proof, if proof were needed, that the only curses on Witching are the curses of obstinacy and silence – as Nicholas Hirst would surely have agreed.'

With the world spinning crazily on its axis in the busy streets outside the phone booth, Witching sounded even more remote than usual when I called home; the action lag made the conversation stilted and sluggish like a record played at the wrong speed. After I had promised to visit soon, and negotiated some unusually wearying small talk, Dad said he would ask around for information about the Ripleys – one of his colleagues on the force was among Witching's keenest local historians – but when I called back, he had nothing to report. My expectations hadn't been high: there was no reason why an ordinary family should have left a mark clear enough to have interested even Dad's encyclopedic friend. Walking home, as a sulky sky promised another thunderstorm, I alternated between thinking of all the people crammed into the dustbin of history, the un-people abandoned by the supposed protectors of their memory, and wishing I had a coat.

Meanwhile Richard, who had recently bought an all-weather jacket worth 700 dollars, was buoyant after his legal tour de force. After congratulating him, I gave him an update of my own case as he prepared to take Donna out for a celebratory meal he had booked fifteen minutes before the result was announced. He listened attentively to my description of the hypnosis, making occasional approving comments. When I had finished outlining my ancestral-memory theory, however, an unmissable rise of his eyebrows irked me.

'I know it's bizarre, but there are precedents,' I said.

'I know,' he said, 'but she's an actress. Don't you think she could just be acting?'

'Of course, but you should have been there. If she was acting, she's a brilliant actress.'

'She *is* a brilliant actress,' said Richard, tying his necktie.

'But the way she behaved under hypnosis . . .' I objected.

'You know what decided the Genelli case?' Richard asked, rhetorically. 'His counsel was going on and on about Stockholm syndrome and at first it worked.' He imitated the querulous whine in which all his opponents spoke when he impersonated them: '"Mr Genelli was terribly afraid. Mr Genelli was mistreated. Mr Genelli had to defend himself." Et cetera et cetera.' He drew these last words out, mockingly. 'But then Genelli started chipping in. "Oh, I couldn't speak the truth because they would beat me up. So I came to identify myself with them. It was a defence mechanism." All that kind of thing. And it was all too polished. He'd got it out of a book. In the end we proved he didn't have Stockholm syndrome; he'd just been very well trained.'

'So?'

'People these days know what symptoms they're supposed to be exhibiting,' said Richard. 'They read the casebooks, they see shrinks in TV dramas, everyone's an expert. I'm meant to have Stockholm? OK, I mention that the cops started to feel like my buddies. I'm recalling the distant past under hypnosis? OK, so I acquire extraordinary detailed knowledge and deliver it like this.' Adopting a glassy-eyed expression, he produced a maddeningly accurate impression. 'And afterwards, I won't remember a thing. You know,'

Richard continued, 'I think I might have mentioned that we knew each other from Witching when I recommended you for the job.'

'What are you saying, that she could have invented the whole story? Why the hell would she do that?' I demanded, rising to the bait.

Richard, with a mischievous twinkle, sensed my indignation. 'All this is pure speculation,' he said, raising his hands like an athlete accused of foul play, 'and if anyone can tell genuine from fake, it's you.' He had always had the trick of pitching his voice right on the ambiguity line between sincerity and mockery. Many psychiatrists, like politicians, make an art form of the non-committal stance, weaving waves of smooth and subtly meaningless sentences into glossy blankets with which they smother their listeners' objections. Richard's skill was not to disguise the absence of opinion, so much as to indicate that he was capable of holding all opinions simultaneously. Although this was a crucial factor in his popularity, it alienated some people and was one of the seven character flaws which Donna listed in retaliation on the last day of their relationship. I found it exasperating.

'Come on,' I pressed. 'Why would she be making all this fuss for nothing?'

There was a second's pause.

'You can't think of a single reason.'

'She *could* be trying to seduce you,' said Richard, ignoring the snort I felt obliged to produce as a response. 'Or she might just love attention. Or it might be a good career move, in the long run. Did you know their box office is up fifty per cent since she started going nuts? They're selling out every night. Bigger audiences and more press attention means more agent attention. She's desperate to get back into the movies, like all of them.'

I was about to tackle his points in order when Donna entered, carrying a bottle of wine. Her hair was tied back in a bow and she was wearing a low-cut maroon dress. The scent of expensive, summery perfume filled the room as she pulled Richard's arm in playful impatience. They were a delightful couple.

Always mindful of the fact that as a guest I was intruding, I made my peace with Richard and wished them a good night. She dragged him to the taxi as he flailed in mock reluctance and the last thing I heard was the two of them discussing favourite Italian seafood dishes. Almost revelling in the pathos, I made myself a peanut-butter sandwich as rain began to lash at the windows.

Inevitably, my thoughts soon turned to the Charterhouse and the performance that was underway. She would be announcing Duncan's murder as I finished my meagre dinner, and beginning her obsessive hand-washing at about the time I stepped out of the shower; this was the moment when the calculations broke down, for the phone started to ring. It was Lily.

'The play's off because of lightning,' she announced.

'It's cancelled?'

She was already on to the next stage. 'I need to . . . can I come to yours?'

'Well it's not really "mine", that's the thing, I . . .'

'It's just that we need a quiet place to do our stuff.'

'Our stuff?'

'I've worked out what we need to do about the . . .' said Lily. Here she was cut off by more fuzz and a groan of thunder rattled the windows as if to corroborate her story. There was no turning her away; I waited for her with the usual mix of fascination and trepidation.

The streets below were dark; car drivers honked

petulantly as if accusing each other of causing the weather. A lightning flash threw a wild light across the scene for a moment and I remembered sitting on Dad's shoulders on the roof at home, happy and indestructible as the storm cracked around us and Dad jovially challenged the Witching devils to do their worst. Looking out in the vague direction of the theatre, I reflected upon the poor timing of this latest coincidence: Lily was bound to find some way to read the weather as another warning from the increasingly impatient spirits of her past. No doubt one of her forefathers had been killed by lightning, or during a storm, or as a result of a play's cancellation.

Lily arrived with a multicoloured string bag from which, as she spoke, she unpacked a stream of peculiar objects: small candles, a box marked 'Energy crystals', and several spherical items of indeterminate purpose.

'It was weird,' she said, as I sat her down in the well-appointed room that was not mine. 'We were just about to go on and there was this massive CRACK! And all the lights were flashing and then, complete darkness. And it just stayed dark.' At this point there was a childish excitement in her voice, but over the next few sentences, yesterday's cold fatalism crept in. 'And they couldn't fix the lights so after a while, this poor guy had to go out and tell them it was cancelled. And he tried to make a joke of it with the audience – "So the question now is, when shall we three meet again?" – but they all took it very badly. And all this time I was there thinking, Shit, another one.'

'Another . . . ?'

'Another warning,' she said. 'And the agents are coming tomorrow, Pete. We've got to lift the curse or . . .'

The sentence faded away. I looked down at my reams of handwritten notes – on genetic information, memory, superstition and hysteria – and wondered if it would all be in vain. Rummaging in the bag as if preparing a conjuring trick, Lily brought out a small book emblazoned with silver stars.

'In this book there's a whole chapter about curses,' she said, handing it to me. It was entitled *Be Your Own Guru* and the introduction informed me that I would soon understand the universe and myself: I had no idea it could be so easy.

'So what do you want me to . . .?'

'You have to hypnotise me again,' she said. 'And I'm going to regress to the incident, become Elizabeth again and apologise.'

'Apologise to Rebecca?'

'Yes,' she said. 'It's the only way. If I can purge myself of the guilt, all the negative psychic energy will disperse. And then the curse will be broken.'

Silence fell; she looked at me expectantly. We were now at a crossroads. I felt that I was the only person left holding out against the flood of anti-rational mysticism. I had to stand my ground.

'I know you're in a hurry to get this sorted out, but . . .'

'You're right,' Lily cut me off, throwing her coat into a cupboard as if in her own home, and tossing her head back to shake hair out of her eyes. 'I'm going to have a shower first, I got soaked in the storm.' As far as I could see she was perfectly dry. 'I'll get mentally prepared,' she said over her shoulder, as I sat staring down at the star-covered book. She had brought a towel with her. I wondered how long she intended staying.

The dilemma I pondered now, as Lily padded about upstairs, was an uncomfortable one. She was asking me to act not as psychotherapist but as a faith healer, and all her talk – of dispersing malign energies, of psychological time-travelling – contravened the very beliefs which formed the anchor of my professional ethics. Indulging the role-play, stage-managing a psychic retreat and apology to Rebecca, would free Lily for tomorrow's performance, giving her short-term peace of mind; I would be able to get on the plane with the plaudits of a 'solved' case in my ears. But this would be only a placebo: and in six months, or a year, even five years, another arbitrary trigger – a psychologically demanding role or just a chance dream – would disturb her anew; and even when this in turn had been dealt with by another spiritual cleansing rite or an embrace with a mystic tree, the cycle would eventually restart, feeding Lily's superstition for the rest of her life (and possibly on into the next one). I would be abandoning her to the will of her overactive unconscious.

The alternative was more difficult but more honourable. It would involve taking an icepick to Lily's beliefs, providing her with a reasoned long-term plan for dispelling her problems. *We can explain this logically*, I needed to tell her, *and work through it properly*. It was my duty to myself and to her, even though:

- it might mean a terrible disagreement; Lily would accuse me of not caring, and worse;
- she would probably leave straight away and might not speak to me again before I went home;
- she would remain convinced that tomorrow's performance was ill-fated;
- she might even go ahead and withdraw from the play, in which case
- I would leave with my reputation badly dented.

And it was here that my resolution began to crumble. I could see Richard's reaction to the papers: SHRINK GOES HOME DEFEATED AS LADY MAC CRACKS AGAIN. I could even imagine that Richard, still flushed with legal success, might take over Lily's treatment and, when she finally overcame her troubles, claim the credit. That would be too much. I had worked so hard to get inside this woman's head. I would never completely understand her or be as close to her as I had hoped, but I could not let her be recorded as my first, public, failure. And so, as Lily returned, I chose the placebo. Instead of screwing my courage to the sticking-post, I screwed up my principles.

'OK,' I said. 'Let's . . . purge you.'

The lights were dimmed, the candles lit, the mystic objects scattered in patterns of Lily's choosing. Trying to lull her into the submissive state required was difficult, this time; she was breathless and excitable, I was fidgety and pre-occupied. Eventually, however, Lily's eyelids grew heavier and expression faded from her face. Having transported her back to the century of her choosing – like the charlatan genius in a time-travel movie – I was unsure what to do next; but Lily had gone into hypnosis (and, indeed, our whole time together) with her own agenda and it soon transpired that all I had to do was wait.

Before long she began to mumble indistinguishable words, some of them possibly names, but I had seen this routine before and Richard's cynicism had, in spite of everything, gone some way towards denting the mystique. Still it was a moving sight to see the tears squeeze out of the corners of Lily's eyes, running down the exact centre of her nose. Crying suited her well and I had an irritating wish to kiss her, to plant a single kiss on her moist lips, as though one moment of physical closeness could atone for the fact that we were worlds apart at heart. Looking right through me, her eyes meeting but not touching mine, she mumbled, 'I'm sorry, I'm sorry.' Then, louder, more urgently: 'Sorry.' I wondered if I was meant to play Rebecca and accept the apology – 'Sure, that's fine' – but Lily's sudden expression of tranquillity gave me my answer.

I saw that somewhere in the crossed wires of her subconscious, she had found forgiveness; I was not so sure I could forgive myself for the route we had taken.

Half an hour later, the set was still in place, the mini-candles burnt down to stubs. There had been no official end to the hypnosis this time, no sudden stealing in of sleep. Instead, Lily sat placidly with her arms folded in her lap, drained but peaceful.

'I really feel different,' she said after a while; and then, 'thank you for everything.'

Before long the sound of drink-fuelled laughter announced the return of Richard and Donna. As the key jiggled in the lock I felt vulnerable. The two came in, Richard leading Donna stridently in a reverse-frame of their exit, glowing and noisy from their evening out. Taking in the scene efficiently without betraying any surprise, Richard greeted Lily like a regular visitor. As she chatted back, I remembered with irrational displeasure that they had met and spoken (albeit briefly) before I even came to New York.

'We've just been working through a few things,' said Lily, and it seemed to me that a sly look passed between her and Richard, as if the whole rigmarole had been *my* idiosyncratic idea.

'Did you get results?' asked Richard. As in our earlier conversation, he succeeded in sounding and even *being* genuine in his interest while incorporating a shade of humorous scepticism too slight to be noticed by an outsider, but too pronounced for me to ignore. When it came to the telling inflection, the catch in the voice, there was little doubt Richard was a genius. For that alone he had deserved the part of Macbeth all those years ago.

'I think we got what we needed,' I said, evenly.

Richard made no response except to ask Donna a quick

inaudible question. As she strode off in search of something or other, he slung his jacket lazily over the couch and asked Lily about the show. She told him of the cancellation and there was a brief, uninteresting set-piece about the weather. Then, as the conversation zeroed in again on the play itself, Richard said: 'I saw . . . is it Victoria? . . . your understudy.'

'Oh, yes?' said Lily with the specific extra-politeness meant to convey strong distaste.

'Something on TV, it was,' said Richard. 'A courtroom thing. I thought she was excellent.'

'I think she has been on one or two shows,' said Lily. 'We don't really . . .'

'She must be waiting in the wings, no pun intended!' said Richard, who probably had intended it; 'waiting for you to give her a chance.'

'Well, she gets a chance if I'm ill,' said Lily, 'or if something happens to me.'

There was a pause. Lily was eyeing Richard with a righteous contempt which he relished. I searched for a conversation-rerouting remark, scrolled through some possibilities – the weather had already been covered, I didn't quite have the stomach for Richard's legal victory – and settled on claiming the headache to which, after all that had happened in the past few days, I felt fully entitled. The moment passed, but Lily, I knew, could not have forgotten it.

Sure enough, in the cab I had ordered to get Lily home, our conversation focused on Richard's inexplicable eulogy of Victoria Dobson. 'That's the last thing in the world I wanted to hear the night before an important show,' said Lily.

'I don't know why he brought it up,' I said, truthfully.

'I think he just wanted to upset me,' she said.

'I don't think so,' I countered, surprised at the compulsive loyalty I still felt for my friend. 'He's a good guy.

Sometimes he can't help seeming . . . kind of condescending, because he knows everything. But he doesn't mean it.'

'He thinks a lot of you,' said Lily.

'Well, we've known each other years and years.'

'But it's not that, he really respects you,' she persisted. I had seen few signs of this recently but apparently it was one of those things women can tell. 'And, I mean, so do I.' She thanked me again for my help as we stood on the rain-dark sidewalk outside her apartment. Then we shook hands, held the pose, hugged with the sheepish familiarity of ex-lovers and almost sank into a fumbling kiss before springing away. Parted, we stood for a while in silence, each reviewing our few days of strange, professional-personal intimacy and searching for a suitable closing line. As nothing seemed appropriate, I wished her good night and good luck and went on my way.

SONGWRITING SHRINK SINKS JINX
USA Today, 26 May 1986

British actress Lily Ripley has paid tribute to the psychotherapist who helped her to beat the stage fright that dogged her in Julian Mackensie's *Macbeth*. Miss Ripley said she feared the show was "cursed" after a number of frightening incidents and sub-par performances. But top performance shrink Peter Kristal, who three years ago helped rid Patsy DiMarco of a stalker by writing a song, rebuilt Miss Ripley's confidence in just one week with Eastern spiritual techniques including hypnosis and energy crystals. "I don't want to go into the details but he really helped me to deal with some things from my past," she said. Kristal, who practices in Chicago, IL, and is a school friend of TV expert Dr. Richard Aloisi, watched as Miss Ripley produced a best-of-run performance on Friday night, less than 24 hours after their final session, in which Kristal performed a psychic cleansing ritual. She is now rumored to be considering a role in the upcoming *Back to the Future* movie. All remaining performances of the Russian-styled *Macbeth* are sold out, but Charterhouse officials say there will be a specially arranged showing to accommodate ticket-holders who attended Saturday's abandoned performance.

It was true; she was great. I watched with a combination of pride and wistfulness as she unleashed the spellbinding performance of a woman freed from all inhibitions. I had certainly achieved that much. During one of the more sensual scenes with Macbeth I caught her eye and the two of us shared what might have been a lightning-brief flicker of triumph. There was no denying the ovation she received this time: as the audience before had spiked their applause with unspoken reservations, now they were excessively generous to Lily, sensing the choppy passage that had brought her to this point. They whooped and screamed as she came smilingly to the front of the stage with her co-star Robert, who was noticeably less satisfied than when he himself had been enjoying the lion's share of audience love. He had done nothing wrong, but it was Lily's night. My eyes roved over the appreciative faces looking for the movie men, but saw only the fat woman who had been one of the naysayers last time, rolling her playbill into a loudspeaker to yell her approval at her deaf companion. 'The way she *uses her face* . . . it's really something special!' I had to agree.

The after-show party that night was my last chance to see that face. Despite the thanks of a quickly drunk Julian Mackensie and the fake geniality of some thespians, I felt horrendously out of place among brash, self-confident actors and theatre staff in awe of their own resilience. There were only two bright spots: the first a game of cards in which I won fifty dollars from the supercilious stage-door janitor, who turned out to be a generous and convivial man (I gave him the money back later), and the second when I overheard two of Lily's castmates discussing the turnaround in her mood and form.

'I heard the shrink really worked a miracle on her,' one said.

'Who was it? Was it him?' I swung around to see the finger pointed, not at me, but over my shoulder towards Richard who had his arm around Lily while Donna returned with an overflowing pitcher of drink.

'It was me,' I could not stop myself from saying.

'Well done!' they chorused, and I felt ridiculously proud, as if I had achieved genuine professional excellence. Only one man could deflate this pride.

'Lily seems to have forgiven you for last night,' I commented dryly as Richard sauntered over.

'Last night . . .?' he strained to remember. 'Oh, when I mentioned the understudy! But that was reverse psychology at its finest!' Richard crowed.

'Reverse psychology?' The phrase was not yet current at that time. I think he might have invented it.

'I knew what she needed was an appeal to her basest instinct: jealousy,' said my old friend sagely. 'I knew if one thing could wake her up for tonight, it would be talking up Victoria. And it worked, didn't it! She said "Thank you for getting some sense into my head."'

'She *said* that to you?'

Richard smiled the smile of a man who can afford to lend out some of his accolades to others. 'She said you were great as well.'

Clipping the article from *USA Today* to send home, I reflected upon a week in which events had controlled me as much as the other way around, and which had culminated in what would become the most publicised success of my career, achieved at the cost of the worst abandonment of my professional ethos. For the sake of three more minutes of fame I had ensured that I would never enjoy complete credibility in my field again. I sealed the envelope and, holding out the newspaper in both hands as if to hide my face, turned to the Personal pages.

5

Christmas with the Kristals

As I had foreseen, the next two years of my career were streaked with a kind of fame so misrepresentative as to be closer to notoriety: at least that was the view of many of my Lakelands colleagues, who never tired of pointing out the discrepancy between the rationalism of my normal methods and the alleged moon-gazing mysticism which had brought my greatest success. Much of the teasing was as light-hearted as the jibes about my romantic failures, which continued to be popular, the two strands running concurrently like new and old seasons of a TV show. I received Guatemalan good-luck dolls as a birthday gift and people would read bogus horoscopes out to me with mock gravity, advising me that I should grasp opportunities while I could because Jupiter had come into congress with Mars, or stay out of taco bars because Venus was on the warpath. As people recognised long before Freud, however, jokes are a good way of expressing an unpalatable truth.

Jealousy of my invitations on to talk shows and solicitations from ever more exotic clients was not the real problem: it was more that, in the course of winning these lottery prizes of my profession, I had changed our patients' expectations of psychotherapy, changed what would today be called our 'brand'. People increasingly expected, even demanded, holistic therapies which cheerfully embraced the facts of their past lives and, instead of delving into their character and upbringing, waded fearlessly over to the other side to bring back newsflashes from the former selves who were casting a supernatural shadow. In a perversion of the cause-and-effect mentality I had fought so hard to foster, patients tried to attach their present malaises to long-buried alter egos with cables of sheer fantasy. Crisis point arrived when Simon Stacy had to drop a client after six months because the man, a dentist with an unremarkable case of depression, became implacably convinced that his melancholic moods dated back to his former life as an Irish embalmer.

Simon was not the only colleague unhappy with the shifting rules of the game and angry with me for seeming to redraw them, despite my protestations that my beliefs were unchanged and the Lily case had been misrepresented in the reports. Although I appeared as little as possible on TV, discontinued the use of hypnosis altogether and published many letters trying to clear my name of the hippy association – including one in the *British Journal of Psychiatry*, after a report which referred to me as 'the Witching doctor now, apparently, turning into a witch-doctor' – the atmosphere was becoming hostile. When the dentist patient walked out to begin a new business as a funeral director, I made the mistake of commiserating with Simon, and the dam of suppressed antagonism burst.

'Thanks for your concern, Pete,' he snarled, throwing his papers into a briefcase and snapping it shut. It wasn't the end of the day but he often used this gesture to imply a contempt so great that it made him physically restless. He was never seen unpacking the papers again and I had my suspicions that they were props brought along especially for the purpose. 'Just a shame you weren't treating him, I guess. You would have understood him better.'

'I'm not saying I would have understood him better . . .'

'*I'm* saying you would have,' said Simon. 'Because he was full of shit.'

I told Simon sharply that in assisting Lily, I had used the time-honoured stratagem of letting a patient believe whatever it would do them best to believe; also – and this was a more contentious point, one I would have argued against in a different situation – we were a business like any other and had to tailor our service to fit our clientele.

Simon suggested that since I loved it so much in Manhattan, maybe I should take my business expertise to Wall Street. The bitterness was luminous in his voice – he had been in the practice twice as long as me without any forays into the limelight, because he had no Aloisi figure to feed him scraps – but the high ground, I knew, was his. And so I left the practice that had been my base for eight years and set up on my own in an office which had previously housed the Chicago Church of Jesus Christ of Latter-Day Saints, until one of their priests was jailed for money-laundering.

A few unobtrusive press cuttings, posted on walls which still bore the marks of quasi-religious iconography when I arrived, quietly recalled my more publicised successes; on the desk, next to a picture of my parents, was a small framed photo taken for a newspaper in which Patsy and I were posing with a microphone. I rarely spoke to Patsy these days beyond the condensed news bulletin of the Christmas card, but the picture gave a celebrity gloss to the operation: like so many office photos its main function was not so much to fuel pleasant memories as to impress prospective clients, in this case with the idea that they might emerge from my office with a head full of brilliant songs. It gives me no pleasure to recall this and other exploitations of my new fame – even at the time I was uneasy with the altered trajectory of my career, which had been deflected by the Lily encounter like a pinball into the higher reaches of the table: more points, more prizes, but less feeling of control.

While the crisp air of self-employment gave me the freedom to take on some unusual commissions, I steered clear of malingerers, time-wasters (however wealthy) and anything remotely connected with 'other worlds'. Becoming comfortably established, I awarded myself reasonable holidays and a reasonable wage, and passed the checkpoint of middle age with everything, to outward appearances, in good condition. But still I was conscious of a hole somewhere, very gradually leaking lifeblood, drying me out at an infinitesimal rate: a gap which I had tried to plug by forming hasty romantic attachments, but whose shape now seemed more ragged and indefinite, needing to be sealed with a clot rather than choked up with a slap-on bandage. How I expected this clot to form, I had no idea, like so many of the thirty- to sixty-year-old clients – nearly all professionally successful – who came to me reporting the same feeling: too vague to be a longing or a craving, but too insistent to be ignored for ever. Perhaps it was nothing more than the gravity pull of middle age, but if this was a hard diagnosis to offer patients, it was even harder to pronounce upon myself.

Dad's lungs, reluctant labourers for years, were now rebelling more and more as each winter rolled around. After the Christmases of '86 and '87 I stayed in England for as much time as I could steal from my schedule, helping and hindering my mother in equal measure. Dad waved away most of the available attention with the determinedly commonsensical, no-use-making-a-scene bustle, which can portend either recovery or impending surrender. For long spells the act was convincing; he could still go fishing, go for walks, keep up his end of a vigorous conversation on the state of the police; but on bad days each breath was a tough catch, hauled up from the bottom of a river, and his lungs were like leaky buckets frittering the air away. In a restaurant one night, after he had been silent for almost the entire meal, an attempt to reassure us of his health set off the log-jam of coughs he had been holding back, a hacking chorus so long and raucous that we had to be moved to a corner to placate two other diners. Doctors made it known, with professional tact, that any measures they could take would be stalling the inevitable, because his real disease was old age: the only one you don't look forward to being cured of, as one of his favourite films reflected.

We heard that he had six months to live; then it rose to a year; then, another ricochet, back down to three months; and finally they told us that it was impossible to predict anything. My mother handled the fluctuating life spans with serenity, weaving her slim fingers between Dad's as the doctor looked up solemnly from charts of bad statistics. This serenity was not something I remembered from my childhood, when she used to flit restlessly in and out of rooms and conversations; in later life she seemed to have developed a calm resolution, as if resigned to upheaval. When Dad became worried that the nights of cough sequences (through which Mum lay patiently awake, refilling his water and diverting him with talk) were robbing him of the recommended eight hours of sleep, she got into the habit of tampering with the clocks to reassure him. On the morning of 21 December, fooled by her own plot, she left the house in a hurry for a hairdresser's appointment, crossed the street into a grocer's shop to pick up potatoes for later, and collapsed. A young policeman was sent round to my parents' house; my dad mistook him for a health visitor and greeted him with a cheery remark; the man informed him that his wife was dead.

Nineteen eighty-eight was our first Christmas as a one-parent family. In an afternoon even quieter than usual, while snow settled thickly on the roofs of happy families on TV and drifted sluggishly around our own real-life garden, I went slowly up the stairs (the third from the top gave a tame creak) which Jennifer O'Hara had mounted more than twenty years ago, to the bedroom still cluttered with the artefacts of my childhood, which lay atrophied on shelves and under beds. I reached into a drawer containing unfinished letters to people I would never again meet, notes for school assignments written for teachers who were now dead, and fished out the one live item: a black leather book with fraying yellow pages. In this book, every Christmas Day for the past twenty-eight years, I had taken time out from the high spirits or drunken apathy of the Kristal family gathering at our home to record a synopsis of the day's events. These were my oldest case notes, the original and longest-running set of bullet points, and by chronicling the mundane details of almost three decades of Christmases, it unfolded into something like a bullet-point summary of my own life so far. With many of its protagonists gone from the stage, its incidents made meaningless, whitewashed by time, and the diary routine itself now on the verge of extinction, I indulged in the shameless retrospective joyride that is the consolation prize for those who have outgrown Christmas's primary pleasures.

As a reedy wind whistled outside I relived, as best I could, the excitements and tensions of our family Christmases. As the diary progressed, the spidery handwriting of youth gave way to the regimented joins of school script, then the mock-careless dash of teenage and twenties, settling around the late twenties into the professional scribble which had supplanted my personal handwriting as my career outgrew and subjugated my social life. Yet the apparent chasm between the ages of ten and nearly forty had wrought incredibly few changes in the actual recording procedure. The pedantic cataloguing instinct, the desire to melt truth down and harden it into as compact a form as possible, wavered as little as the Christmas routine itself. I don't know anyone else who would have adhered to what began as a kid's hobby for half a lifetime. As the years flew away like the leaves of the book, I could almost understand how the long, flat expanses of time had folded up between the annual markers. One Christmas looked very much like the last, like two seascapes seen from the deck of a ferry; but the ocean was rushing away all the same, and one day we would grind into the shore.

PETER KRISTAL'S CHRISTMASES 1960–88

KEY (written 1960)

- Dad   Robert Kristal
- Mum   Linda Kristal
- Uncle Frank   Frank Kristal (Dad's oldest brother)
- Aunt Dorothy   his wife
- Uncle Tom   Tom Kristal (Dad's brother, older than him, but not as old as Frank)
- Aunt Sally   his wife
- Jemima (14), Rose (13),

  Johnny (9)   my cousins, who are the children of my aunts and uncles. As you can see from their ages, Johnny is younger than me, but the two girls are older. The girls' Dad is Frank, Johnny's Dad is Tom.

1960

MY PRESENTS

This diary, comics, sweets, a shirt, pen, clothes (boring!), book on photography (but I don't have a camera!), train set (the most expensive present)

WHAT PEOPLE TALKED ABOUT AT DINNER

Elvis who is a rock and roll band, Dad's cough, my grandfather (his Dad) and how he died, communists. I don't know what these are. Uncle Frank said elvis was a communist plot to take over the world, I think it was a joke as most people laughed, plus it wouldn't make sense. What everyone thinks of black people, there are more around than before.

Dad and Mum had a big ~~arguement~~ argument about something, it went on for a long time, I had to go and play with Johnny. We did a few things. The girls were rude to us and made fun because last year Johnny slept in my bed but there stupid.

1961

MY PRESENTS

Camera, football boots, sweets, money, five books, racing car game, mini pool table, I'm lousy at it, that means I'm no good.

WHAT PEOPLE TALKED ABOUT AT DINNER

Frank said a few things about communists who are people from Russia who killed a lot of people. It's a race America against them to get into space, I would think whoever drives the rocket faster will win. I said so 3 times, in the end Mummy said "it's not that kind of race" and Rose looked pleased.

Rose won a prize for writing at school and Jemima won some stupid contest about who is most beautiful. She wouldn't eat the chicken or duck because they were animals. Frank made a joke about it, saying let's hope if you are in the jungle the animals are as kind to you. It was funny but Jemima and Rose left the table and Frank was told off by Dorothy. I don't know why girls don't laugh at jokes and why they just stand round and whisper stuff.

THINGS THAT HAPPENED

We played with my pool table but Johnny, who is a year younger beat me 5 times and I only beat him once. Dad told me not to worry, he said if I ~~practice~~ practise I will get better and no-one is just born good or bad at sports. But also he said there's other stuff you can get into. I hope so because I think I might have been born bad despite of what he said, I'm no good at ping-pong either. Tom taught me a trick where you can get 3 balls in your mouth. He said it would make me famous. I got good at it but Mum hated it and Tom got into trouble for showing me. Mum thinks I'm about 4 and everything is about to kill me. When there was a thunderstorm and Dad took me on the roof and made jokes about how the Witching curse wouldn't get us, she was so angry you wouldn't believe, well you would because you are me!!.

1962

MY PRESENTS

Swimsuit (why!?), clothes, nine books, chemistry set, bike (the best present)

WHAT PEOPLE TALKED ABOUT AT DINNER

There was a big argument because there was nearly a war with America and Russia this year, and Frank blamed it all on some people, I didn't understand who they were but homosexuals was one. Tom and Frank both called them faggots or fags and homos and my Mum told them to be quiet very fast, I think it was in case I heard, but I know what homosexuals are anyway.

THINGS THAT HAPPENED

I couldn't ride the bike because there was too much snow outside so we went for a walk. I talked to Johnny about lots of things, he is a good friend. In the evening there were carols on the television, Frank and Dorothy sang along, Jemima looked at them like they were stupid. Dad listened to the carols with his eyes closed and looked pleased and I thought he was asleep but then he put his hand on Mum's shoulder and said something and they went outside.

1963

Mostly stuff for the bike. A new saddle which is better than the old one, and new tyres and a puncture repair kit! Also got a book about cycling, and one about the moon.

WHAT PEOPLE TALKED ABOUT AT DINNER

JFK who was the American president who was shot by a man who was shot by a man called Jack Ruby. Everyone discussed motives for the crime. Frank said some people who he thought were suspects, most of them were people I didn't know or stupid ones like the Beatles. Tom said the man who shot him was just crazy and you can't do a lot if a fellow is like that. Dad argued with both of them, he explained some things about why they would shoot the President. He sounded like he might be right. Tom said that was Dad, always swimming against the tide. He said it in a quite friendly way but I don't know what it meant. Mum looked like she wanted to leave and Aunt Dorothy asked them to stop talking about the shooting for now. Mum hates hearing about shootings and guns or anything violent. She's boring (see last year).

THINGS THAT HAPPENED

Jemima and Rose hardly paid any attention to anyone else. I took Johnny for a bike ride. He had to ride Dad's bike which was too big for him so I had to go really slow. I told Tom about how Richard Aloisi can do four balls in his mouth. Tom said "you'll have to kill him". I really like Richard though, he's my best friend this year (for the whole top 10 see school diary).

1964

MY PRESENTS

A heap of books about all kinds of things. Novels, some mystery books and thrillers, an encyclopedia. The encyclopedia had "To prepare you for the university of life, Dad" in it. Of course this isn't a real university, it's a way of talking about the fact that you learn more stuff as you go on. At university I'm going to study psychology. And I got a board game called Private Eye where you have to solve murders, we played it and I solved eight, Johnny didn't solve any. Dad got three, he said I was "too hot" for him. He may have let me win a few but I don't think so. Jemima wasn't there and Rose didn't play. Mum played but didn't do that well.

WHAT PEOPLE TALKED ABOUT AT DINNER

Jemima not being there. She is spending Xmas with her boyfriend whose name is Charles or Chas. She's 18 now, which makes her an adult. They talked about how quick she'd grown up and how beautiful she is. I don't think she is very grown up but she is a bit beautiful but I wouldn't want anything to do with her.

THINGS THAT HAPPENED

I was in the bathroom and heard Tom saying "but she's got to forget it" and Dad saying "I know but she never will". I don't understand what any of it meant but it was to do with Mum I think. While I was in the bathroom I noticed the door didn't lock right, so later when Johnny was in the bath, I tried the door and it worked and I saw him there with no clothes on. He was shocked and yelled out but then he saw the funny side and we laughed about it for a while and had fun.

1965

A guitar, plus books on how to play it, plecs, and a strap to wear it. Frank said I'd be like one of the Beatles but I would need to get my hair cut. The Beatles isn't really my scene. You see all these women who love them and wear badges and scream at them. It's a great guitar. Dad and Mum looked happy that I was so pleased. I sort of knew about it because I let on that I wanted one for a while, I'm 15 now and maybe Christmas isn't so much about surprises as you get older. Also got several books and a game like Private Eye last year, called Cluedo. This one has only one murder but it's different every time. I played it with Dad and Mum and Johnny, and Uncle Frank. Uncle Frank kept saying stupid people had done the murder like Lee Harvey Oswald or the Reds (Communists). He doesn't change. I won the game but other people weren't trying as hard.

THE DINNER CONVERSATION

There were no arguments this year. It was quite quiet. Dad coughed a lot and Mum said she was worried about him, when he wasn't in the room. Frank said he wished <u>he</u> could get his wife to care for him just by coughing and most people laughed. Rose won a load of prizes at school. She mostly just talked to Jemima who came again this year, I don't know what happened to her boyfriend, Chas. The adults talked about blacks like Muhammad Ali who do stuff to get in the public eye. Most people thought it was a bad idea. They talked about Rhodesia, it was complicated.

WHAT HAPPENED

Jemima and Rose went off to do something in the afternoon so I was left with Johnny. We talked for ages about what we thought of women. Johnny asked me if I loved Mum. It was a weird question so I said "I think so". Later I thought about it and I definitely do love her but sometimes I don't understand her, the things her and Dad argue about and the way she is with me.

1966

MY PRESENTS

A Fender. It has an electro-acoustic switch but you need an amp. A book on psychology called Understanding Understanding, it's about how the mind works and what it does. Richard has had it for years and he's read all of it and he found three mistakes and wrote to the publishers, they wrote back thanking him. We're both going to be psychoanalysts or therapists. We'll probably live in the same house or flat – it makes sense because you save money and it would be good to see Richard around all the time. It might have to be in the US though because that's where a lot of the action is.

THE DINNER CONVERSATION

There was a guest, Jemima's new boyfriend. His name is Steve. He's very tall and he plays rugby. He's good-looking and people asked him questions about his life all thru dinner. He looked pleased every time someone asked him something and he made a whole load of jokes, most of them weren't all that funny but everyone laughed a lot. Even Mum laughed quite a few times and seemed quite happy. We talked about how England won the world cup. Steve went to the match but I think it's just as good on the television.

WHAT HAPPENED

Steve took me and Johnny to play rugby outside. Johnny better than me, he's got much stronger and faster since last year and he's in all the teams at his school, I can't believe how much he has grown (maybe it's drugs!) Johnny talked about wanting to go into the Army and Steve was impressed. He asked what about me and I said I was more into being a psychologist. Steve seemed to like Johnny a lot more than me so I got pretty jealous and went inside after a while.

1967

PRESENTS

Records mostly. Tom and Sally gave me a guitar strap – they obviously weren't told that I had given up. I noticed that communication between my Dad and his brothers has died out a bit. I also got all the psych books I asked for and a cool book called Flowers For Algernon. I haven't finished it but it's about how a human could be made super-intelligent – I wouldn't mind doing that kind of thing. I called Richard, he has most of the books already but he doesn't have Further Inside The Mind and I tried to make him jealous. It sounds like he's having a good Christmas, though. I also got £50 quid from Dad because it's harder to buy things for me now.

DINNER CONVERSATION

Steve was here again with Jemima. Steve has had a promotion so he bought an expensive ring for her, everyone admired it and asked him about his job. He is a lawyer as well as a coach for kids' sports. Frank and Tom had a kind of argument about the government. I used to think Frank knew everything but I realise now although he does know a lot, he also makes generalised comments and doesn't study events closely. Rose wasn't here – she is at university and had gone to visit friends in Manchester. Mum said that it was good to get away this time of year. A strange comment because we've never been away for Christmas except one time which I don't remember. People asked me about applying to university and everyone went on about Harvard, I said that I would be happy to go anywhere with a good course. Frank said "yes but Harvard really <u>would</u> be something" like if I go anywhere else, it'll be irrelevant.

WHAT HAPPENED

Johnny wasn't there this year. He has gone to a kind of training camp for kids who want to be soldiers. He's only 16! If he went to Vietnam or somewhere he'd be shot to pieces. It was weird without him. I was all ready to play rugby with Steve if he asked, but he went off for a walk with Jemima.

1968

PRESENTS

Since Frank forgot my 18th birthday this year because of his problems, I got extra money off him and a jacket. More records, Grateful Dead and Janis Joplin. Another James Taylor LP from Dad. He himself got a new record player this year from Mum, which was a sort of peace offering I think because they sometimes argue about him having his music on. She bought it a while ago and we kept it a secret, which was fun. I also got a number of American-themed presents, like a book all about the differences between the countries, and a little Union Jack for my desk.

CONVERSATION

Dorothy left Frank this year so nobody talked about that. He seemed the same as usual, in fact laughed and made jokes more than usual. I think this may have been a 'defence mechanism', to make sure everyone could see that he was managing fine without her. He mentioned her a few times; one time he said she had been abducted by the Communists which was like old times. Everyone laughed. He talked about how much older his kids have got, too. Jemima was sitting there with Steve, the two of them are considering marriage. I still can't imagine doing that. Steve hardly looked at me all day. Rose also had a boyfriend with her this year. His name is Abo and he's black and he campaigns about things like abortion and mercy-killing. He was very polite. He asked me what I was doing in the States – I told him about my course. Frank asked if I could psychoanalyse him. We all laughed but I think I can. He's a man who makes jokes and attacks everything because he's not sure what he believes. And he has a need to dominate – conversation, relationships, everything. I didn't say this.

Abo made a mistake. Martin Luther King came up in conversation and they talked about the Kennedy curse, which is the explanation for why Kennedys keep getting shot. Abo said he'd heard Witching was cursed. This is Mum's least favourite thing to talk about, and one of Dad's too. There was a long silence and it wasn't hard to psychoanalyse Abo: he felt like a doofus.

EVENTS

With Rose and Abo, and Jemima and Steve all going out after dinner, I was left alone with Johnny for the afternoon. He seemed to be ignoring me. In the end I had to make him talk to me. We went for a walk, a long walk all around these snowy fields and into a kind of wood where we sat for hours just talking and stuff. I asked him if he knew anything about the Hirsts, because Tom (his Dad) was talking about it with my Dad again, but he said he didn't. It was dark even when we set out, by the time we came back it was pitch-black and he had to go. Tomorrow I'm going to have to work hard, I have tests as soon as I get back to college.

1969

PRESENTS

The emphasis isn't so much on presents these days, of course; all I really need is books for the course. I got the ones I wanted and money to buy the rest. I talked to Richard; he got $5000 from his family to help him at Harvard. I guess you can be more motivated by <u>not</u> having what you want but I envy him, even though I'd like him to be successful. Dad does the best he can for me though, both of them do.

The Moon landing. Tom said it was a great day and everyone seemed to agree. Then some trouble broke out. It was Rose's fault, but Abo got the blame for the second year running. He has all these leaflets that say 'It's a child, not a choice'. Steve (who flirts with Rose all the time) asked Abo what they were about, to impress Rose, and it turned out it's an anti-abortion campaign. Mum and Dad exchanged a look which I couldn't miss and she slipped out and didn't come back for ages. It went very quiet and Abo looked like he wanted to stab himself with his fork. I wish I could understand why Mum gets so upset about so many things. Could she have had an abortion – before I was born or when I was too tiny to remember? Surely I'd know! But the truth is I just don't know much about her. Still, though, you can't keep a secret like that covered up.

EVENTS

Johnny is in the army now, in Northern Ireland. It's hard to believe how recently we were hanging out. I tried to call him a few times, he didn't get back to me. I miss him. Talked to Dad most of the afternoon, about how strange it is to come home having been in Michigan.

1970

PRESENTS

Well, things are a bit different this year, Dad and Mum have gone to Italy for a bit of sunshine and I'm spending Christmas with Richard and the Aloisis. I hadn't been to the house for at least a couple of years, since the party to see us both off. Richard's brothers and sisters are here with all their boyfriends and girlfriends, dozens of well-off and content people everywhere. Can't write much because it looks weird. We're meant to be playing a game where you have to discuss another country's political structure in the accent of that country. It's stretching me.

CONVERSATION

The dinner went on for hours and we talked about everything: Northern Ireland (I thought of Johnny); the American Presidency – not just a few jokes but a wide-ranging analysis of Nixon and his people . . . then the political situation in Italy, where some of the Aloisis still live; then sports, briefly; then microcomputers, which Richard's uncle said would be as big as television, though they didn't sound exciting to me. All kinds of other things, too. The debate, the exchange of ideas never stopped – it was tiring. I drank a lot to try to keep up.

EVENTS

Richard and I played tennis in the afternoon, on his family's indoor tennis court. He's very good these days, it wasn't as even as when we used to play. He talked about Harvard a lot. He's done a lot of stuff which I've barely heard of and he reeled off the names of theories and experimenters like they were old friends. He is well on his way to being a professional. The guy his father knows in New York is going to give him some work experience and from there he'll get a foothold and go into practice. It was a lot more fun when we talked about friends from school. Jennifer is talking about getting married (!!) to the Australian.

1971

Useful stuff for my place at college and the (uncertain) future. It's a shame when presents you want are just 'useful' things but . . . kitchenware and cooking equipment. Books and book vouchers. You can never have too much knowledge. Richard already knows more than Einstein.

CONVERSATION

Looks like I didn't miss much last year, most things are the same. No Abo though, he and Rose aren't together anymore, so he missed his chance to continue his run of embarrassing mistakes. Steve and Jemima dominated the conversation and offered a few reasons why it didn't work out for Rose and Abo (she wasn't here, of course). S+J looked very self-satisfied. Maybe after they're married they won't come here so much. Or at all. People asked me what I was going to do after I finish at Michigan. I tried to give them convincing answers.

EVENTS

I don't know when Christmas became this dull. I got some books but I couldn't really read them because I've got too much reading to do for the course so I can't start something else. Dad and Mum slept for most of the afternoon. They suddenly looked quite old, like when you see old people dozing off in the park, although in actual fact they're only middle-aged. I was quite glad when it was over, this year. I worked in the evening.

1972

PRESENTS

A clock from Mum and Dad – ironic as I was writing about encroaching age last time I had this book in front of me. It'll go on my desk. And I'll get another one for the wall when I'm editor of the <u>Journal</u>.

David Bowie (me and Dad aren't sure about him) and other new acts. Tom and Frank both said modern music was unlistenable. Dad kept quiet on the subject, which pleased me. It saddens me to see Frank and Tom showing their age – I mean they were always kind of the wrong generation for rock-and-roll but still, they were young men with a thirst for the new at one time; now the new threatens them. But then I guess Dad (the youngest) was always the most daring of the brothers. Sometimes they still tease him about it: Tom, most often, will say something like "trust Robert to tell us what's in fashion" or "well, that's more Robert's generation . . . we didn't think like that when Frank and I were young". As there's only three years between Tom and Dad, I think these sort of comments must refer back to some incidents before I was even born, one of these running jokes that no-one else can quite tap into. I suspect in Tom's case, jokes like this defend him from worrying about his age and the fact he's becoming out-of-touch and his only son is God-knows-where intervening in some war or another.

EVENTS

I just tried talking to Mum about her childhood and her family, who she doesn't see anymore. Don't know why; I just thought I'd risk having a real talk rather than spend another Christmas Day watching the television. Every time I have a real, deep conversation with Mum, it's a huge relief, it reassures me that we <u>are</u> related; but it's just so hard to get started. She was evasive as usual but did mention some boyfriends she'd had before Dad, which was a bit weird. There was one she was really close to, "could easily have married <u>him</u>", she said, which was too strange to think about. I could have had a completely

183

different personality. Maybe I would have been better-looking. Mum was beautiful to judge from the picture of her singing – you can still tell from her eyes and the way she sometimes cuts her hair – but I don't seem to have got a lot of that beauty.

1973

PRESENTS

A new coat, and a record player from Dad. This is like a coming-of-age gift. It's a kind of admission that I won't be at home so much from now on. I'm settling down. I never planned it this way but it's all starting to make sense.

CONVERSATION

Meandering. No-one quite felt like starting a meaningful discussion. They say television is killing conversation – maybe as I'm quite a poor talker, I should be grateful. Although I can't see myself being a television personality either.

EVENTS

We watched a carol concert – Dad's idea. Beautiful music; Tom and Sally held hands by the fire. There were times when I forgot everything but the music; it reminded me of the old days at home (I bought Dad the new Taylor LP this year but there aren't many chances, these days, to sit around together like we used to).

1974

PRESENTS

Just odds and ends for the home.

CONVERSATION

My career. Everyone was quite impressed by the fact that I've been published, even though it's only stupid stuff. When I mentioned about the sex survey everyone pressed me for details, and strangely I felt embarrassed in front of Mum and Dad. I don't know when I'm going to get over that. Richard walked in on his parents 'at it' when he was 15 (he mentioned it on the radio not long ago), and at the time I was relieved it had never happened to me but I think maybe it would have helped. Knowing Richard's parents they probably did it deliberately, to 'liberate' him or something. They bought him that sex book when we were about four. Sick!

Richard came up in the conversation – everyone's heard all about his exploits. My career sounded a bit lame by comparison but Mum spoke up for me; nothing gets her excited like family.

EVENTS

We played a game of charades which, despite some hilarity at the beginning, soon became tiresome. I had a vague sense that this is what it would be like spending Christmas in an old people's home. I think Dad enjoyed it, though, and he certainly was proud of himself when he managed to mime Attack Of The Sixty Foot Woman.

1975

PRESENTS

A few books, including I'm OK, You're OK and Zen And The Art Of Motorcycle Maintenance, which everyone loves. I've already read it though and I thought it was mostly bullshit. It's all head-in-the-clouds stuff, lots of speculation and philosophical jargon you can do without. And you get so sick of hearing about the guy's son. Maybe it's better if you have a motorcycle.

CONVERSATION

Dad reached 50 this year so there was a lot of teasing. Tom said it was amazing he could get out of bed in the morning,

Frank made one or two lewd observations about the brothers' declining powers and some tasteless comments on mortality, e.g. "Who's gonna go first then? Who's it to be?", and arm-wrestled Dad and Tom as if to settle the question. Dad still looks and sounds young compared with Frank and Tom. There weren't any jokes about my career this year. By staying in the USA I think I'm starting to convince them that I am serious.

EVENTS

I found myself in a bad mood this evening and drank quite a lot of whisky to get rid of it. Reading the first 30 pages or so of I'm OK, You're OK, I began to wonder if I was missing something. It's based on something called 'transactional analysis' and as far as I can see, the guy's main point is that every conversation or relationship is a 'transaction' in which each person wants something, and if they each get what they want then it's a 'successful transaction'. I mean all he's really saying is, if both people are OK, then that's a good thing. How hard can it be to come up with that?

1976

PRESENTS

A new stylus for the record player – pretty funny as I got the exact same thing for Dad.

CONVERSATION

This year I thought maybe there would be some talk about my career, as I'm earning more money and have generally moved up the ranks, so I was prepared for a show of modesty, but it turns out Steve and Jemima have something to celebrate once again. The under-18 football team that he coaches won the cup or the Nobel Prize or something and he won an award for Services to Youth Sports. I shouldn't be so bitter towards Steve, I think he just reminds me of something I would like to be. Like Richard.

EVENTS

I went out for a long walk right after dinner. I could tell it was going to be one of those Christmas Days where everyone becomes comatose once the eating is over. To be fair I guess it's what you'd expect now, everyone being well over fifty (except Sally who is 50 next year, I think). I wish there were people my age around. Johnny would be best but I haven't heard from him for years. Next Christmas I'll make a real effort, I'll ask Tom where he is in the world and even if it's the middle of a jungle I will write him a letter. I thought about him this year because some marines who were stationed in Ireland are after compensation for mental ill-effects. Richard was asked for his opinions on a chat show.

When I came back from walking – I went to the place in the woods where Johnny and I went, back in . . . (wait while I turn the pages) Jesus, 1968! . . . when I came back, they were playing a mock game of rugby in the living room with a rubber ball. Steve threw to Dad who made the catch and then Tom tackled him and down they went in a heap, laughing as if they were kids again.

1977

PRESENTS

Because I've been here ever since the funeral, I was able to pretty much specify what I wanted, and sure enough got it all. Of course, this meant it was no fun at all.

CONVERSATION

Without Tom, it was pretty subdued, as Sally didn't say a word for the whole meal. Tom was less vocal than Frank and less astute than my Dad, but he provided the link between them. This year nobody could get a conversation started.

I have to admit I was hoping Johnny would make it this year, to keep Sally company, but I guess he couldn't get the time off. To judge from Tom's funeral, he wouldn't have spoken to me anyway. Maybe it was the army that did it to him.

It hardly seemed right to go back to the Hirst research on Christmas Day, but I thought about it all evening. I just think it'd make an interesting story. It's too late to actually help Nicholas Hirst and not many people care but since when did journalists have to do good?

1978

PRESENTS

A suit. Mum and Dad framed an article about me in the <u>Psyche</u>, about how Dr Rice praised my work. I'd sent it to them because it didn't make any mention of the Hirsts. I walked by the old Hirst house the other day, and the experience shook me up much more than I'd expected: it was like seeing a 'based on a true story' movie and then visiting the site of the true story. I felt I could see the twins running around, playing games like me and Johnny used to.

CONVERSATION

I talked as much as I could about my bullet points thing and the monthly feature, without mentioning the details of the article that started it all. There was some talk about Richard, he was interviewed in the Times last month, but I didn't feel too demeaned by it this time. Anyway, I'm not sure everyone remembers who Richard is. I've noticed the conversations getting more and more samey as the years go by. I think sometimes it might turn out like a sci-fi movie and everyone except me is stuck in a time-loop.

EVENTS
The suit doesn't really fit; I've been putting on weight. It doesn't look as if I'm going to inherit the lean build of my father in his thirties. Again I feel a bit let down by my genes.

1979

PRESENTS
A warm sweater. I'm nearly 30.

CONVERSATION
The reappearance of Rose after God-knows-how-long provided a bit of interest this year. I got the feeling that Frank doesn't really know how to talk to her now, so he treated her like an honoured guest who might be called away at any time. He was eager to please her, agreed with everything she said and went out of his way for her. It was touching, in a way.

EVENTS
Interesting to see how Rose and Jemima got along, although that was something I was never really able to assess when we were kids and there's no guarantee I am better at it now, trained psychiatrist or not. They spent most of the afternoon talking and it seemed to me that there is antagonism on both sides. I felt a bit like the awkward kid who used to follow them around fifteen years ago and long to be part of their conversations. They probably weren't that interesting then, either.

1980

PRESENTS
Every year I think I'll quit this. But . . . I don't know, the longer this goes on the more absurd it becomes in a way, but

also the more sentimental I become about doing it. It's stupid to keep doing it but it would be stupid to stop. Provides me with some kind of link to my past, and . . . it's hard to believe that the kid talking about playing the guitar and being scared of girls was me, yet in some ways little has changed. Dad still definitely seems to enjoy these Christmases; Mum still wears the mixed expression of forced cheer and patient endurance that she always has. This year's gift was an office chair. I was pretty proud when I realised I did have an office this time.

CONVERSATION

"So, Peter, 30 . . . how long before you're bringing a family here?" Frank doesn't soften his confrontational remarks with humour quite as subtly as he used to. I told them all about my new job in the practice, but the fact I'm still single seems an admission of failure to some people. Sometimes the family get-together feels like going before a panel to discuss my progress.

I asked Frank what he thought of the Moscow Olympics boycott but he seems to have lost interest in the USSR.

EVENTS

I talked to Dad about the fact that I'm already 30, not married, no kids. He and Mum were in their early twenties when I was born, and it's an odd thought when you know you're older than your father was – I feel like I'm not keeping my side of the bargain or something. Dad said not to be ridiculous, some people didn't start a family till they were 50. He said it was different for the two of them, they met, he got Mum pregnant (he seemed to find it a bit strange talking like this to me, but manfully overcame it) and that was it. "But you've got twenty years before you should panic, my boy," he said. "If you get to 50 and still no joy, then run for the first woman you see". We laughed about that and played chess and listened to records like the old days.

"Twenty years before you should panic", though. Twenty years have gone by since I started writing in this book. Reading back through the pages, it doesn't feel like much at all. It's as if it has all been one long Christmas.

1981

PRESENTS

The Neuropsychology Of Everyday Memory, by A.R. Luria. A reminder that it's best to keep a little perspective; there are some men of genius in my business. One day maybe I'll write a casebook – the whole thing could be in bullet points as a gimmick. The less time it takes to read a book, the more it'll sell. Richard and I used to say we'd publish a joint book but I don't think he needs what I can contribute. He's already seen enough celebrities to fill a hell of a book. He's probably writing one now.

CONVERSATION

One topic of conversation, unwelcome as it was, dominated this year – Dorothy's new love life. She has a new man, a Greek or something, a multi-millionaire with a mansion in the South of France. Jemima and Steve have gone there this year, and so has Rose. Frank talked for most of the dinner about it. He is finding it harder and harder to lighten his complaints with wit like he used to. I guess it was a pretty demoralising occasion – just him, Dad and Mum, Sally and me. And Sally, since Tom's death, has become even more taciturn if possible. I don't know if she will ever speak a word in our presence again. I couldn't wait for dinner to end.

EVENTS

An awful day. I don't know what happened to Mum but she just snapped this afternoon, stormed out of the room during a conversation and afterwards started shouting at Dad. He had to take her outside. As usual I found myself straining to pick up bits and pieces. She kept asking Dad how he thought it felt, making all sorts of references to things I couldn't hear or interpret. He was trying to calm her down but they were both very upset. It's a terrible thing to watch your mother crying and know you just don't understand enough to do anything about it.

1982

P

So finally this year I persuaded Dad and Mum to come out to Chicago. It was my present to them, but also theirs to me. I felt very proud showing them everything.

C

We had dinner in a restaurant. I paid for everything, in spite of how hard Dad tried to object. I persuaded them that it was less expensive than it actually was, by lying about the rate of exchange.

E

Mum – who seemed to enjoy being alone with "you boys" as she called us – went for a nap when we got back to my apartment and I was left to talk to Dad. We put the TV on – it was It's A Wonderful Life. One of Dad's favourites. "It's a great film," he said at the end. "The moral of the story, you know, that everything you do rubs off on someone or sets off a chain somewhere – I see that all the time." And he told me about a recent case in Cambridgeshire where someone ran over their boss because he made them work such long hours that they were too tired to drive properly. We recalled the psychologist with his 'cause and effect' thing: apparently Dad heard from him this year, he's a farmer now.

I wish people had the chance to see alternate worlds opening up before they took important decisions, like in the film.

1983

P

The video of It's A Wonderful Life from Dad. The second time he's given me something I was about to give <u>him</u>. It's nice when that happens. Also several gifts relating to the Patsy case. Sally gave me a copy of her album – as if I wouldn't have it already! – but a nice gesture all the same. The first time I've achieved something in the real world important enough to be the inspiration for gifts.

C

It was an unusually lively affair this year, partly because of last year's break, partly because of my short flirtation with fame (and with a famous singer), which impressed everyone, but mostly because of Steve and Jemima's new baby, Ami, who is a beautiful little girl. Frank was delighted that they chose to come here rather than going out to see Dorothy.

E

Ami dominated the attention. It's refreshing to have a kid around. Mum asked me if it made me want one; I was stuck for an answer. Not surprisingly, we spent the afternoon entertaining her (or maybe the other way round). She was almost drowned in gifts by Steve and Jemima. Her presence harmonised the adults; Jemima was very friendly to me. The absent Rose provided a common-ground topic: we agreed that she was sulky, hard to communicate with.

1984

P

A food processor. An 'I'm With Stupid' mug.

C

Everyone knew this was the end of an era. With no Frank, the only reason for all of us to congregate was as a kind of tribute to him. Mum and Rose cooked. Jemima and Rose were polite to each other, Steve and I got on well. Dad played with Ami and enjoyed himself enormously. We talked about Frank, what a generous man he was. A few times I could see people looking at Dad, wondering what he thought of being the last Kristal brother standing. Whatever he thought, he wasn't letting on. As usual.

E

I had my first ever real conversation with Rose. I think I have misjudged her badly. She was very quiet during dinner, didn't join in with Jemima's eulogies of their father, nor with the politically-suspect banter that was conducted in his honour. After dinner, she announced that she was going for a walk. On a whim I asked if I could join her. She was surprised but didn't seem to mind the idea, so we went out over the fields. She seemed like she might cry (I should be able to spot the signs by now). I asked what was wrong, and managed not to butt in with any professional opinions. She told me that she'd never been able to say goodbye to her father. She said that she'd intended to come last year but other things got in the way: "in fact all kinds of things always got in the way" she said. As we headed for the spot where I once had a 'heart-to-heart' with Johnny, she said that she'd always felt in the shadow of Jemima, and the feeling had only intensified as they got older.

"It's easy for her to tell me what to do . . ." she said,

"with her amazing husband and little girl . . ." The thought of this familial bliss was what broke her. It was easy to sympathise with her troubles: no partner (she's older than me, too; she said she has trouble finding a man she can trust), no career stability, and a terrible inferiority complex. "You're a psychiatrist, why did she get all the good genes?" Rose asked, poignantly. I thought of poor Nicholas Hirst asking almost the same question about Richard around this time 35 years ago. I said one or two comforting things and gave her my business card, trying to make it seem like an offer of personal, rather than clinical, help. I'm not sure how well I expressed the last part, though. I've never found it easy to discuss things with women outside the office.

When we got back, Richard phoned from New York. He is publishing a book in the New Year. There are good advance sales.

1985

P

A new suit; it doesn't seem long since the last one. They sent me to get measured for it so not much of a surprise, but hell, I'm 35. And I feel it.

C

Just me and Mum and Dad, same old same old. I spent most of the afternoon with a Rubik's cube. I'm expecting the call from NY to tell me Richard has cracked it any minute now.

E

I don't really feel like doing this. Maybe this'll be the year I grow out of it. I didn't really feel like coming home this year but I didn't have the guts not to.

1986

A CD player. Mum and Dad have never stopped being generous even though I can afford things like that myself these days, especially now I'm dream analyst to the rich and fabulous. I'm tempted to give it back to them so Dad can use it – not because I don't want it – but then, I'm not sure he ever would. He wrote on the gift tag: "this is, of course, not intended as a replacement for your record-player".

We talked about the nuclear tensions still hanging around. Apparently thousands of troops are on day-to-day standby in the UK as well as America, probably including Johnny, although if Gorbachev launched a nuke I'm not sure even a very neat line of soldiers would be able to block it out. Johnny's old enough to be a sergeant now or God knows what else. It's unlikely that I will ever see him again.

Other than that, it was all about the Lily thing. I gave them almost the whole story. I underplayed the extent to which I went along with mystic bullshit that Dad would have disapproved of, and compromised my principles . . . I also left out some of the bits where I almost deceived myself that I was in love with Lily and then found, once again, that it wasn't quite right. It's the festive season, after all.

I found a good present for Mum this year: an exercise bike. In the afternoon, as luck would have it, Mr Imperfect was on TV and there was the younger Lily, head cocked on one side, staring out from the screen. I realised I have more chance of seeing her on TV than in the flesh, from now on. Looked for that huge mole on her chin she talked about but it wasn't visible, maybe you need a big screen.

1987

P

The most predictable present this year was a copy of Richard's book Affairs Of The Mind, now out in paperback and still number 12 in the bestsellers. There was an epilogue with a description of the Genelli case which alluded briefly to my witch-doctoring. Closest I'll come to the bookstores for a while. Richard sent it along because I excused myself from the New Year party which he is combining with a shindig to celebrate his success. I could go out to New York but there are all sorts of reasons not to. I had the book already, of course. I bought it as soon as it hit the shops.

C/E

Dad and I bought an unusual gift for Mum this year: a week in a health farm. She's become kind of a health freak over the past year but as Dad says, "at our age if you're going to have a new interest, it might as well be your health". Normally it would be a weird time of year to go away, but in view of Mum's lifelong unease with the festive season it seems to have been a good plan. We spoke to her on the phone in the morning, then went for a drive through deserted streets.

After lunch we just drove round some more, not knowing where we were going. We talked about the ways the landscape had changed since I was a boy but, considering it's 30 years (incredibly) since I was really young, perhaps the most surprising thing is how much is left standing. Thirty years is almost half a man's life but so much of Cambridgeshire and East Anglia has just stood still. It's a creepy thought in a way, as if your life barely registers, but equally creepy when you see everything changing. You can't win unless you stop thinking altogether.

We came home and had brandy together with Joni

Mitchell playing. Her new record isn't so good, her voice is all fouled up now from smoking. We listened attentively all the same and when Dad coughed over the first minute of a song, we went back to the start of it. Towards the end the record jumped and I went to re-set the needle, and Dad was fast asleep.

1988

A new computer.
We went to see Mum in the chapel of rest. Then we had a long talk.
I think this will be the final entry.

Little more than two years later, my father was dead too. Once the lungs had given the signal, the other links in the chain of command capitulated readily, shutting themselves down in sequence like dominoes. His death was as protracted as my mother's had been sudden. Her collapse in the grocery store was a final taste of the abruptness of action with which I could never quite come to terms; my dad's decline was an orderly chain of cause and effect. In that respect, their deaths suited them well.

Where Mum was concerned I didn't know whether to take comfort in this or not. Certainly she could never have stood to be tossed about in the grip of a slow murderer of an illness, as Dad was. And given her dependence upon him for happiness and stability, she would have made a bad widow, so perhaps there was a kind of expediency in her going first, although he didn't last long without her: perhaps inevitably at such an advanced stage of love and life, they needed each other equally. In any case, however apposite, hers was an immensely frustrating death, leaving in my guts a sense of waste, of knots left untied, normally associated with the death of a younger person. However much you might think about it, and even plan for it, trying to simulate the loss of a parent in the mind is as futile as trying to convince yourself that a limb is missing, and for the same reason: the habit of a lifetime is more than mere habit.

Time and again, patients who came to me suffering from grief-related depression have complained (as Rose did) of something left unsaid. 'I didn't get to tell him . . .' 'I never had the chance to say . . .' The lament is always in the same tone, combining self-reproach with a sense of injustice, and it has been more than adequately echoed in the countless poems and songs that urge us not to leave the important stuff until it's too late. But all those patients of mine failed to learn the overfamiliar lesson, and in 1988 I found I had failed to learn from them.

So, fittingly perhaps, it was my Dad – my closest, most trusted source – who had to fill in the large gaps of understanding that still lay gaping between Mum and me at the time of her death. On Christmas afternoon, after the visit to the chapel of rest which we both treated as if it were as well established a part of the Christmas routine as any other, he broke the silence by initiating the 'long talk' which, that evening, I would record as the last ever incident in my yearly diary. He began by talking in businesslike terms about the funeral, scheduled for the day before New Years' Eve, which I took to be his way of demonstrating that he had got used to what would have been an unthinkable idea just a week ago. I thought back to the funeral of his brother Tom, which he had also had to organise.

'I'm expecting a number of your mother's relatives to come,' he said, 'people you haven't met before.'

'Well, whatever you need me to do . . .' I said, wondering where this was going, not that I could ever have guessed.

'So there's a few things that are bound to come out now, things that haven't really come out before,' Dad continued, with a lurch into romantic-thriller territory. And like the key links in a good murder plot, these 'things' he referred to, these heavy hidden facts, were no sooner out of the bag than they glinted with a light so harsh that I felt I should have been able to guess them several commercial breaks ago. But my vantage point had been all too close: ornamental details had clogged my viewfinder and left no room to focus on the wider picture. The guy inside the tower struck by lightning is the only one who doesn't see it happen. This is my defence against the smug reader who has already deduced that:

- Mum was brought up in Lincoln;
- It was she and not some untraceable woman who slept with Richard Hirst on the night of 27 December 1949;
- It was she who pulled the bedclothes up over their naked bodies and watched in terror as Richard's brother Nicholas, returning unexpectedly to the house, entered the room, surveyed the scene with what almost looked like amusement, turned a loaded gun on them and then, shouting down his twin brother's incoherent pleas, pulled the gun away from the lovers, jammed it in his own mouth and squeezed.
- My mother's scream rebounded around the empty spaces of Richard and Nicholas's Cambridge flat on that night, setting off a chain of echoes in her own head which would remain, muffled but never quite silenced. For decades to come, her sleep would be ruptured by vivid remembrances, her peace of mind snatched away by loud noises (real or imagined), stories of brotherly love and hate, violence, sudden death – signs of all kinds that whirled into a perpetual action replay, an unending comment upon her one night of indiscretion.

And as she and Richard lay in guilty pleasure together, Richard not knowing that his brother and lifelong companion would be dead within the hour; as she tore her face away while Richard recoiled from the shot as if it had entered his own head; while all this was happening, incredibly, a tiny subplot was hatching inside her, where – in one of the gods' perfectly timed, elaborate practical jokes – the fruits of their short union were already growing. With a much-needed stroke of bathos the child, symbol of the most terrible and significant night of my mother's life, was given the undemonic name of Peter.

And Richard, with his haunting lead role in the old Witching-curse story I had helped to bring into the open, was Dad. No. Richard Hirst was my father, but he was not the man I spent my whole life loving as my dad. That man, Robert Kristal, who recounted this bizarre story now with steady eyes gazing out of the window as if watching a reconstruction, befriended my mother shortly before I was born. She had given up all dreams of a singing career and moved to Witching to look after the devastated old Mr Hirst. Robert quickly became devoted to Mum and accepted the mantle of proxy father, and everyone assumed I was his, although, in a way, I was nobody's. It was as close to father-hood as he was to come: she would never conceive another child.

'I only wish we'd all been able to talk about it a long time ago,' Dad concluded, 'when we were . . . so to speak, a three. But, you know, there was never a good time for Mum, and I suppose the more we felt ready to talk about it, the less we saw of you, and . . . well, the less important it seemed. I felt you *were* my son, and that was what seemed to matter.

'Well. I don't know if you'll be able to look at me in the same way now that you know,' Robert Kristal finished up, examining the fingers that had slipped the ring on Mum's slim hand four decades ago. 'Maybe you won't be able to, as it were, feel that you love me in the same way, and suchlike.' Even with Dad's stone-faced delivery, the monologue sounded Hollywood-scripted. The word 'love' announced itself awkwardly, like a celebrity with a scandalous past. All that it needed was for Dad or 'Dad' to continue by urging me not to blame my mother, and the scene was a wrap.

Instead he took a deep breath and answered the putative

critic: 'But well, I'd say you certainly *should*, because I've done pretty well. And if you want someone to blame . . . well, blame everyone, I suppose. You know the whole story now. I just tried to carry on *after* the story.'

That was all. By Dad's standards it was a long speech. I could almost hear the insipid film music welling up behind him to soundtrack the solid embrace of two men, parted and now united by the truth. Instead there was a flat silence as we each hoped for the other to say or do something; then a faint hissing noise in the background gave way to a mechanised scream as the smoke alarm went off in the kitchen. The first word spoken after my dad's great revelation was a muttered profanity as he leapt up and went to inspect the damage.

How did relations alter between me and the man whose surname and whose ideas I inherited, but whose gene pool I now learned I had never shared? In the two years that were left to us, far more remained the same than changed. Dad (as I was neither willing nor able to stop calling him) was right that in almost every way that mattered, he *had* been my father, and I had certainly been his son. In some ways the final twenty-something months were a time of refreshing candour and clarity. Every question I had ever wanted to ask about their past or my own could now be brought into the open: the truths I learned after Mum's death didn't just open the barn door, but ripped it off its hinges and blew a gust of wind inside so that all the contents were thrown into the air and tossed about. The artificial but imperishable father/son bond that had hardened over a lifetime could not be blasted apart by even this bombshell; instead it was gilded with real objectivity. We could discuss personal matters like contemporaries. Details of the Hirst case which had puzzled me for years were now cleared up;

half-remembered incidents from my early life acquired a shape and a significance.

And, objectively, I admired him more as Robert Kristal than as Dad, because with the shackles of duty and habit at least slackened if not removed, I could see him in a light unrefracted by filial devotion. The formidable patience and understanding and devotion of the man shone through. Like a born-again believer trading the cosiness of long-held assumptions for the more substantial reward of recrudescent belief, I 'rediscovered' Dad, and both of us were enriched by the process. In his last year, when his besieged body began to give notice that it might not see another winter, we made the natural reversal, whereby the son becomes a dad to the declining father, more easily than most. The knowledge of his sacrifices made the task of attending to his needs seem trifling, and he was never made to feel like excess baggage – a feeling, subconscious in some, acute in others, which hastened the deaths of a good many people in his hospital ward. Dad and I remained partners and co-conspirators right up until the stalemate between body and spirit was broken, a few weeks into 1991.

When his death was close enough to touch, I felt a certain relief insinuating itself: I had kept my promise, this time, to leave nothing unsaid or undone. Admittedly it had taken the death of one parent to make sure I cleared my debts with the other, but half-closure is better than some people manage. We even staged a mini deathbed scene when, in the last hour, Dad looked back over his life with the standard mixture of satisfaction and regret. 'You know, Pete,' he said, 'all the business with your mother – I never really intended it to be some enormous secret.' A salvo of coughs. 'It just happened that way, it was meant to be, so to speak.' I looked into the half-closed eyes for a final time and told him it didn't matter. Those were my second-last words to him. The last words were to tell him that I had brought him the cup of soup requested with what turned out to be his last ones. In the two minutes it took me to tear open the packet and prepare the lukewarm drink, he slipped away, a death as gentle as a limousine door closing.

'You seem to be coming to terms with it well,' said the doctor as I watched with clear eyes the covering of the body. The man who had often reflected upon the interconnectedness of all lives was now a single bullet point in the indexes of a tiny handful of remaining individuals. He would occupy the space between mouthfuls at the doctor's dinner table that night; news of his passing would stall a few conversations by a few minutes each.

In my life summary, however, he was the source of every stream. I was his ambassador now, and it was my responsibility to prolong the life of his influence.

These grandiose thoughts did not occur in the surprisingly ordinary first days and weeks after he was lowered into the patch of ground warmed up for him by Mum. Nor was I troubled (as, for example, Lily would have been) by the implications of the knowledge that I was a child of the Witching curse, the symbol of a tragedy that had blighted the lives of its protagonists; that I had never known my father and never been wholly loved by my mother; that I had lived my whole life under false assumptions. All this was swept into corners as I busied myself with what a therapist might call the beginning of the rest of my life. But 'coming to terms' is a slippery phrase; where it hints at conquest, it means assimilation, a temporary truce. I had not thrown out the intruder, the truth I had to deal with, but found a cage for it in the loft, where it would prowl, scowl and scratch away at the ceiling. As time wore on I would hear it shuffling through long series of almost sleepless nights; insomnia blunted my senses by day and patients merged into a blur.

I was living with the sound and contrast turned down. I took time off, but my unoccupied mind ran loose among the empty hours and sent me into worse confusion. I should have sought professional help, but pride barred the door: I was a doctor, not a patient, and so I carried on with the rounds, prescribing treatments which would have been better used if I had taken them myself. Richard called from time to time and got the idea that something was wrong, but I didn't tell him the whole story; it would have to wait until we met. I had no idea when that would be.

Eventually I took at least a partial hold on myself. I closed my office for a few weeks and flew to England. In a silent Witching I threw out nine black sacks of my parents' things and my childhood memorabilia, and began the process of selling the house in which I grew up. The last thing I removed from the shell of my adolescence was my late mother's photo from the bathroom. When I stared at it from the toilet for the last ever time, the look of aloof reproach which had fascinated me for years (and marred so many bathtimes) now seemed more akin to embarrassed amusement, as if she had been standing there watching me. We were bound by the closest of ties and yet had never achieved intimacy; it was as if we had been miscast together in a play which ran and ran. It was no easier to return her gaze than it had been before. I stared down at my feet.

When the house was sold, I bought a new one in a desirable area just outside Chicago; bought a fabulous car, a future holiday, bought anything I wanted. I joined fitness clubs, book clubs, clubs for people who had no particular interests but liked to be a member of something. Then I had my office renovated and reopened for business. Meanwhile, the beast in the loft peeped through the bars and prepared to play its part in the next, and darkest, major case of my career.

6

Sports and Games

For all the popularity of the sporting-misfortune videos to which I alluded earlier, which milk amusement from the vaudeville antics of colliding fieldsmen and pool cues tearing baize, nothing beats the truly unexpected. There is one clip, a classic vignette of eccentric drama, which never made it on to a howlers tape but which I often used to replay in my mind in dull moments. It's the late eighties and the runners are lining up for the hundred-metre dash in a youth track-and-field competition: they are all boys about to be young men, with tight muscles straining through flimsy string vests. The starting gun cracks and from the outside lane, a black kid springs out of the blocks and into the lead. In comparison with some of his opponents he appears wiry rather than powerful, but his graceful strides seem to take him further away from them with each split-second. Halfway to the finish, although the eye struggles to keep up, he looks to have the race in his pocket. Then, unbelievably, he angles his run so that it cuts into the lane to his left, and deliberately collides with the other runner, sending him sprawling; he shimmies away from the prostrate form and lurches into the next lane, where he repeats the trick, again felling the oncoming sprinter before gliding away; and so he makes his way across the lanes, taking two more victims, leaving a trail of bruised and furious runners splayed out like traffic-accident casualties behind him, before jogging over the finish line for fourth place: behind the runners he couldn't reach in time, ahead of those he cut down.

Asked to explain himself, he said: 'You only gotta finish fourth to make the final.'

The sprinter, Webster Bruce, then sixteen years old, was banned from competition after the incident, and narrowly escaped the courts after a fight with the mother of one of his hapless opponents. The ban lasted for two years: enough time, the committee said, for him to 'develop maturity' before returning to compete in a 'decent and respectful manner'; also – the subtext – a long enough period for him to take his destructive habits safely away from track and field, a sport desperate to preserve the paltry credibility still left after the doping frenzy of the 1980s. Instead of joining the likes of Ben Johnson[20] in the trashcan of sports villains, however, Bruce served his time and returned a stronger and better athlete, and worse still, as crazy as ever. In between notable track successes he continued to find time for the occasional party trick. In one race he simply failed to respond to the starter's gun, remaining crouched and ready on the blocks until the others had finished; another time he arrived on the track on a bicycle claiming that he had 'gotten the sports mixed up'.

Feared and disliked by other athletes, despised by purists, Webster Bruce looked certain to land a more permanent ban; and when he finished second in the trials for the 1992 American Youth Games, a task force was set up to engineer

[20] The Canadian sprinter Ben Johnson was stripped of his 1988 Olympic gold medal after being found guilty of performance-enhancing substance abuse. His associates defended him saying 'cheating was something no one else was doing'.

his disqualification before he made it any further. But, as the authorities plotted to catch him on a technicality, they realised that he had made an important catch of his own: the public's imagination. For one thing, he was talented; also, he was hugely entertaining, a larger-than-life performance artist in a sport where for some years the main appeal had been trying to distinguish between male and female competitors. Above all, his was a rags-to-riches tale of the kind so often sought by sportswriters but rarely realised in the ruthless real world of billion-dollar contests. He came from a squalid home in the Bronx; after his dad had shot himself, his mother had abandoned him; and he had grown up in the child's equivalent of a dog pound, developing his nimble feet by running away from cops. By breaking into a sports club one day and proving his firecracker speed before he could be turfed out, he had created an opening which he now exploited by taking on and beating college kids and forging a name for himself on ever bigger scoreboards.

The American Youth Games would give him an opportunity to cement his status and confirm his position: to the fans, a brilliant new talent; to the critics, a glorious example of the levelling power of sports. The only problem was his habit of doing something so absurd that it bordered on insanity.

Although I had played tennis with Richard in our school days, until he went for coaching with a former Wimbledon finalist and began to pull away from me, I was never much of a sports fan myself: Dad took me to see a football match once at Cambridge, but it was such a poor game that we never went back, and all the fishing trips gave me a taste for solitude which dampened my interest in team games. I had happened to catch Bruce's lane-jumping stunt whilst channel-surfing. From then on, however, I followed every unpredictable step of his career, fascinated by his behaviour and intrigued by its possible sources. Something about the look in his eyes on the news clips, triumphant but haunted, made me thirsty for a glimpse inside his head. Bruce wasn't eloquent and gave few interviews, but in one rare and brief TV appearance he made a teasing reference to a man called Michael Streissman who, he claimed, was responsible for 'telling me to do everything'. It was Streissman's idea to run the other sprinters off the track; he was there on the sidelines instructing Bruce to stay on the blocks or run only part of the distance; and he had come up with the stunt in which Bruce produced an egg and spoon from his pocket and ran unsteadily along with it. Pondering this morsel of information or misinformation, I came up with three hypotheses:

- Streissman, whoever he was, had motives for disturbing Bruce's performances, and was preventing Bruce from offering anything more than hints about him, perhaps by using threats;
- Streissman, whoever he was, had an influence which Webster Bruce either greatly exaggerated, to give himself an excuse, or misinterpreted in his own mind;
- Streissman did not exist.

Although it is not common practice for a shrink to chase after patients like a football coach at a draft pick, I began to plan ways in which I could meet Webster Bruce. I started attending track meets where he was running, and hanging around locker rooms like some kind of seedy voyeur. In the end I was introduced to his coach, Frank Macguire, and offered to give Bruce a free consultation – I even suggested that I could pay his way to Chicago, if that would help. Macguire, who had long been worried that Bruce would make a mockery of his hard work and faith by blowing his chance at the Youth Games, agreed to broach the subject, though he doubted that his protégé would cooperate. To his surprise, however, Webster seemed almost as keen on the idea as I was. I thought it could be a perfect match.

Bruce, Webster

- born, New York, 1972
- third of five children
- youngest brother, Aaron, dies in accident at home
- deterioration of relations between mother and father
- cuts school regularly from age six
- challenges white kids to street races for money; wins $350
- establishes reputation as 'fastest kid in Bronx'
- parents argue over WB's long absences; mother levels various accusations at father
- father commits suicide, February 1983
- mother suffers series of nervous breakdowns
- runs whole day of races, winning $750 to support brothers and sisters; loses eighteenth race of streak, to 22-year-old; vandalises victor's car; eludes police with two-mile run
- returns home to find mother committed to 'crazy house'
- children dispersed among foster and care homes
- WB placed in Kennedy Onassis Home for Disadvantaged Youths
- first meets Michael Streissman, 1986
- first sexual encounter, aged 13, with 25-year-old
- remains at Kennedy Onassis
- appears at track-and-field club, gaining admission by vaulting fence
- resists expulsion, impresses coaches with extraordinary sprint performances

- despite opposition, becomes bona fide member of club
- represents club in local track meets, recording many victories
- selected for New York State championships; causes fracas with illegal lane-crossing suggested by Streissman
- banned from competition for two years; remains member of club thanks to support from head trainer, Frank Macguire
- continues training under Macguire's supervision
- leaves Kennedy-Onassis, rents apartment in Brooklyn from friend of Macguire, funded by sports club
- abused by Streissman on grounds of:
    race
    inadequate parenting
    lifestyle
- threatens to kill Streissman
- returns to competition, winning eleven races in streak (disqualified from three due to unorthodox behaviour)
- entered by club for American Youth trials
- runs personal best time, qualifies for event
- continues to be troubled by Streissman
- receives offer of help from psychiatrist

The story of Webster Bruce, like many from my casebook, was a two-hander rather than a monologue; it was also the story of Michael Streissman, this mysterious puppeteer who stalked every move and appeared at unpredictable times, pulling the malevolent strings, weaving them into rope for Webster to hang himself. Surveying my office with quick nervous glances, cradling a glass of water which would later smash on the floor after a moment of wandering concentration, my young client described many encounters with

Streissman in detail – the sniping and cajoling, the psycho-logical abuse targeting his colour and upbringing, the disruptive plans which Webster felt compelled to obey. However, completely absent from the account was any shred of actual detail about Streissman: his appearance, age and connection with Webster remained unexplored. When I asked Webster to describe his nemesis, he produced such a jumble of physical detail that Streissman sounded like a fantasy creature from a child's book, made up of assorted animal parts. The only description he could furnish was an imitation of Streissman's voice rasping instructions at him.

The non-existence of the mystery man as a physical presence in Webster's mind was suggestive, as was the discontinuity of Webster's manner, which shuttled from amiable to suspicious to outwardly hostile within thirty seconds. I quickly became convinced that Webster was suffering from diagnosable schizophrenia, and that Streissman was the product of a subconscious urge for self-destruction. Webster almost admitted as much himself when I asked if he thought there was any way of ridding himself of Streissman: 'He goes away sometimes, if I concentrate.' It was as if one half of Webster's brain were tormenting the other, intercutting illusion with flashes of the truth, so that he simultaneously wished to live by and reject the myth of his mental jailer. A 'split personality' is the common, but clumsy, term for this phenomenon; of course it presupposes that most people have a single unified personality, something which I came to doubt more with every year that went by and every Lily Ripley who passed through my attempts at care.

Some schizophrenics are deafened by the cacophony of imagined voices, and if Webster only had the one, that at least was something to be grateful for; but the lively imagination which he showed, even in a tentative first meeting, had given

Streissman an unusual, dangerous vivacity. The brutality of Webster's upbringing would have been enough to bring about the separation of mind and (what we loosely call) soul which somehow implants these voices; and the more he spoke to me, with neurotic defensiveness and loose-tongued confidence trading places at disarming speed, the more tempting the diagnosis became. The question was how the phantasmagoric visitor could be killed off, how the voice could be silenced, without damaging the host mind it was inhabiting and inhibiting.

I went step by step with Webster through the history of his supposed relationship with Streissman, trying to gauge the extent of the control which the invisible mentor exerted upon him. Had Streissman ever told him to give up running altogether? 'Yeah.' How often? 'All the time.' (A hesitation; his eyes seemed to focus on six targets at once.) 'After I win, first he's quiet and doesn't say nothing, then he starts on — *What you gonna do next? You think you fast? You slow for a black guy.* If I run ten-two, he says you gotta run ten seconds. I run ten seconds, he says you gotta run nine-ninety-five, still too slow, you better give up. He's like a coach gone crazy.'

'And the stunts . . . ?'

'Sometimes he just says, don't run the race. Do this. Run into people or do something dumb, whatever. And I have to do it.'

'Why?'

Webster shrugged. 'I always do what he says.'

'But why?'

(Silence. Webster was suddenly uninterested in the subject. He stared down moodily at the gold ring on one long finger and shrugged, glancing up occasionally with childlike truculence in his eyes to indicate that it was my responsibility to make the next move.)

'What would you do', I asked him steadily, 'if Streissman told you to do something really . . . stupid and dangerous?'

Webster shot me a contemptuous look which I parried by holding his gaze. Coolness in eyeballing contests is, with a few exceptions, one of my most dependable weapons; I was staring down reticent patients when he was still a baby. He shifted in his seat.

'What does that mean, stupid and dangerous? More stupid and dangerous than when he got me to smash the store window and run six blocks dodging cops?'

'I mean stupid and dangerous like harming yourself.'

He shrugged again.

I took the initiative. 'Then I'm going to have to recommend a treatment.'

I sent him away with a prescription note which, I felt, had as much chance of achieving its purpose as a message in a bottle. Even if Webster returned home without losing or discarding it, it seemed unlikely he would go to the effort of seeking out the drug, and even if he did make it to the pharmacist, I wondered if the pills would get further than a medicine cabinet. The prescription was for a neuroleptic which would calm the schizophrenic impulse by limiting the transmission of dopamine, one of the accepted roots of the illness,[21] but at a cost. There would be one certain side effect, not clinical but professional: he wouldn't be able to run a

[21] As there is still no unanimous neuropathology for schizophrenia, the precise influence of dopaminergic neurons is still open to debate. For opposing views of schizophrenia, try Michael J. Turner, *The Divided Self* (McGill University Press, 1980) and Broad, *Schizophrenia: The Mind-Myth* (McGill University Press, 1981): two books from the same stable which differed so radically that the authors reportedly came to blows on campus, with Broad the winner, although student bias against the misogynist Turner may have distorted accounts of the fight. The chapter on schizophrenia in Aloisi's *Affairs of the Mind* is also very useful.

race while under the treatment, because it contained several substances affected by the blanket ban on chemicals in the aftermath of the eighties' cheat-fest. Taking the pills to subdue the schizophrenic voices would require Webster firstly to admit that he needed treatment, and secondly to resign himself to sitting out several months without a competitive race. Only if he allowed the medication to do its work would we be able to phase it out in time for the Games.

I explained the situation to a blank-faced Webster, and to his coach Frank Macguire in a covering letter. This at least was successfully delivered: Macguire, a genial man, called to thank me for my help and said he'd be encouraging Webster to try the treatment, but without much optimism. 'I'm the person who knows him best,' he said dryly, 'and I don't have any idea what he'll do at any time. I'm his coach, and most races I don't even know if he'll run, swim or skateboard down the track, so . . .'

So I told myself to be content with my bit part in the Webster story and looked forward to telling people I had treated him when he won Olympic gold in four years' time and failed to show up to collect his medal. It was a little frustrating that many of my clients now saw me on this kind of basis, a visit here and there when the mood took them; the money made it worth my while (although in this case, none had changed hands) but the process was an unsatisfactory race: a couple of hours to strip away what might be years of psychological moss, a time trial of fact-finding and lightning conclusions, the whole thing nestling neatly in the schedules but bearing as much resemblance to the slow, patient probing of classical psychotherapy as a home-run contest to the regular season. Instead of giving me weeks to weigh up the situation, clients were asking me to swing the bat and hit every problem out of the ground. However, the mental agility required by the frequent changes of tempo kept my mind too busy to grapple with personal worries, and, besides, I was becoming well practised in fast-food therapy: since mid-1989 I had been answering one bite-size concern a day for a column in the *Chicago Herald* called 'PK's Couch'.

Dear Dr. Kristal,

I have been on medication for depression for two years now. Although I'm feeling a lot better, I am worried that the drugs might have permanently changed my character. These days if I'm happy, I can't be sure if it is genuine happiness or just a product of the drugs. Or even what "genuine happiness" is.
—Unsure in Portland, OR

PK's PROGNOSIS: You're right that "genuine happiness" is very difficult to define. The drugs you've been taking have worked chemically on your mind to alter your perception of what is normal, and so in a sense your character *has* been permanently altered. But character is just as hard to define, and besides, drug-assisted joy must be better than sober misery. Many of us would trade places with you!

I had become sick of the column very soon after beginning it, but however hard I tried to get it discontinued by discouraging my correspondents, I could not seem to arrest its popularity. The more abrasive and pessimistic my answers, the more my mailbag swelled and the more of a following I gained. I was praised for my 'tough love' by other agony uncles, and for my 'arch critique of mainstream therapy-bynumbers' by smart-ass commentators. Once again, apparent career success was masking an unfulfilling lifestyle in which I handled more and more patients with more and more superficiality. I wondered if Richard, in New York, had experienced the same discontent at the times when I had envied his impregnable position; but then Richard had taken a more controlled path to fame and sidestepped its pitfalls more efficiently. He also had more of an out-of-office life, and – for two years now – a beautiful wife, Christy, the former style journalist now editor-in-chief of a six-magazine syndicate and fashion consultant to a Hollywood studio.

Dear Dr. Kristal,

I have been married to "Joanna" for five years and we are very happy. Recently, though, I have become worried that loyalty to her means writing off other areas of my life. Last week an old female friend of mine knocked on our door asking for a bed for the night— she had been mugged and left on the street with no possessions. Naturally I offered my friend our spare room, but "Joanna" was furious and glowered at her all through breakfast. Later she explained, "Any woman who's your friend is my enemy." "Joanna" is worth the trouble as she satisfies me mentally, spiritually and sexually, but does marriage really mean cutting ties with everything and everyone else? —Devoted Husband in Detroit

PK'S PROGNOSIS: It shouldn't, but it so often does, in practice. One of my best friends got married a couple of years ago and it's now even harder than before to get a word with him. I'm sure it sometimes saddens him, but (as you said

yourself) the reward is worth it. The three satisfactions you listed are beyond most of us, most of our lives. Be grateful!

Late one afternoon while I was cooking up another column of sad soundbites for page 34, the phone rang: it was Frank Macguire with some news surprising enough to shake me out of gloom for the whole weekend. Webster had acted on my advice and taken a course of the pills, and the results were already visible. Communications with Streissman had dwindled in frequency and harmful potential; Webster had become more predictable in his movements and constant in his moods. He was training conscientiously and had run one of his best ever times last night. And – contrary to my expectations – he wanted to see me again. 'He got a lot out of talking to you last time,' Macguire explained. It was very satisfying to reflect that even a faltering, battle-of-wills consultation had made some long-term progress. We arranged a second appointment and I left the office that night in a rare mood of self-congratulation.

The Webster Bruce who made a return visit to my office was very different from the original fidgety, untrusting customer. He gave me a wide smile and flicked my hand in a complicated handshake which I was only confident enough to join towards the end. Where improvement was concerned, his words matched his appearance. 'I feel a whole lot better, doc,' he said, spreading his arms expansively over my easy chair where he had previously pawed at the upholstery and chewed his fingernails. 'The drugs have done great.'

'And you're running well in training?'

'Sure,' he said, grinning again. 'I guess I'll probably win the Youth Games. It's just whether I can compete. It's so nice in here with my new drugs, I don't know if I want to stop them.'

But he did want to win gold at the Games: a platform to recognition on a near-international scale, a tribute to his father, an act of revenge on society (and perhaps Streissman, although this name was gratifyingly almost absent from this session) . . . all these motives were touched upon as we discussed Webster's ambition to come off the drugs in two months' time and claim a landmark victory over the college-scholarship crowd. I told him that, if the progress continued, there was no reason why he could not withdraw from the treatment by the time of the Games; but we'd need to be absolutely certain he was in the clear. His psychological future was at stake and that was a greater, if less glamorous, prize than those available on the track. Our eyes met as I stated these grown-up truths, and by an invisible wire I communicated the less responsible side of the argument: Webster had to win that medal. For both of us.

Was I falling into the trap of personal involvement once more? Perhaps I was, but then, despite its unfortunate repercussions, 'personal involvement' in Lily's case had brought us a long way and provided a shortcut to some insights even if it had diverted us from others. In any case I found that 'not getting too close' to the people whose psychological states occupied my days was unrealistic. I had to *want* them to get better rather than simply trying to bring it about with efficient detachment. In Webster's case, I found after only two meetings that his welfare was a personal mission. He had had me hooked right from the start with the lane-crossing fiasco and now that we were acquainted, an attachment was definitely forming.

At least this time we could not call upon the deep well of common interests which had fooled me into thinking that Lily and I were ideally suited. Webster and I clearly had very different backgrounds and mindsets; and he was still in diapers when I began consulting (although he could have beaten me in a race even then). All the same, our time together extended well beyond the formal boundaries, and after a drink in a café, I ended up inviting Webster back to my apartment. We sat up into the night discussing his heroes (Muhammad Ali predictably appeared) and mine.

'You know a lot of shit, but it's a weird kind of shit,' Webster concluded after I had given him a not very interesting account of some psychologists I admired. 'I'm a weird kind of person,' I admitted, cheerfully.

'I didn't mean that,' said Webster, as if I had insulted him rather than myself.

Seeing Webster into a taxi (he was staying in a hotel, something which would have been considered a risky idea even a couple of months previously), I felt a flush of pride in my role that was almost paternal. It was hard to avoid the idea of fatherhood as I pondered Webster and tried to rationalise my great wish to help him and be respected by him. Although the knowledge that Dad wasn't my dad had helped to insulate me against the chill of loss, in the longer term it was making the landscape bleaker: I felt as if I had lost him twice. The pangs of solitude I now felt were partly down (I believed) to the feeling I alluded to more than once in my Christmas diary: that I should now be taking my place as father, continuing the cycle, growing my section of the family tree. And here, walking into the middle of my suppressed but real desire to be a protector and an inspiration, was Webster, a talented, vulnerable kid who needed someone to replace the fallen idol of his father.

If it had been a movie I would have adopted him. Instead, I thought about him often, spoke to him or Frank Macguire every week for updates, and succumbed too easily when Webster made a request I had been secretly yearning for: would I come to the Youth Games with them, and be on hand to help him? It would create a disrupted appointment book but also, far more questionably, another instance of extra-curricular work with a patient. I weighed it up for about ten seconds.

> Dear Dr. Kristal,
> Is it true that you are treating Webster Bruce and trying to get him fit for the American Youth Games? If so, what is your involvement? Are you connected with his physical performance e.g. how fit he is to run or is it all about his mind? Is he crazy or just a little strange and unhinged? —Curious in LA

> **PK'S PROGNOSIS: Again I feel I should remind readers that I cannot use this column to divulge personal information about my clients. On this one occasion, to end speculation, I can reveal that I am treating Webster for a minor neurological condition. It shouldn't stop him from running everyone else out of the race—although not in the way he did once before, hopefully . . .**

As the Youth Games neared and the hype-wagon rolled obediently into gear, fuelled by an endorsement deal with a major athletic-goods company, anticipation grew. A nation normally apathetic to track sports recalled Webster's conduct of past years and waited with a mixture of fascination and alarm to see if he could triumph. He was paid 100,000 dollars by a fast-food chain for a commercial in which he shoulder-checked people out of the line: 'Get there any way you can' was the slogan, delivered with a huge, winning grin to the camera. But before Frank Macguire, Webster and I could start planning our victory lap, there was an important stage in the recovery to be negotiated: withdrawal from medication, in time to pass the blood and urine tests now as routine at the end of the race as the starter's pistol at its beginning.

When Webster visited me for the third time, just weeks before the Games and days after coming off the drugs, the fear of a comeback by the malign side of his brain was weighing heavily upon him. Even in the same breath as he stated that Streissman was 'nobody really – he never bothers me now', he expressed concern that he could still relinquish the ground newly won by his treatment. 'I worry what if he comes back,' was how Webster put it. It was upsetting to see him so able to spy the self-inflicted danger on the horizon and yet not fully confident of his ability to elude it as he had eluded New York City cops a few years back. Webster's body language this time was the language of uncertainty, reflecting his frailty since the drugs stopped contributing their magical ingredient: his hands trembled on the glass, and he toyed with clothes and hair as in our first meeting.

Speaking to him and Macguire together, I explained that allowing Webster to compete in the Youth Games without assurance of his complete recovery would be un-professional of me, but it was not my place to make career decisions for him. 'In the end, whether Webster runs has to be down to him,' I concluded. This was both cowardly and rash. Where somebody's mental health was endangered, it *was* my place to intervene. I could have made him withdraw from the Games: it might have meant waiting a while longer for big-league success but it would have been the responsible verdict. Maybe I just didn't care about professionalism, any more. In any case, Webster made the only decision that made sense to him: competing in the Games and leaving the rest to chance.

'If I do something stupid, hell, at least I'm there and not at home,' he said.

And I would be there too.

I took a week off and flew to Florida, where the event was being held. Blistering sun beat down on the hot red track as Webster showed me the arena where, over the next few days, he would run three career-shaping races. Around the stadium, the smart white brick buildings of a university campus provided the athletes with a small Olympic village of their own, 4,500 miles from Barcelona where the real Games were being held that summer. In another four years, Webster's generation would get their chance. Those who impressed at the Youth Games would be enrolled on to a development programme and groomed for the next Olympics, where the peaks of sporting renown beckoned. Those who missed this opportunity to shine, and were not picked for the programme, would be herded along a rockier path, trying to break through an ever thickening field of jostling wannabes with no sponsorship and little official funding to help them. The air around the athletics park was dense with desperate hopes, tensions, rumours; smiles were strained, conversations fizzed with unspoken rivalry; track-suited coaches prowled around monitoring the eating, drinking and probably defecating patterns of their protégés. Every night brought a thunderstorm, after which the stuffy Floridan air would thin briefly before reprising its muggy grip; it was like a microclimate especially engineered for the Games, perhaps by one of the sixteen corporate sponsors whose ubiquitous names, suggestive of lucrative deals placed tantalisingly at the competitors' fingertips, jacked up the pressure even more. The commercial kitsch festivities of the opening ceremony could not dissipate the feeling that it was only a matter of time (as they say) before someone cracked.

When the head of the organising committee heard that I was at large, he approached me to ask if I would consider running a daily drop-in session to deal with athletes' problems, occupying the post of 'Games psychiatrist' which had been hastily set up in response to the unprecedented demand from competitors. My instinct told me not to volunteer for more work when I could be enjoying leisure time, but fifteen minutes by the pool trying to enjoy the midday sun was enough to change my mind. Watching a gaunt young sportswoman thrashing up and down in the water, head tossing to one side and the other, I realised some truths: that the more I could stretch my brain, the less likely it would cruise on autopilot towards the cliff edge of my past; that however lucky in some ways, the athletes labouring under the logo-ridden banner of American youth deserved some protection; and that, in spite of all my complaints, I enjoyed psychotherapy more than most leisurely uses of my time. Brought face to face with this last, comforting realisation, I broke out into a smile of satisfaction, misread as salaciousness by the swimmer who grimaced at me and hauled herself out of the pool before scuttling off sheathed in a towel with a contemptuous half-glance back.

The Games paid for my hotel and expenses; I set up the drop-in time to avoid any clash with Webster's heats, and opened for business. Most athletes simply wanted to talk at me about the weight of expectation (coaches', parents', their own), or complain about the tight security procedures. One long-jumper asked sardonically if I would be taking a urine sample. A volleyball player asked me if I knew how he could improve his technique at the net. There was something refreshingly pure about these patients' worries compared with my usual round; or maybe they were easier to help and more grateful. Either way, I felt genuinely useful.

Webster's first race was on the Tuesday afternoon; after a brief talk with him in the morning, I headed for the arena, heart quickening. Our consultation had not been a completely happy one. Webster was quiet and detached, and neither Frank Macguire nor I could get enough out of him to reassure us. Macguire confessed to me that he had had nightmares about Webster disappearing before the race or throwing it away with another of his eccentric routines. It was difficult to know whether to mention Streissman; the power of suggestion might open the door to an adversary who would otherwise remain forgotten. I decided to gamble on it.

'And have you spoken to Streissman?'

Webster aimed a brief flicker of disdain in my direction in a similar manner to the self-conscious swimmer. 'No use talking about him.'

We had to be content with this. At least there were no signs of a physical reaction to withdrawal from medication. My second-worst fear was that his performances this week would be blighted by some side effect I had failed to predict. I was reserving the worst fear for a scenario too strange to occur – Webster poisoning himself by accident, announcing he had had a sex change, or giving up the whole thing on a whim – so that I would not feel outpaced by events if he sprang one of his surprises. This was a weak safety net and, as the runners skulked around on the start line, I felt jittery and helpless, unable to drag my eyes away from the lanky figure in the fourth lane who was making his way through gentle warm-up exercises. What it must be like for Macguire, who sat simultaneously smoking cigarettes and chewing gum, his craggy face half concealed by the giant peak of a baseball cap, I could only imagine. The runners crouched; the gun cracked and a blur of limbs whizzed down the track. For a long time there didn't seem to be an inch between any of them; then in the final three seconds Webster breezed away from the field, lurching over the finish line before decelerating smoothly like a car, one arm slightly raised to acknowledge a comfortable victory. People around us cheered; photographers snapped; Macguire nodded calmly as if he had predicted the whole thing and Webster loped over to us with a vacant but bright smile on his face. He had won his first race as a reformed schizophrenic and one more good run separated him from the finals. I slept soundly that night.

Midway through the week there came a tentative knock on my door and in walked the attractive swimmer who had suspected me of voyeurism. My heart skipped as harassment-case thoughts flooded into my head. I began defending myself.

'Oh, it's not about that,' she said, amused. 'Anyhow I didn't think you were spying. I just don't like to be looked at, I feel ugly.'

She was fifteen or sixteen years old, short, blonde, with an easy poise counteracted by a shifty demeanour. I asked her to sit down.

The girl introduced herself as Kirsty Reid and explained that she was in the tennis tournament. This was an understatement, I knew; she was one of the top three under-sixteen women in American tennis and slated to make the jump to the pro circuit within two years. A glance at the official guide to the Games, open on my desk, provided her vital information in a hyper-distilled form I might have designed myself:

KIRSTY REID	**born Kansas City, 8/8/76**
• **EVENT**	Tennis (ranking: 2)
• **SPONSORS**	Nike, Budweiser, Calvin Klein
• **LOVES**	Horseriding, pizza, vacations, Michael Jackson
• **HATES**	Losing, intolerance
• **SOUNDBITE**	"I can't wait to get out there!"

'My parents gave them all that information, I was out when they called,' said Kirsty, shuddering at the photo that captured her in a gawky smile as she collected a trophy. 'And "intolerance" . . . I think the organisers put that in.'

'So can you give me a more accurate picture?' I asked.

She turned the shiny brochure towards her and leafed through until she found another entry. The picture was of a tall girl with bronze skin, clad in a flattering white dress and arching her racket like an example from a coaching manual. Pushing the booklet back to me, Kirsty sighed.

'All you need to know is, I have to play *her* in the finals.'

LOLA VERDINI	**born Long Island, 4/24/76**
• **EVENT**	Tennis (ranking: 1)
• **SPONSORS**	Nike, Budweiser, Calvin Klein, TDK, American Airlines
• **LOVES**	Playing tennis, reading, music, dancing, traveling, nature, going out, movies, understanding other cultures
• **HATES**	Green vegetables, restrictions of freedom of speech
• **SOUNDBITE**	"Whoever wins, the American Youth Games is a great opportunity for us all."

Lola and Kirsty: another archetypal case of an inferiority complex created by comparison and competition; my old specialist subject revived for the nineties. Two outstanding young tennis players pitted against each other again and again, publicly sparring in the gladiator fishtank of the junior circuit, each game picked to pieces by sharp-eyed experts and ignorant parents alike: spectators so close to the sidelines, Kirsty said, that she sometimes felt like presenting one of them with her racket and inviting them to demonstrate the shot that had met with their disapproval. The two of them, a league above most of their contemporaries, met in the late stages of competitions everywhere – Key Biscayne, Des Moines, Las Vegas – and their respective techniques, skills and (in Kirsty's view) looks were relentlessly compared and contrasted. A familiar theme, given a sharp twist by the breathless timewatching of junior tennis – professionals, after all, join the tour as young as sixteen, and anyone over twenty-five is finished – but also by a cruel quirk of the form book. The two had met fourteen times; Lola had won every match.

'And it wouldn't be a big thing if it was just the tennis,' said Kirsty, no doubt seeing my eyes light up at the prospect of a sporting rivalry, 'but it's everything. I mean look at her profile. What a golden girl. "Understanding other cultures"!' She laughed with an almost affectionate despair. 'She's incredible.'

'So are the two of you friends?'

'Not really,' she said. 'She's a nice girl, I just don't have a lot in common with her except that we always have to play in the finals and she always always beats me, like, six-three six-four.'

'Why do you think she always wins? I mean . . .'

'She is a good player,' said Kirsty reasonably. 'But she isn't fourteen matches better than me. It's just, when I'm

231

playing her, I just get, like, overawed by the whole thing. It's like playing against Jessica Rabbit.'

'Jessica . . .?'

'From the *Roger Rabbit* movie. She's a kind of perfect character.' She sighed gently. 'Lola's just, like, this perfect person. Everything you want to be but never could be. You know, tall, thin, beautiful skin, all the right friends, always in the right place . . .'

I glanced down at the brochure. 'I wouldn't say she was especially beautiful.'

Kirsty raised her eyebrows contemptuously. 'Of course she is. Look at those cheekbones. And the hair.'

'I suppose, but . . .'

'And look how thin she is,' Kirsty persisted, tracing Lola's skeletal frame on the paper with a forefinger as if admiring a work of art.

I looked at the logo on her tennis shirt and then down at the same logo, emblazoned across an advertising feature on the page opposite Lola's profile. The ad featured a girl so skinny she could probably have been scanned directly into the magazine.

'So how can I help you?' I asked.

'Well, I think you might be able to, kind of, psychologically prepare me for the game,' said Kirsty. 'Lola has a mind coach who gets her in the zone, and it seems to work because when we play, she's always, like, mentally stronger.'

'Who is this . . . "mind coach" of hers?' I asked.

'His name's Richard Aloisi.'

And there he was again. Bobbing up into view every time I landed in fresh water, with an exasperatingly reasonable expression on his face: *Sure, I was here first, but you're welcome to stay*. Even in territory I thought I had marked out as my own, even when I had an office confirming beyond dispute that I was the official Games psychologist, he hovered into view as the mental mentor of the infallible Lola Verdini. Mr and Mrs Perfect. I was left to work with the nearly girl, the gallant silver-medal prospect who had suffered as many brave defeats at Lola's hands as I had experienced setbacks trying to keep pace with Richard. As can be imagined, I warmed to Kirsty immediately. The instant bond of a common neurosis extended across the table. We arranged to meet on Friday night, the evening before the final: her fifteenth clash with Lola. Meanwhile I kept a look out for Richard.

I saw him, as so often, at an inopportune moment, while I was pursuing Webster across the parking lot. It was Thursday, the day of Webster's semi-final, and he was still acting in a nerve-eroding fashion, spending the morning wandering aimlessly between points dictated by nothing more solid than his shifting, unreadable mind. 'I just need to get my head straight,' he had explained, but once his meanderings were into their second hour, Frank Macguire and I were becoming increasingly concerned. Spotting Webster from long range, I shouted his name; he changed direction as if to shake me off. I shouted his name again, surrendering my dignity like a hack photographer looking for an exclusive snap, and at this moment Richard emerged from his luxurious hired car, leading his wife Christy by the arm. We exchanged hasty greetings and arranged to meet the next afternoon. It was his idea to play tennis and the aptness appealed to both of us. 'I'll see you on court!' Richard shouted after me as I continued after Webster, following him out to a shady corner of the site, glancing back as I heard a peal of laughter behind me.

In the minutes before his race, Webster apologised for his conduct. 'I just don't feel myself today,' he declared. 'Really strange things going on in my head.'

'What kind of things?'

'Just, you know, strange thoughts,' he said casually, while Macguire gnawed his sleeve, his underlined eyes suggesting that retirement could not come soon enough. 'I kind of can't concentrate on the race.'

Webster had been pacing tirelessly up and down the corridor in a small-scale retracing of his earlier walk, so I settled him down and, questioning him as much as I dared so close to a race, ascertained that Streissman was not the problem.

'It's not the schizo thing,' he said, 'or maybe it is, 'cause I wouldn't know, would I?' He laughed. 'It's just . . . without the pills it's hard, you know?'

I told him I did know, but he could go back on them in a few days. Just two more races, two more draining routines of tension and release.

Frank Macguire and I watched with an effort at impassiveness as Webster went through the motions of preparation all over again for the semi-final race before at last poising like a panther waiting to spring. The gun went off and then repeated itself; a false start. After some discussion a red marker was placed, with slow ceremony, on Webster's blocks. One more mistimed burst and he would be disqualified. No one breathed as the gun fired again; this time, though, a clean start. And then the same smooth sequence: Webster biding his time before stretching his legs and exploding away from the pack, not even looking around at the finish; he had won by such a margin that, while he slowed down after the white line, his nearest rival had to continue for ten yards at full pelt before he could offer his congratulations. This time Webster was given a generous ovation by the crowd – even Macguire lifted his baseball cap into the air and shook it gently – and as he embarked on a swift circuit of the stadium to receive the adulation, I felt a defiant stab of pride. *Are you watching, Richard?* I almost heard myself ask.

He wasn't, I learned, the next afternoon on the tennis court, but he had been following Webster's progress like everyone else and was intrigued to hear of my work with him. After a preliminary discussion about the tennis tournament – Richard, it transpired, had been doing 'confidence work' with Lola for the past year, in which she had won seven titles and 95,000 dollars in prize money – we soon moved on to my main client, now one of the most talked-about athletes at the entire event. It was Richard who made this observation and I realised with some trepidation that it was true. While we smacked brand-new tennis balls to and fro on beautifully maintained carpet courts reserved for the use of staff, Richard asked me how I had gone about treating such a threatening condition as schizophrenia without removing Webster from the competition.

'He was out of competition for a couple months,' I responded, angling my racket to play a topspin winner that deceived Richard with its altered bounce and whistled past him: a shot, I felt, that no player in the world could have returned. 'I had him on —[22] and another neuroleptic and he improved very quickly.'

'And then . . .?' Richard asked, pausing to take a long swig from a bottle of water. I observed with silent satisfaction that marriage had already taken its toll upon his fitness.

'Then he went off it,' I said.

'He went *off* it?'

'Yep.' I tried to keep my tone light and seized a handful of balls to serve the next game, but a sick feeling was

[22] Editor's note: The brand name of the main drug used by Webster has been deleted from this edition for legal reasons.

gathering around my stomach. Richard considered whether or not to voice his thoughts and, vexed as usual by his combination of quick thinking and measured response, I tried to pre-empt him. 'I know it's normally a six-months minimum, but he's perfectly . . .'

'That's dangerous, Pete,' said Richard, returning my serve imperiously while scratching his head to summon up a memory I was not anxious to hear. 'Wasn't there a guy who . . .'

'He's perfectly stable,' I interrupted.

Richard was obviously thinking back to yesterday's incident, in which he had observed me chasing an unstable-looking Webster across a parking lot. He refrained from comment though; and his silence communicated more than a reproach. I began to defend myself again but the sentiments shrivelled in the stuffy air.

We continued the game, Richard gaining the upper hand, and civility reasserted itself; but I was fuming with the terrible self-righteousness of a man furious to have his wrong exposed. What did Richard know about Webster, anyhow? It was easy for him to propose by-the-book divisions of drugged and non-drugged time; I was the one who had to balance Webster's health with his ambitions, the desire to fulfil his enormous potential before the spotlight shifted on to another newcomer. Richard understood none of this. Achievements had always floated into his life in neat rows like prizes on a conveyor belt, inviting him to shoot and claim them at his leisure. It was different for those of us who had to tunnel every mile of progress through solid rock. As I chewed over these unconstructive thoughts, my body obligingly illustrated my point by withholding my tennis skills: shots slid or ballooned off my racket, scudding into the net or sailing impotently over the back line; Richard performed the role of surprised, reluctant serial winner to perfection, watching the skewed balls respectfully, as if even the most woeful of the shots had missed the mark by a mere fraction. His courtesy and my incompetence were acid drops into the self-inflicted wound of my anger.

By the time I conceded defeat and trudged off court with sweat sticking my shirt to me and Richard offering friendly platitudes ('I hardly noticed who won – the whole point was just to see you'), I was in an evil mood. Perhaps the one thing that could have multiplied my grievances then occurred. As if scripted into a play to symbolise the hero's folly, Webster appeared from around the corner. He was in the middle of a furious argument, but there was nobody with him: his cries and counter-claims, flung into the air where an adversary should have stood, lingered there before dissolving in embarrassment. And nobody on the whole campus, perhaps in the whole state of Florida at that moment, was more embarrassed than me.

Of course Webster was beyond reason for the time being, but then so was I, in my own diluted and rather pathetic way, and the two wrongs collided to make a greater, grotesque one. As he raved against incomprehensible targets – unseen enemies trying to 'cut him up' or 'fuck him up', it was impossible to know who or how – I tried calming words which floated into the air as lamely as my tennis shots earlier. When these failed, I grasped his shoulders as if steadying him physically would calm the evil spirits in his head, stop them from jerking and chattering him into a cave of madness. He writhed out of my grasp; I struggled to regain it, repeating his name over and over.

'What's happening, what's the matter?' I yelled, while Webster shouted back: 'I don't trust you, you're just like Streissman, I don't trust you.' Richard watched the miserable scene from his discreet distance. Finally the pantomime antics provided some violence; on my third or fourth attempt to clutch at Webster, his arm shot up in self-protection and landed a blow to my nose, not hard but sudden enough to burst a few off-guard blood vessels. Richard, advancing unobtrusively, held out one of his white tennis towels with a smile of genuine empathy. I took it with barely a nod, mopped the trickle of red off my shirt with the ruined dignity of a child covered in sick at his own birthday party.

After that, Webster calmed down and began to talk more coherently. I coaxed him down from his ranting into a submissive whimper and, with Richard's assistance, escorted him back to my office. It was six o'clock and in twenty-eight hours he would run by far the most important race of his life; here he was in my supposed care and in a mental state too perilous to be entered for a sack race at infant school. To my brooding mind it only made matters worse that, once Richard had slipped away apologetically with a remark about seeing me at tomorrow's tennis final (Jesus, I thought, that too), Webster regained surer footing and began to speak with the togetherness that had deserted him in the past hour.

'I don't know what I did,' he kept repeating. 'I just felt like getting at you.' He hung his head penitently, but my pride demanded more. After expending considerable time, energy and – yes – love on Webster, I now felt disposable and ridiculous. My trip to Florida, and in fact the whole Webster project, were being mocked by his behaviour. Perhaps it was my fault that he had taken an irregular course of drugs, but it was the only way he could still compete: I had taken my reputation into my hands by tailoring a 'treatment-lite' to suit his needs; and in exchange for this courageous gamble he was sticking the knife into my public image and – the grand slam – showing me up in front of Richard. In the space of a few moments Webster had become scapegoat for years of frustration. I let him have it with both barrels.

'You don't want to be helped at all, do you?'

'Well, yeah, but . . .'

'You're more interested in just making a scene.'

'I didn't know what I was doing . . .'

'You knew. It was there in your eyes. You wanted to show that you could still make me look stupid. Well, you have. I look stupid because I thought I could do something for you. I can only help someone who wants to be helped.'

Webster shrugged, his old trademark. This goaded me on to greater heights of stupidity.

'I know what's wrong with you – you're scared to win, scared things might be going right for you at last. You're pulling yourself back because you're so used to living with the problem, you don't know what you would do without one. Am I right?'

(Shrug.)

'Tell me I'm right.'

(Shrug. My fury was wavering, without the oxygen of response.)

'Webster, do you care at all what I say?'

A third shrug from Webster, who was now removing non-existent dirt from his fingernails. The more impassioned I became, the less notice he took. I gathered up strength for a last stroke of melodrama.

'Then I don't see why I should care what *you* say,' I said resoundingly, as if this meant winning the argument. I left him in the office, still occupied with his nails, busy with thoughts that I might never be allowed access to again.

When the creeping knowledge that I had probably made a mistake met the residual scraps of anger from the afternoon of humiliations, what remained was a clammy, festering feeling of wrong that lay in wait for a vent. I called Macguire, but he didn't pick up; almost called home, then realised my parents were dead; even called Lily's new number (she was back in London these days, appearing in *Les Miserables*, married to the lanky actor called Liam), which I had torn from the corner of a Christmas card, hanging up before it had a chance to ring. I went for a walk to relieve the burden, but as once in Central Park every insignificant pointer had marked out a path to happiness, now every triviality seemed a stage in a plan to inconvenience me. My anger and despair kept flaring up at chance happenings as if they were rubbing against a sore, and I was alarmed to see the extent of the negative energy I had been repressing; when a small dog ran across my path yapping and sniffing playfully at my toes, I had to stifle the urge to swing my leg and boot it high over the hedgerows like a field goal. Resettled in my office, I awaited Kirsty, whose final was, like Webster's, tomorrow, and wondered what I would say and do next.

Although the meeting with Kirsty began politely, it was not long before her demeanour – a proud lack of self-esteem, a triumphant pessimism – sparked me up again.

'Why the hell do you care about Lola?' I suddenly demanded of her, mowing her down the first time she breathed the name of her rival. Kirsty shrank back in her seat.

'Well, because I'm playing her tomorrow and she's the best, and . . . you know all this, because she's beautiful and . . .'

'There you are, because she's beautiful!' I almost yelled. 'Well, that's bullshit! You believe she's beautiful because people tell you so . . .'

'How else am I supposed to judge?'

'. . . because *people tell you so*, and because she looks like one of the toothpick women they get to do the commercials. OK, fine. If that's beautiful, then she wins on that count. But does it make her a better tennis player? In fact, even more than that, does it make *you* any worse?'

She hesitated.

'Does the fact that Lola has all these amazing qualities, does it make you worse?'

Kirsty pondered this for a second. I had now lowered my voice and was behaving more like an adult.

'Well, yes, because you have to compare yourself to . . .'

'Listen, Kirsty,' I said, suddenly conspiratorial, beseeching. Her voice cut out as quickly as if I had turned the radio off; my constant shifting of tone seemed to be mesmerising her and she was paying me full attention. 'If you want to win tomorrow – and even if you don't – you have to remember this. Comparing yourself to people might be inevitable, especially in the game you're in, but it's one of the worst things you can ever do. I know you might say, Everyone compares me to her, just by playing against each other we're setting up a comparison.' (Kirsty nodded and I gave myself a small mental clap for anticipating a response, one of the skills of the champion orator.) 'Well, maybe. But that's a comparison *other people* are inflicting and you can't do anything about that. The moment you start making your *own* comparisons, you are sunk. And do you know how I know?'

(My hands were poised to provide a rhetorical gesture, but my office was an unpromising forum; there was no picture of Richard to point out, for example. I left them suspended in the air as if I were about to offer her a papal blessing.)

'Because I've been doing it all my goddam life,' I answered. 'And however much I know I've been successful and whatever, there's always . . . certain people who make me feel my own achievements have been completely worthless. And however many times I learn that lesson, I forget it again at the important times and it really screws me. But maybe you'll learn it better than me, Kirsty. If you do, you could really go a long way. It's never too late to stop thinking of yourself as inferior. I'm going to try. You should try.'

As the passion of the speech gradually spent itself, tapering off toward these final words which were spoken in restrained tones, I was distracted by a cleaner who came in to empty the garbage with a thin smile on his lips, and realised that I had been too frank and certainly too animated: my tirade could have been heard by anyone. But I felt at ease for the first time that day. I had given voice to something important and, moreover, it seemed to have worked on Kirsty. Fifteen years of ambition and attainment gazed up in respectful silence at forty years of ambition and frustration. I was not just another cosily detached shrink getting 'right behind her' for an hour before getting back behind the desk; and at the same time I had (narrowly) steered the right side of the line that separates the well-applied personal touch from the maudlin don't-be-like-me routine. I could almost see the words sinking into Kirsty's mind and setting to work like antibodies.

Careful not to overplay my hand, I asked Kirsty to talk me through her preparation for tomorrow's match. Together we devised a schedule that would take her from the morning shower to the afternoon encounter with Lola in a focused manner without allowing over-concentration to tense up her muscles and mind, as it had in the past. I advised her not to think about her opponent at all, but if the subject appeared, not to wade into the trap of glamorising her. Focus on Lola's problems and put her own advantages into perspective, I said. Even if Lola wins tomorrow's final and every other trophy on the junior circuit, turning pro will be like being a goldfish dropped into a fast-flowing stream, and glamour will only hamper her; the renowned locker-room rivalry of the women's tour, which suffocates many blossoming talents, will burn all the more fiercely against her. 'And, you know, I spoke to Richard Aloisi about Lola today,' I said, venturing a lie to clinch my point. 'He says she's really stressed and unhappy. Not just about the game – about everything. She's got all kinds of issues. So don't feel inferior. It sounds like she envies you.'

This tailored untruth, this fast-acting balm, worked its magic on Kirsty's face. However worthy the axioms about valuing yourself and the warnings about invidious comparisons, I should have known that nothing gratifies a fragile ego like news of a rival's struggles. Maybe all Kirsty needed to beat Lola was to know that she too was prey to fears and insecurities (which, despite the mild dishonesty, I had no doubt was true). On the other hand, maybe what she needed was a stronger backhand or more of a serve-volley game: I had never seen either of them play and if the gulf in talent were unbridgeable (as her 0–14 record suggested) then, however strong her psychological condition, only a sporting miracle would see Kirsty claim the gold tomorrow. But I hoped and believed, as she rose and thanked me enthusiastically, that I had helped her towards a slightly revised conception of success and failure: one that did not begin and end with the balance sheet of win and loss.

It had been an eventful afternoon, one in which I had watched chunks of my professional self-respect sluice away before clawing some of it back in the final hour. If I could have found Webster or even Macguire, I might still have been able to put myself into credit for the day by making my peace with the patient who had served as my punchbag. But they were nowhere to be seen in the village, not in their chalet nor in the social room, where small packs of athletes sat conversing in low tones. The sight of their dazed faces and the flickering TV screen made my own eyelids heavy and I stumbled back to my room, wondering if I would see Webster before his final (which, as the showpiece event, was not until tomorrow night) and how Kirsty would fare in hers.

The air on finals day was, appropriately, even more muggy and thick; the sky, dark blue all week, had turned white; the site already heaved with spectators as I approached the stadium, still hazy after a long sleep full of ominous, half-remembered dreams. Huge electronic billboards at every turn spelled out the two events that would determine the fates of my two patients and the success of my efforts: 1PM WOMEN'S TENNIS FINAL, and then, a few races and slogans later, 9PM MEN'S 100 METERS FINAL: SPONSORED BY EAST COAST AIRLINES, BECAUSE LIFE'S TOO SHORT TO WAIT AROUND. It was coming up to noon already; Kirsty would now be replaying our conversation as she made her final preparations, running through superstitious rituals, double- and treble-checking racket strings and equipment, trying to block out thoughts of the previously invincible opponent separated from her by the thin wall of a locker-room stall. On my way to the tennis courts I made a hurried search of the stadium area and found Macguire on the practice track, where he was contemplatively watching two of Webster's rivals trotting through warm-up runs.

'Webster's still asleep,' he explained, offering me a cigarette as he always did although aware I did not smoke. 'He asked me to let him sleep in this morning, so . . .'

'Did he say anything about what happened last night?'

'He mentioned some kind of altercation,' Macguire reported with a knowing smile. 'But it didn't seem to be worrying him. Nothing much seemed to be worrying him, really. Most calm he's been all week.'

Good news, then, although I would have given a lot for a reassuring glimpse of Webster, five minutes to apologise for the harshness of my reaction to his unfortunate appearance last night. The more I recalled the incident, the worse the criticism I received from the studio analysts in my mind. The antagonism had been clearly written on Webster's face as he swore and shook me off in front of Richard; but now, in the reconstruction, his face was blocked out and all I could see was my own rage and resentment spilling out like the blood from my nose. I told Macguire that I would meet Webster that afternoon, after the tennis, and (after hesitation) asked him to pass on my apologies if I had caused any offence. Macguire nodded, staring out over the fence that separated the training area from the main arena. Whatever had passed between me and his man failed to prick his curiosity: all he could see was the lined tarmac on which, in a few hours, Webster would have the chance to skyrocket both of their careers.

The tennis court was almost full, Lola and Kirsty already patting polite practice shots over the net, as I took my seat in the staff enclosure, separated from Richard by a handful of officials shielding their eyes from a now menacingly bright sun. They say any deterioration of playing conditions favours the outsider, and it was Lola who cast occasional wary glances up at the heavens as the umpire announced the start of play. Lola returned to her chair for a last gulp of the energy drink provided jointly by three of the sponsors, and I scrutinised the 'perfect' body that had hacked such holes in Kirsty's self-image. Lola was certainly finely constructed, three inches taller than Kirsty and as evenly proportioned as a statue. Above her, at one end of the court, a gigantic banner thanking various corporations displayed the very similar physique of a well-known player, so that it could be imagined that the banner was advertising Lola herself. There was a calm and a correctness about her manner that contrasted her with Kirsty, who was hopping and twitching about at the other end, adrenalin sending blasts of energy through her limbs.

As had perhaps happened every time they had played, the adrenalin quickly became an oil slick for Kirsty's technique: in the opening games she ran too fast and hit her shots zealously, her impacts producing strained, unnatural noises that alternated with the easy regimented clicks and clocks of Lola's smoother groundstrokes. Kirsty soon trailed 5–2 in the first set, and as her opponent prepared to serve the game that would take her halfway to another victory, Richard chatting jovially with her coach and applauding loudly, I scanned Kirsty's face uneasily for signs of resignation. Instead, glancing up into the grandstand, she met my eyes and flashed me a wicked, unexpected smile of self-assurance. Of all the tiny moments of collusion I had shared with female performers, this was the most definite and the most enjoyable. For the next minute I felt as happy as if the scores were reversed. And then, amazingly, they were.

Kirsty's mother, who had stayed away from the final at her daughter's pleading (on the grounds that her presence was bad luck), but who nonetheless saw most of the game on the TV highlights show, would later say that it was the best she had ever seen her play. It started with small psychological boosts – a surprise winner here, a mistake by Lola there, giving her the game and cutting the deficit to two – and these became the building blocks for a tower of confidence which, ascending hesitantly then smoothly, eventually brought her level. As her lead was whittled away, Lola's composure was perceptibly shaken. Her face at the changeovers between games was telling; she darted anxious short looks up towards us and appeared dissatisfied by Richard's thumbs-up and array of other soothing gestures. Meanwhile Kirsty was balancing her racket on her knees and twirling it with dexterous fingers loosened by self-assurance. She had reached the top of the tower and now saw her rival in a clearer light. When the set went to a tie-break, only one player looked psychologically prepared to win it. As Lola sliced the decisive shot into the net with a cry of disgust, Kirsty's surreptitious fist-clenching brought me out of my seat in excitement. Applauding wildly, I glanced across and drank in the sight of Richard regarding the court uncomfortably. His face and that of Lola's coach were united in confusion; Lola looked up again in search of guidance which was not forthcoming. The balance had shifted.

I wondered if Kirsty might choke on the advantage in her haste to taste glory — my own heart was thumping with the scent of success and I felt, in her position, I would certainly be dazzled into errors by the gleam of the trophy. But it was Lola who began to break down as the atmosphere thickened and the sun, still hanging high over the bleachers, sent down a steady shaft like a spotlight. Lola's reflexes were still crisp, but her judgement was ebbing away, deceiving her into overhitting shots as Kirsty had done at the beginning; and even her Aloisi-refined temperament was starting to show cracks. When a questionable call went against her midway through the set and she halted the game to issue petulant, pointless comments at the line-judge and umpire (who smiled genially back like school librarians), Kirsty could be seen turning her face away to conceal a gratified smile of her own. Outbursts against officials might be powerful psychological tools for the McEnroes of the world, but escaping the polite lips of a normally placid (and smug) player, they rang with the tones of impending defeat.

Having won the mental battle, Kirsty had only to remain

disciplined and watch as a string of errors by her increasingly disenchanted opponent propelled her close to the finish line. With the score at 4–1 to Kirsty, there was a shuffling to my right as Lola's coach departed, preparing to console her before the sharp post-mortem that would come later. Richard remained in his seat, an unusual glumness creasing the face that had made many an acceptance speech. The glitter was fading from his client, and the less fashionable Kirsty – now wielding her racket like a weapon as she backed Lola into a corner and readied herself for the kill – was exorcising two sets of demons. When the final winner exploded past Lola, who had long ceased chasing the difficult shots, I sprang out of my seat with a shout so loud that four rows of officials turned to look at me with curiosity or annoyance. The dutiful pitter-patter of their applause was drowned in my yells of acclaim as Kirsty trotted delightedly over to the sidelines. Lola dressed at double speed and sloped off bemused, bag slung heavily over shoulder and head bowed, the pose of unexpected defeat. Richard's face and body language did not mirror hers – this was no more than a drop of piss in the ocean of his career successes – but mine certainly mirrored Kirsty's. We were winners.

Outside, murmurs of the sensational result were already dispersing from the departing spectators out into the wider world, the news racing around the site, the horizon humming with the knowledge of a new champion. Every conversation I passed sent one of its participants away with an expression of shock or, in more than a few cases, dejection and amazement. Lola had had many fans on the campus and, beaming benignly at the passers-by, I felt I had beaten them all. Only gradually, by searching the pale faces of hurrying crowds and straining to catch the ends of fraught conversations, did I begin to suspect that there was another drama afoot, another news item creeping like a disease from one carrier to the next. Somebody was sobbing by the concessions stand; an official was repeating 'I don't know what to do, I don't know what to do' into a walkie-talkie as if the gadget would supply the answer for him; sponsors' reps, with their logo-plastered T-shirts, were congregating in ominous bundles. All indicators of disaster, but not fully threaded together by my mind until, within a hundred yards of my hotel, an official placed a hand on my shoulder: 'Are you Dr Peter Kristal?'

And suddenly, without his having to say anything, I knew.

All around the perimeter of the building where Webster was staying, a throng of people – police, spectators, athletes, photographers – was being marshalled by a flustered committee member who tried to wave me away like a greenfly. When I identified myself, he led me without a word through the packs of voyeurs and along the network of corridors to Webster's room. The door was wide open and a cop was keeping watch. The official turned, still without a word, and left me on the threshold. Inside the room there were two people, one alive. Maguire sat mutely in an armchair, staring at nothing. Webster was sprawled across the bed, partly covered by an orange sheet which had become discoloured as it absorbed a seeping dark red stain. Still nestling lightly in his left hand was the gun he had fired just once, an hour and a half previously, into his brain. Christ knows where it came from, how he got it on to the site. That was my first thought.

There was no note. You don't need to explain when you've got a psychiatrist.

I had studied, and researched the causes of, suicide for a large part of my almost twenty-year career. But this was still one of the first times I had stared into the white eyes of a man so recently deceased that the room struggled to catch its breath. It was certainly the first time I had felt directly responsible for a death. It should have been the first time I cried in public in adulthood, but, as at Dad's funeral, emotions would not run to order. The first sight of Webster's handsome black body lying as if on a mortuary slab numbed me. The tears came later.

Doctors kill people all the time, of course; firemen drive to the wrong address, army sergeants get their own men blown up; I had treated an escapologist's assistant who lost concentration during a stunt and left his man to suffocate. Among the professions that routinely deal with life-and-death issues (either in theory or practice), psychotherapy is unusually kind to its practitioners in some ways. The comparative vagueness of its science opens up a number of escape routes: he would have done it anyway, it was caused by something that happened when he was a kid, by the time I met him he was too far gone to help. Compared with the body blow of a dead patient to a doctor, the shrink is left with something more like a brief illness: a creeping sensation of guilt accumulating in the veins, eventually being discarded as professionalism claps its hands and moves everyone along to the next potential disaster site. The afternoon that Webster shot himself, I found escape routes blocked and was forced to confront the rush of instant horror felt by the fire crew who should have been there five minutes earlier, while at the same time knowing in my stomach that the slow nausea, the bitter aftertaste of remorse, would plague my future. I wanted to throw up and keep retching for days, weeks, till the whole thing was out of my system. Instead I joined Macguire in his blank vigil for the boy who brought us together, whom between us we had allowed to die.

★

I didn't cry at the funeral; I wasn't there. They flew him back to New York for a ceremony attended by more than three hundred of the people he had charmed in his short career. Across the coffin was draped a flag signed by all the other athletes in the Games; Kirsty's name was there somewhere, a heart serving as a dot over the 'i' as in the 'thank you/with sympathy' card I received from her. The flag had to be removed before the service itself because the vicar objected to the sponsors' logos. Before all this had happened, I was back in Chicago; I flew back at the first opportunity after helping the police with their enquiries. On the aeroplane I tried to write a letter of apology and explanation to Webster's remaining family; three lines in and I was choking on tears, one splashing on to the paper. The woman in the next seat offered me her 'motion-sickness receptacle' to wipe my eyes. I had one of my own, but appreciated the gesture of support. No one on the plane would meet my eyes once it had been established that I was emotionally insecure; everyone was embarrassed by my presence.

The air hostess didn't bother to wish me a nice day when we landed. She could obviously see it would be wasted.

And even when I got comfortable with crying, when I could let myself collapse without a moment's notice, welcoming the sudden onrush of despair that reared up during *Seinfeld* or in the shower; even when I knew I was 'working through the grief' like a model post-traumatic depressive, I could not abandon myself to it without turning the cause-and-fucking-effect over and over. If I had dealt properly with finding out about Mum and Dad, I wouldn't have felt the intense loss of a protector and the need to protect which made me get too close to Webster. If I had rationalised my Richard complex, I would have been able to control the envious anger and the bilious pride which made me scream at Webster for undermining me in front of him. If I hadn't been so hung up on reputation and eager to associate myself with a future Olympian, I probably wouldn't have let him compete at all. I would have put him into safe hands and told him there were plenty of years to run races when he had cleared his mind of Streissman and the rest. Tracing back from the moment Webster's hand closed around the trigger into time I had spent with him, and from there back into the past that had made me what I was, I could name ten things I could have done differently, any one of which might have set us on a different path, one that bypassed the worst-case scenario instead of hurtling headlong into it; one that opened out on to green fields – a lifetime of achievement for Webster and a fulfilling relationship between us – instead of juddering to a violent stop in a student room and sending me crashing through the windshield.

It was only *might*, of course. You couldn't prove it. Patients kept coming. Colleagues sent their sympathy. No one blamed me. They didn't have to; I knew. And I knew also that all this analysis didn't matter a damn. All my theoretical knowledge of suicides had not been enough to intercept one as it happened: a million bullet points couldn't cancel out one real bullet. I understood now what tragedy meant. It wasn't about the details after all; all that mattered was the brutal pay-off. The people who thought Nicholas Hirst was killed by a witch's curse had more idea than I did after all, because at least they *felt* something, some dread of the inescapable, some powerlessness that I in my arrogance had denied. That's tragedy: not something you think about until you can write it down like a recipe, but something you feel all the way through your body. I had never been able to feel properly. Now it might be too late to start.

7

Effects

Chicago Herald – March 3, 1994

Dear Dr. Kristal,
I was wondering what you thought about Razomide, the new drug being developed which may provoke a slight, deliberate weakening of the memory, and which may (if it is judged to be safe) be used in controlled conditions to aid some trauma sufferers in overcoming painful memories. Should it be welcomed as a compassionate treatment for those whose lives are torn apart by terrible recurring memories, or condemned as another example of "playing God".
Interested In Psychological Developments, Ohio

PK'S PROGNOSIS: **Thank you for drawing attention to what will become a very important debate. The "playing God" issue calls into question what the purpose of psychotherapy really is: how far should we go to palliate the victims of trauma? Should drugs be reserved for the "mentally ill" or given also to the mentally disadvantaged—and is this even a meaningful differentiation now? Is the memory a logbook from which we should feel free to tear a painful page here and there, or a black box, unchallengeable in its workings? Given** the mysterious trellis that binds all our memories together, can we remove individual pieces of data without causing the whole edifice to collapse like a house of cards?

The two questions—what is the memory really for? and what is psychotherapy really for?—are each big enough to fill a book, one that would demand a greater intellect than mine to write. I am grateful to the *Herald*'s editors for giving me the extra space I need this week to tell a story which may or may not throw some light on them.

I turned 43 years old last year. Middle age. Life expectancy is 78, plus a couple of years because of my wage bracket, minus a couple of years because I'm overweight and depressed. I have reached the midway point in my life, and beyond, without ever meeting my biological father. His name was Richard Hirst, and his involvement in a family tragedy drove him to leave the UK before I was born. I was raised by Robert Kristal, my mother's lifelong lover and protector, whom I took to be my father until five years ago. He died in early 1991.

Since then, goaded on by constant reminders of the gaps in my self-knowledge, I have been tracing my real father. I looked up emigration and immigration records and traced the red line of Richard Hirst's escape from Witching, over to Australia, then—after a twenty-year interval—back to England. I made dozens of calls to missing-persons organizations, placed adverts in newspapers nationwide, scanned telephone directories. I spoke to two or three Richard Hirsts who quite easily supplied an alibi to prove that they had not fathered me. Then, at the end of last year, I learned that a man called Hirst was a long-term resident of The Glens, a rest home in Blackburn, Lancashire. I made a long-distance call, my hands shaking even as I reminded myself of what a long shot this, like all the others, would be.

"I'm looking for . . . Richard Hirst," I said, spelling out the name, which suddenly sounded impossibly far-fetched, like a ridiculous character in a play. "Do you have him there?"

"No-one called Hirst here," said a far-off voice, and I had almost put the phone down before he went on. "We do have someone called Horst. I mean, that's not so different from Hirst." There was a pause as I digested this. "Just an 'o' there instead of the 'i'," the man observed.

Barging aside his remarks on the ironies of the alphabet, I asked a series of quickfire questions about this Mr. Horst, which were calmly deflected. They knew very little about him. He had been committed to the home by a cousin many years ago; he had no visitors these days. All this vagueness was quite promising. I had to try my luck.

"Can I talk to him?"

"It's a bit late . . ." the man hesitated. 'May I ask what it is in regard to?"

"He could be my father," I said.

"I think he's having his bath," replied the man.

"Well, can I come in and visit him?" I blurted out.

I know all this sounds ridiculous, almost self-parodic—the shrink trying to get to the bottom of his own personality, the amateur detective trying to exhume his own past—but I'm past the point where I can analyze my actions with self-awareness, or rather past the point where it seems worth doing. What I wanted was what people are always asking me for these days: "closure". Closure is the new denial. Once upon a time people wanted to bar the door to any upsetting thoughts; now they want to invite them in and question them until exhaustion kills them off ("them" being either the thoughts or the individual, depending on the success of the procedure). At least, in my defense, I had a reason to be poking around among the debris of my family history: the prize of a meeting with my real dad, however far off and speculative, was too great to be ignored. If it was stupid to chase the dream, it would be doubly stupid not to pursue the one thing that might give me peace of mind. I got on the plane to England last week.

On the way I asked myself what I was expecting to find, what would satisfy me. Richard Hirst could not live up to the stand-in father who had done such a consummate job, and I didn't want him to. He didn't have to embrace or even touch me. A sentence would suffice, just enough to confirm that this was the man whom I had thought about so much over the past twenty years: as the bad guy in a local horror story, and then belatedly as my mother's lover, the man half responsible for my existence. All I wanted was confirmation that I was his, even if saying it appalled him, even if he screamed at me to get out of his sight. My quest was to see the last piece of my life's jigsaw fit into place, even if the picture it completed was hardly any different, and no more beautiful or coherent than before. For a man who had spent a lot of his life slotting such puzzles together, it was a natural wish, I guess. I asked my way to The Glens in a pub, and got an easy answer; ordered a drink out of politeness but found I couldn't swallow a drop; hurried into the men's room and, sitting in a stall, tried to impose some order on the sweaty palms and watery guts, unite them into a person who could handle the truth about his past. IT'S NEVER TOO LATE! said a yellow sticker on the inside of the door inviting people to stop smoking and fend off death for a little while longer. The words stuck in my head.

The place was neat but smaller than I had imagined; the atmosphere was tidy, unthreatening, and there was still a light on in the reception area. Frightened and excited, I tottered through the doors, perhaps the most nervous individual ever to enter this home of professional reassurance. A balding man offered to help me; I explained my mission. The man led me through a rabbit's warren of wide, gently lit corridors with creaking furniture and amateur landscape paintings, and the musty smell of old age in every corner. I was led into a dormitory and given fifteen minutes with the old man perched on the bed nearest the door. This was Mr. Horst, or Hirst.

It took me two of my fifteen minutes to sit down, shake the limp hand offered to me and make a stumbling introduction. I gabbled an explanation of the possible link between us. Mr. Horst, who had large, enquiring eyes of a very light blue—the same color as my own, but paled by the watery patina of age—listened with what looked like interest, nodding very slightly from time to time, his face and body otherwise motionless. As I gave a few particulars, Cambridgeshire . . . Witching . . . 1949 . . . (and then, finally) Nicholas, his expression never wavered for a second. It was that of a kind grandparent listening to an improbable tale from school. This was encouraging, in a way— he didn't feel threatened by me—but painfully ambiguous. At the name Nicholas, however, a faint light flickered in his eyes, no more than the on-off clicking of a cigarette lighter, but enough to give me a pulse of hope. The name had had an impact, for certain. I looked at the old, reddened, lined face, the immobile frame, and tried to believe that this man had once slept with my mother. I thought I could see realization dawning in his eyes. I tried the names again; saw the slight spark again. I waited for him to say something, in vain. I would have to do all the work.

"So . . . so as you can see," I stuttered, totally

unsure of the right mode of address, the right tone for such a one-off topic, "I, uh . . . well, there are reasons to think that you might be . . . that you might have been my father."

There was a pause that felt as long as the four decades I had waited to meet him, then the tentative progress of a smile across his face. In the strange mishmash accent that came out as, finally, he spoke, I could hear a note that chimed with mine.

"Where've you been?" he said.

I was oblivious to the other people in the room, to other sounds, to the environment; I don't know if I could have remembered the name of the place. I certainly had forgotten my time limit—it seemed irrelevant next to the length of time we had been apart—and I took a slow minute to study every detail of his face, not knowing how to react to it, to anything. The delaying instinct was perhaps the same one that, in my youth, made me spin out the job of opening Christmas presents over as long a period as possible. I wanted to savor this late present, this grown-up adventure.

"Where've *you* been?" I said at last.

"I've been sitting here all this time," he replied.

"I've been in Illinois till the day before yesterday," I said. "I live in . . ."

"Where are my other boys?" he asked, looking right at me.

This caught me off-guard. The prospect of new half-brothers had never even occurred.

The thought of finding myself part of a living family again was swaying tormentingly in front of me.

"I've no idea," I said. "I came on my own. When did you last see them?" His eyes narrowed; for some reason this question made no sense. "The boys," I persisted. "Were they here recently?"

"Why, yes!' said Mr. Horst impatiently. "Didn't I send the three of you out to get the groceries?"

This rang the first real alarm bell, but I persevered. "No, you've never seen me before. I just came in tonight. I've come all this way."

"Well, who went to get the groceries, then?" demanded the old man. "And what did you say you came for?"

"I came to find you," I insisted, urgently, but with my hope already shriveling. "I think you were my father – *are* my father – remember what happened in Witching? With . . ." (I was in too far now to care) 'with your brother, who killed himself?"

"My brother?" he repeated in puzzlement. "Well, now, I haven't seen him for a good couple of years. But Witching . . . why yes, I went there. In fact we used to go all over. Cambridge, Sussex, we even visited the—what was it called—the Isle of Wight!" He laughed a wheezy half laugh and continued his amble through an increasingly cloudy landscape of recollections. "And do you know, wherever we went, really, people were all the same. Of course the world's a different place from what it used to be . . . I can't remember whether you were there at that time . . ." He paused, losing the thread, and looked around as if someone might show him a cue card. Then his large eyes fixed on me and for the first time I forced myself to see that they were empty. The light which I had taken for the fire of remembrance was really just the arbitrary flashing of a faulty bulb.

"You're the dentist, then?" he asked me.

The memory I had hoped to rifle through, salvaging precious clues to my own identity like sentimental treasures from a bonfire, was no more than a heap of charred, jumbled remains; the fire had burnt out some time ago. Whatever had once been there was so overgrown with weeds that it would never again be possible to identify it, except in fleeting random glimpses. I walked out through the gates feeling idiotic and disillusioned, having left my possible father talking himself around and around in endless mazes (his last words to me were an order for six chicken legs). Three days previously at a seminar, I had been voicing my provisional support for Razomide, a drug which might subdue the clamor of the traumatised mind by allowing for "memory editing"; now I found myself confounded by a memory all too much like an editing suite, in which images had been cut, mixed and grafted on top of one another until only amorphous clumps of data remained. After God knew how many years of solitude, not only had the man's short-term memory atrophied, but his long-term memory, left to compare notes with no-one but its own reflection, had tangled itself into the intractable knots of senile age. The one disease you don't look forward to being cured of. IT'S NEVER TOO LATE! danced mockingly in my head.

I checked into a dingy hotel where honeymoon suites were advertised by a heart-shaped neon display which flashed its message to an empty street all night long. In the room separated from mine by a paper-thin wall, a willing couple were noisily taking advantage of the facilities. They returned to their exertions at intervals of about an hour, with what seemed a joyless punctuality, as if satisfying the terms of a special offer. I didn't mind the disturbance; it didn't matter.

Sprawled heavily across my own bed, I took an inventory. My parents were gone and my original father was either unhinged or in some other place where I would surely never find him. I had no family of my own. My faith in my professional methods had faded and my job no longer seemed important. I had no religious or philosophical belief to sustain me; all I had inherited was a commitment to the cold logic of questions and answers, which now left me pinned against a barbed-wire fence of fact. I could think of few possible things which would improve my hopes for the future and couldn't even muster much interest in the question. I needed help and there was only one man who could do it. He was the man I once blamed for my problems, but now I saw the problems were all my own.

Editor's note: PK's Couch will be folded away after this week. Peter Kristal thanks all those who have written to share their problems. He will return to present a special edition of the column at Christmas; in the meantime he can be contacted c/o Dr. Richard Aloisi, Aloisi Surgeries, New York.

So here we are in the final chapter, the part where you find out I've been writing the whole thing from the nuthouse. The old *Catcher in the Rye* trick. At least Holden Caulfield knew who his parents were. But let's not go down that path again. Knowledge comes with its own traps. After the effort it has cost me to write this book, the painstaking work of putting my past into sequence and rationalising the results, I feel quite comfortable with ignorance. I just wish I had discovered it sooner. I know enough to thank God I don't know any more. I read that in a book somewhere; can't remember which one. I've had a lot of time to read books in the past eighteen months. I'm allowed to, because of course I'm not really in a nuthouse; I'm living with Richard.

Richard always said that writing my memoirs would be a helpful experience, and he was right, if only because the process of sitting down and doing it has brought a certain routine into my life. The rowdy chorus of unanswerable questions has been at least partly silenced by the methodical grinding out of words. A thousand today. A thousand tomorrow. Clear targets to be met; little time to think about other things. For the past year Richard has been working on his latest book, an anthology of sixties psychology called *Understanding 'Understanding Understanding'*, and the two of us have spent many pleasant evenings in creative activity, almost reminiscent of the evenings, now yellowing in the memory, that I once shared with Dad.

Christy Aloisi, Richard's beautiful wife, takes time out from supervising her empire of fashion magazines to bring us cocoa and cookies with a few indulgent words, as if we were a secret society meeting in the attic. Perhaps she's using me as practice; before long there may be young Aloisis entertaining the intellectual cream of their school classes in upstairs rooms. The first one is due early next year. 'You can be Uncle Pete,'

Richard sometimes says in moments of sentimentality. I will have moved on by then, of course. It takes only two to raise a child, sometimes fewer: I'm sure they will manage.

Before long Christmas will come round yet again and Richard has invited me to spend it with him and his ever patient wife, as I did last year, but I can't be in their way for ever.

Now that most of the story is down on paper, at least it makes a kind of sense, although it's not the most warming of tales: a guy • graduates from an average university; • toils away in the penumbra of a more successful friend; • achieves minor successes only to see some failure counteract them; • tries to change the world in his own small way, only to watch it spring back into its original shape as if it were a rubber ball he had squeezed between his fingers; and • watches his personal history mock him mercilessly as soon as he gets close to it. Still, it's my life and I can't disown it.

I don't know what was the decisive blow, the scene when audience members exchanged meaningful looks and students underlined their texts. The part where I found out Dad was not my father, and I was the bastard product of a meaningless fuck which drove a man to suicide? The part where I finally tracked down the 'real' Dad and found his brains turned to soup? The moment when I sat down with all these facts and saw how it made sense that I was a psychologically mixed-up wreck; and that after years of smugly dismissing talk of tragedies and curses, I had walked into exactly the kind of trap – part fate, part background, part own errors – whose existence I once scorned?

No sense now in splitting hairs, trying to pinpoint the moment of collapse. The bullet points all joined toward a predictable conclusion, or as normal people say, one thing leads to another. Or maybe everything just happened randomly, maybe the whole idea of bullet points is as misleading as the straight line tracing the route of an airplane. It's for other people to work out, now. I don't need to explain myself. I have a psychiatrist.

PK

APPENDIX

by Dr. Richard Aloisi

Kristal, Peter

- conceived, 1949
- father, Richard Hirst, disappears
- mother dates, marries Robert Kristal
- born, 1950
- mother's aversion to baby; never entirely dispeled in later life
- PK a solitary, studious child
- develops lifelong suspicion of/awkwardness around women, fueled by uneasy contact with:
    mother
    cousins
    school headmistress
    classmate, Jennifer O'Hara
- meets Richard Aloisi; friendship develops
- feels inferior to Aloisi, complex amplified by:
    Aloisi's superior performance in tests
    Aloisi's musical/sporting abilities
    Aloisi's prospects
    progress of Aloisi's career
- possible homoerotic feelings toward Aloisi
- influence of teacher Leonard Paulson sparks:
    interest in psychology
    fear of failure
    feelings of homophobia, becoming disgust of own sexual instincts
- first homoerotic experience

- brief sexual experiment with cousin, Johnny; attempts to discuss incident with Johnny; ostracised; vows never to mention it
- studies at Michigan 1968–72; maintains contact with Aloisi, at Harvard
- begins job as researcher and feature writer for *Michigan Psychiatric Journal*
- researches Hirst case
- dawning interest in "bullet point" life-summaries
- enjoys job; hardening convictions about power of psychology to predict and rationalise human behavior
- gains post at Lakelands Institute, Chicago, 1980
- establishes good reputation, enjoys measure of fame
- difficulties with physical contact; confused sexual urges; increasing repression
- Lily Ripley stage fright case:
    romantic ambiguity
    successful, but scientifically unsound, "treatment"
- leaves Lakelands, sets up own successful practice
- death of mother sparks revelations; profound shock
- death of father
- represses initial grief
- yearning to find biological father surfaces
- strikes up friendship with Webster Bruce
- suicide of Bruce
- grief; guilt; self-reproach; severe depression
- follows slender lead to biological father; hopes dashed
- depression resumes; consults Dr. Richard Aloisi
- begins writing book, *Bullet Points*, while living with Aloisis
- gives preliminary drafts to Aloisi
- attends Thanksgiving celebrations with Richard and Christy Aloisi, in good spirits

- retires early
- takes massive overdose of pills
- discovered too late

For a long time—more than five years—even the thought of preparing Pete's book for publication was repugnant. Handling and collating his scripts felt like what it was: rifling through a dead man's property. Pete left no note, no last wishes or apologies, just like Nicholas Hirst and Webster Bruce—unless of course the whole book is seen as a monstrously extended declaration of suicide. But I don't believe that is the case; I think his decision only crystallized as he wrote it.

But why? Was it the failure of his principles that finally broke him, or the fact that the more rigorously he applied them, the more sharply they illuminated the painful facts of his own nature and nurture? Was it ignorance or over-knowledge that he found unendurable, or a little of each? I have no *Death of a Psychiatrist* epitaph to deliver. I will limit myself to a few professional observations.

Firstly—and this will go with me to my own grave, at the risk of overloading the reader with yet more melodrama—it is clear that, rather than allowing Pete to reconcile himself *with* himself as I had hoped, the idea of making him write his memoirs was dangerously flawed on two counts:

(1) It belabored him with an overwhelming sense of failure;

(2) He remained blind or semi-consciously oblivious to the most important factors in his depression.

The most important of all was his homosexuality. I'm not sure if Pete ever took full possession of the fact that he was gay, even though it will have been suspected by a careful reader at an early stage of his memoirs. The close and

269

troubled nature of his attachment to me, to the exclusion of nearly all other friendships, is one clue;[a] his lifelong difficulties in dealing with women, another.[b] And the homophobic prejudice kindled by the chance remarks of his

[a] As with many such attachments, the idolization of the object provided a canvas for the self-loathing of the ego. Throughout Pete's manuscript, excessively flattering references to me give notice of an obsessive perception of inferiority which – although he alludes lightheartedly to it early in his manuscript – was never satisfactorily tamed and underscored most of his life. Freud's contention that every suicide is a sublimation of a desire to kill an "other" has been exhaustively debated elsewhere; it will simply be noted here that his uncle Tom's remark that Pete will "have to kill" me (in the 1963 diary), though humorous, may be seen by Neo-Freudians as an ominous prediction.

[b] A taste of this can be gained from his diaries, which also contain various more unpleasant references to his cousins Jemima and Rose which have been omitted here at their request. The lack of warmth shown him by his mother provides an obvious explanation for the deep mistrust of women which was the concomitant of his attraction to men. Pete's recollection of feeling threatened by his mother's picture in the bathroom, as well as the meaning he attributes to it, is suggestive of a pathological, and specifically sexual, unease regarding women, which manifested itself throughout his life.

The "romantic ambiguity" in his dealings with Lily Ripley seems to have been more pronounced on his side than hers; she was surprised to read the account and claimed that, in her memory, there was no "fumbling kiss", nor did they share a bed; nor does she recall having answered the door to him wearing only a negligee. She says she always thought it likely that he was gay. Pete describes her eyes as being green (the color of his mother's eyes), although in fact they are brown.

Patsy DiMarco would not comment upon whether she and Pete flirted with each other at any point but accused him of overestimating the "affection" which she showed him on his first visit to her house. It seems that as a necessary part of his denial of the homosexual side of his character, Pete invented or exaggerated some heterosexual affairs. Whether he was seeking to deceive the reader or to delude himself is not clear.

teachers, relatives and peers (which, again, can be spotted at intervals throughout the text, beginning with Mr. Paulson's onslaught on me) offers one reason why he might have shut out the knowledge and continued to seek heterosexual attachments long into his adult life, yearning for the familial model of monogamy for which he was unsuitable genetically. In short, Pete was so horrified by the prospect of his homosexuality that he locked it away for what seems an unbelievably long time. But there it stayed, and even if (in Pete's terminology) it might have seemed just one bullet point among many, its influence was to shadow his every move.

The real pointers are in what Pete doesn't say. In the opening pages of his manuscript, for example, he describes our first meeting as having been at "the birthday party of someone I no longer remember". But Pete remembered, all right; the host's name was Martin Crown[c] and, when they were fifteen, he and Pete had a brief homoerotic experience after a football practice at school, when Mr. Kristal was very late to collect his son. No-one but Martin knows any more details than this; unless he chooses to reveal more at a later date, nobody ever will. Nonetheless, seeds had been sown, and Pete was to repeat this experiment with his cousin Johnny. The two had long been friends and, sharing the experience of growing up but coming into only periodical contact, they developed an attraction and curiosity for each other which (as a reading of the young Peter's diaries confirms) quickened into sexual excitement. At Christmas 1968, the eighteen-year-old Pete performed a sex act on his cousin during what his diaries describe innocuously as a walk in the woods. Johnny afterwards refused to acknowledge the

[c] This name has been changed.

incident in Pete's presence and the two never spoke again, except at the funeral of Pete's uncle Tom nine years later, when Johnny told him to get out of his sight.

I was able to uncover proof of my suspicions regarding Pete and Johnny after the death of the latter from a sexually transmitted disease. According to friends, Johnny picked this up after a sexual encounter at an air base during the late eighties. He blamed Pete for first implanting the homoerotic impulse which flared up again during his time in the military, and held Pete responsible for his death. According to the friend I spoke to, Pete was made aware of this by letter in about 1991.

Whether or not he accepted responsibility, there was one death which certainly did hang upon Pete's overactive conscience: that of Webster Bruce. Pete describes this in his manuscript, but again seems deliberately to steer the reader wide of the truth. Though he did have an argument with Webster which may be said to have precipitated the suicide, at the root of this argument (although perhaps neither of them ever acknowledged it) seems to have been the quasi-sexual relationship which had sprung up between them. In Pete's mind, with its by now confused view of familial and romantic ties, the paternal bond he enjoyed with Webster became a sexual one. Either Webster disagreed strongly with this, and Pete made him feel guilty; or Webster was acquiescent and Pete, suddenly horrified at himself, snubbed him. Whichever way it happened, Pete believed he was a crucial bullet point in the death of the schizophrenic sprinter. As Pete himself notes, in such an extreme case it would be impossible for anyone to speak with certainty of his guilt; but, as he goes on to say, "they didn't have to; I knew".

And this, as Pete suggested without perhaps ever fully understanding its implications, was his greatest problem:

knowledge. Knowing his true background undermined everything he had held onto; knowing his true self was a task he shied away from and, when it became inevitable, dodged by dealing himself the final blow.

But as I have said, the moral of all this is beyond me, and I don't wish to do any more damage to Pete's reputation. Perverse as it may sound, I am publishing this with the same intention as once drove Pete to publish the Nicholas Hirst bullet points: to salvage honor. I hope that with a sensitive consideration of the factors underpinning his words and actions, the reader will see Pete not as the failure he came to think he was, nor as a "psychologically mixed-up wreck" who destroyed himself, but as a victim. A victim of what exactly, I'm not sure it is possible to say. There is, after all, no single reason for anything.

Dr. Richard Aloisi
New York, January 2001

ACKNOWLEDGEMENTS

I would like to thank the following people, without whom the book wouldn't have been very good or, in some cases, would never have existed at all:

- REBECCA CARTER
- ED JASPERS
- RICHARD PROCTER
- KEVIN CONROY SCOTT
- ROBIN WADE
- PATRICK WALSH
- CHRIS WILLIAMS
- ROSE SILLENCE

Also special thanks to:

- MY PARENTS, PAUL, EMMA, LUCY and EMILY

A NOTE ON THE TEXT

With the obvious exception of the books of Oliver Sacks – which I apologise for plundering in a haphazard way – almost all psychiatric, sociological and literary sources cited are imaginary. Fact and fiction have been freely crossbred throughout the book, though, so it's probably best not to take anything too seriously.

FIND OUT MORE AT

themarkwatsonsite.com